continued . . .

MONA LISA CRAVING

"Suspenseful twists promise more heart-throbbing surprises in the next installment of this haunting erotic fantasy series."
—*Publishers Weekly*

"[The] series is unique, captivating, and sexy . . . Everything you've come to expect from Sunny and more . . . Another remarkable addition to Mona Lisa's saga . . . Those who are following this amazing series are going to be shocked at the degree of intensity this book takes on . . . I love not only the eroticism of the story but also how the plot and characters are constantly evolving."
—*Romance Reader at Heart*

"The latest chapter in the Monère series is a pulse-pounding erotic adventure . . . narrated in first person by the heroine in a strong yet emotional voice. Sunny creates a fascinating world that's violent and sexual."
—*Romantic Times*

"Fans of this erotic fantasy saga will appreciate this powerful entry . . . Once again it is the secondary characters that provide strong support to the plot, which makes this an endearing tale . . . Another winner."
—*Midwest Book Review*

LUCINDA DARKLY
Book One of the Demon Princess Chronicles

"An awesome story populated with endearing and sexy characters. This unabashedly sensual gothic story will feed your need for something new and fresh. Readers will be loath to put the book down until the final page is read . . . The ending will leave you hungry for more."　　　*—Romantic Times*

"An emotionally intense, sexually charged gothic romance between a dead demon princess and her men . . . The last chapters in this book are phenomenal . . . If you're in the mood for a different kind of paranormal read that is superbly written, marvelously told, and extremely sensuous, look no further."　　　*—Romance Reader at Heart*

"[A] superb, fast-paced urban fantasy in the tradition of Laurell K. Hamilton."　　　*—Midwest Book Review*

"Full of paranormal passion, Sunny's fast-paced first in a new erotic fantasy series, the Demon Princess Chronicles, introduces Lucinda, a six-hundred-year-old demon princess who's getting bored with her long unlife."
—Publishers Weekly

MONA LISA BLOSSOMING

A NOVEL OF THE MONÈRE

SUNNY

BERKLEY SENSATION, NEW YORK

THE BERKLEY PUBLISHING GROUP
Published by the Penguin Group
Penguin Group (USA) Inc.
375 Hudson Street, New York, New York 10014, USA
Penguin Group (Canada), 90 Eglinton Avenue East, Suite 700, Toronto, Ontario M4P 2Y3, Canada
(a division of Pearson Penguin Canada Inc.)
Penguin Books Ltd., 80 Strand, London WC2R 0RL, England
Penguin Group Ireland, 25 St. Stephen's Green, Dublin 2, Ireland (a division of Penguin Books Ltd.)
Penguin Group (Australia), 250 Camberwell Road, Camberwell, Victoria 3124, Australia
(a division of Pearson Australia Group Pty. Ltd.)
Penguin Books India Pvt. Ltd., 11 Community Centre, Panchsheel Park, New Delhi—110 017, India
Penguin Group (NZ), 67 Apollo Drive, Rosedale, North Shore 0632, New Zealand
(a division of Pearson New Zealand Ltd.)
Penguin Books (South Africa) (Pty.) Ltd., 24 Sturdee Avenue, Rosebank, Johannesburg 2196,
South Africa

Penguin Books Ltd., Registered Offices: 80 Strand, London WC2R 0RL, England

This is a work of fiction. Names, characters, places, and incidents either are the product of the author's imagination or are used fictitiously, and any resemblance to actual persons, living or dead, business establishments, events, or locales is entirely coincidental. The publisher does not have any control over and does not assume any responsibility for author or third-party websites or their content.

MONA LISA BLOSSOMING

A Berkley Sensation Book / published by arrangement with the author

PRINTING HISTORY
Berkley trade edition / February 2007
Berkley Sensation mass-market edition / November 2008

Copyright © 2007 by DS Studios Inc.
Excerpt from *Mona Lisa Craving* copyright © 2008 by DS Studios Inc.
Cover photographs: "Woman's Back" by Sara Valentini/Getty Images. "Moon & Sky" by Mia Klein/
Getty Images. "Trees" by Altrendo Nature/Getty Images.
Cover design by Annette Fiore Defex.
Interior text design by Kristin del Rosario.

ISBN: 978-0-425-22494-6

BERKLEY® SENSATION
Berkley Sensation Books are published by The Berkley Publishing Group,
a division of Penguin Group (USA) Inc.,
375 Hudson Street, New York, New York 10014.
BERKLEY SENSATION and the "B" design are trademarks of Penguin Group (USA) Inc.

PRINTED IN THE UNITED STATES OF AMERICA

10 9 8 7 6 5 4 3 2 1

To Da,
who loves me, encourages me,
and lets me bloom.

AUTHOR'S NOTE

To describe the full catastrophic effect Hurricane Katrina wrought upon New Orleans is beyond the scope of this story, and this author's ability. The story only briefly mentions the great devastation this city suffered and continues to recover from. My heart goes out to all whose lives were affected by this disaster.

O N E

WE WERE IN a private jet winging through the darkness of night, flying to New Orleans. My new territory. I was dressed in a black gown. Full-length, formal. Not my usual style or taste. But at least this one fit me, not like the hand-me-downs from Mona Sera, which had gaped and gathered at my modest bosom. My mother was lushly built. Not so, me. Too bad I hadn't inherited that physical aspect from her. Or maybe it was a good thing that I hadn't inherited more of her traits. Not too nice, my mother.

All I seemed to have gotten from Mona Sera was my black hair, high cheekbones, and a jawline that was both delicate and strong. Oh, yeah. And the Monère blood that ran strong and true and dominant in my blood. A quarter of me is human. The other three-fourths is of another species, from another world: Monère—children of the moon, stronger and faster than humans. And more powerful. We are the truth that the legends of werewolf and vampires are based upon.

Beside me sat Gryphon. He'd been unusually quiet. We

weren't touching, but I felt his presence, his power, like a hand pressing delicately against my skin. I turned to look at him, to gaze upon him, this beautiful creature descended of people from another world who had fled their dying planet over four million years ago. His extreme loveliness struck me, as always, like a blow to my chest, knocking the very breath from me. But who needed to breathe when you could drink in the richness of his beauty instead? The midnight blackness of his hair that fell like a silky curtain of darkness, brushing across his shoulders. The alabaster purity of his skin. The startling redness of his cupid-bow mouth. Such unearthly loveliness, such lips, should have only graced a cherub. In fact, the first time I'd seen Gryphon, the thought had whispered in my mind that he was a fallen angel tumbled to Earth, kicked out of heaven. I hadn't been too far wrong. Only their heaven had been the moon.

Haunting sadness swam like a living thing in his sky blue eyes. Sad eyes that had seen too much, done too much. I hated seeing that look once more in those crystalline depths. Feeling my caressing eyes, Gryphon turned to me and I watched the sadness that seemed so much a part of him fade away, and watched something else rise up from deep within to take its place. In his blue, blue eyes, I saw my dream come true. Hot passion, sweet adoration. Love. Everything I had wished for all my life and never thought to have. Gryphon. My dreams made flesh, an arbiter from another world who had come to me, alone and injured by his own Queen's hand, dying. Saving him had freed me from my loneliness and initiated me into my real life.

The memories and the pull of emotion between us swelled and I wondered why we were not touching. I wanted to touch him, feel him, caress that sweet skin, to reassure myself that he was real, not a vision that would fade away. That he wouldn't leave me.

A movement drew my attention away. Ah, yes. Coming down the aisle toward us was the reason why I wasn't touching him. Amber, my other lover. Tall like a majestic mountain, solid with hefty bones and even heavier muscles. Powerful like a massive oak tree, grand and rough-hewn. His beauty lay in his ruggedness, in his battered heart, with his raw strength and even rawer emotions that he normally hid behind a cold wall of reserve, a wall of control—his normal façade. A life-preserving habit that he had honed under Mona Sera's cruel rule, so that one was fooled into thinking that he didn't feel much . . . until he looked at me, like he was doing now.

I swallowed against what I glimpsed naked and intense on Amber's face, what he allowed me to see. There was nothing cold or reserved about him now. His dark blue eyes had changed to fiery gold, glittering yellow like a bright, shiny jewel; the same color as his name—Amber. The eyes of his beast. They heated and glowed with this extraordinary color whenever he was gripped with passion or power.

I watched him walk toward me with those glowing, molten eyes filled with desire and devotion intertwined, and was torn between running away and throwing myself into his massive arms. He had saved me, brought me back from the brink of death, protected me from a band of kidnapping rogues, and had loved me. When we returned from our ordeal, the bond between us had been forged strong and true, and I loved Amber now as dearly as I loved Gryphon. My two Warrior Lords. My two lovers. I still hardly believed that I would not have to give up one or the other. That I could keep them both and allow them to share me, as they called it.

Amber lowered himself into the aisle seat beside me, his trim waist and hips fitting easily. Even the great sword he wore at his waist found a space. But his shoulders were so wide, so broad across that we touched. And with that small contact, a sigh of relief rippled through us all. The tension between us eased, the strain ebbed. My left hand naturally, without thought, reached for Amber's broad, callused hand as my right hand twined with Gryphon's long, slender fingers. Gryphon raised my hand, brushed a kiss across the back of it, and pressed it to his heart. A courtly gesture that was as natural and graceful as the man himself, triggering a rare fluttering feeling within me— happiness. And being this happy, having things this perfect made me nervous. Why? Because I knew it couldn't last. Not for me.

"The pilot said that we shall be landing soon." Amber's voice was so deep, so dark, so low, it made my spine shiver. "You look beautiful, Mona Lisa," he said, and my name was like a caress upon his lips.

I grimaced. Amber was no doubt referring to my long hair that I had left loose and unbound, and my long formal gown . . . swirling black lace over black silk lining. One of several dresses I had bought in Manhattan, not because they were to my taste—oh no, not that. Jeans, T-shirt, sneakers, and ponytail were more to my taste, and what Amber and Gryphon had become used to seeing. But the long black gowns were what Monère Queens wore, and that was what I was. A Monère Queen. The newest one.

Monère men were a bit primitive in tastes when it came to their women—long dresses, loose hair, and even looser morals—especially their Queens. No doubt they'd love to throw in barefoot and pregnant if they could manage it. Problem was, very few could. The Monère were not a fertile people. It was difficult, rare, for their women to become pregnant. I wondered if it was a natural state to balance out their longevity—they had a typical lifespan of three hundred years—or if it was a condition they had become afflicted with on this foreign planet, their new home. Briefly, I wondered if it was a condition that had cursed me as well.

I'd worn the dress as a concession, one of many I'd

probably be making as I entered my new territory for the first time. As the first Monère Mixed Blood Queen ever, I was strange enough as it was. No need *not* to wear the usual Queen trappings . . . at first, that is. We'd see about later, after they'd gotten more used to me. They, being my new constituents, the local Monère. And not just in New Orleans. New Orleans, it turns out, is just the seat of my throne. My new province expands far beyond the French Quarter, beyond the bayous with their dark waters of chocolate. Its tentacles of reach sprawled outward like an octopus throughout the entire state of Louisiana and a little beyond.

I looked to the front of the airplane where the rest of my people sat, to what I had thought would be the entirety of people I would rule until Gryphon had corrected my misconception. My eyes softened as they landed upon Thaddeus's dark straight hair, so like mine. Thaddeus, my brother by true blood.

Jamie and Tersa's red hair gleamed like ruby exclamation marks beside Thaddeus; they were the brother and sister of my heart. All three are Mixed Bloods like me—rare, few, and unwanted. Jamie and Tersa's mother, Rosemary, a Full Blood Monère, sat alone in the row behind them. She was a gifted cook who had left her coveted position at High Court to follow me blindly to whatever territory I was assigned. I had been the only one to step in to save her daughter, Tersa, when she was being raped by a Monère warrior. No one else had interfered because it's not against Monère law to rape, kill, or do anything your little black heart desired against Mixed Bloods. In fact, their laws were skewed against Mixed Bloods. We couldn't kill Full Bloods.

Yeah, their law sucks. Luckily it had been amended once I became a Queen. I, the sole Mixed Blood exception, could kill a Full Blood. In self-defense, that is. A cold smile touched my lips. Any killing I did would be made to look like self-defense, of course, whether it was or not. Because, no question about it, if I killed them, it would be because they richly deserved to die.

Rosemary had followed me because she believed I would protect her Mixed Blood children, being a Mixed Blood myself. Shrewd woman. She was right. I would do whatever I could to keep them safe. Hard to believe, as I gazed at the stout, dark-haired cook who was as tall as an Amazon, that Rosemary had given birth to Jamie, reed thin and slender tall, and tiny petite Tersa, whose bones seemed as light and as delicate as a dove's. Made one wonder—or not want to wonder—who their human father had been. Redheaded for sure and slight of build. I shook my head, clearing my thoughts. The odd, mismatched mating was not something I even wanted to try imagining.

In the third row sat Tomas and Aquila. With soft brown eyes, wheat-colored hair, and a Southern accent that flowed warm and thick as molasses, Tomas was as straight and true and loyal as the sword he had sworn to my service. Aquila, on the other hand, was an ex-outlaw rogue, one of those who had kidnapped me, in fact. You'd never have guessed it to look upon his very proper and precise person. He was not much taller than my five feet eight. The hair of his neatly trimmed Vandyke beard was crisply straight in contrast to his brown wavy hair. He was older, like Amber. Over a hundred years was my guess. The only one in our little group besides me who knew how to drive . . . in a jerky "at least half-a-century since he'd gotten behind a wheel" manner of fashion. Aquila's knowledge and grasp of commerce and business was a nice boon for us all, although perhaps not so surprising considering the orderliness of his nature.

Behind them sat Chami, the last and least wanted of my warrior guards. The most dangerous. I had taken him because Mona Teresa, a nasty jealous rival Queen, would have taken him had I not. I'd taken him because he had humbled himself and begged me with his deep violet eyes not to let her have him.

Chami had curly brown hair like Aquila, but with a whipcord-lean, greyhound slenderness to his build. The press of his power was like an invisible kiss against your skin, light, barely there. Until he loosened the shield and let you sense the fullness and weight of it. But his real gift was not in the cloaking of his full power, although that was a nifty trick. No, his real power lay in his ability to cloak himself. Actually, not cloak per se, but rather the ability to blend in with his surroundings and background so that he was invisible. Chameleon. He'd been an assassin, killing silently, an unseen hunting shadow, his nature as dark and complex as his gift, his loyalty less sure, although he had stood true thus far, even when we had come up against a demon dead.

My family. My inner circle.

Unknowingly, unconsciously, we had sat in reverse order of power. Mixed Bloods, traditionally—and true in Jamie and Tersa's cases—are not much more powerful than humans. My brother, Thaddeus, and I are the exceptions. But then we are more Monère than human. Our father had been a Mixed Blood, identity unknown. Dead according to our mother, Mona Sera, although I rather thought that she had lied at the time.

Thaddeus was the curious exception in our unconsciously seated hierarchy, which had the strongest sitting in the back to protect the weaker among us. Thaddeus, might in fact, prove to become the strongest of us all with time, if we could grant him that. He was certainly the most unique, even more so than I. Thaddeus, you see, can call down the life-prolonging rays of the moon. He can Bask, something that before this only Queens could do. My brother, Thaddeus, was the men's precious hope for the future. I can see it in their eyes when they look at him . . . Aquila, Tomas, Chami—all warriors sworn to my service but whose allegiance, perhaps first and foremost, conscious or unconscious, was to my brother. And that's okay. It was my desire as well. I'd rather they see to his safety first. I can look after myself.

Two

THE PRIVATE JET bumped down on the runway of Louisiana's Lakefront Airport, a small domestic airport we'd deliberately chosen instead of the busier Armstrong International Airport, named after their beloved New Orlean's native, jazz legend Louis Armstrong.

We stepped out onto the black tarmac and took our first breath of the deep South. The air was sultry, tinged with the sharp taste of water, both salty and fresh. Beneath that, far away in the distance, was the fecund aroma of moist, fertile earth, and the promise of forests and land, plenty of land. The soft glow of our mother moon fell upon us in welcoming benediction and the night air was cool and comfortable, surprisingly so. Or perhaps not. It was winter, after all. A few weeks before Christmas and not a snowflake on the ground. Okay by me. Monère weren't big on building snowmen, I don't think.

Two men stepped forward to greet us, smiles on their face, and all of my senses locked onto them late, carelessly late in what really was new, uncertain territory. I registered their slow heartbeats the same moment I felt that tingling brush of awareness of like to like. Monère. Full Bloods.

They froze, we all froze, as unconsciously I unleashed my full force upon the strange men, sending out a wave of power to brush up and test theirs, an invisible, unerring, seeking force rippling through the air like a tense arrow unleashed. An answering surge arose ... was pulled from them ... and I knew the exact moment when our two opposing forces came together, and I tasted them. Power, yes. But not much.

A strangled sound escaped one of the men. Greeting smiles had disappeared, completely gone, and their eyes were wide and wild, their bodies quivering tense.

"Mona Lisa," Gryphon murmured from slightly behind me. They were all behind me, I realized. Unconsciously, I had stepped forward protectively to meet the unknown threat. And my men had let me. Begging the question: Why?

Behind me, I felt the presence of my men, relaxed and easy, deliberately so. Mmmm ... belated realization: Perhaps because there was no threat.

Oh.

"Please, milady." Amber's deep baritone came softly from my other side and I hastily called back my power, my force, whatever it was. It came flying back to me like a bird called to hand, wrapping around me, sinking down into the depths I had called it from, disappearing.

See, harmless.

The smaller man, who had involuntarily gurgled, took out a handkerchief—jeez, did people still use those things?—and wiped the sweat off his face, blotting his trim little mustache carefully. He didn't bother blotting the other little thing down below that had popped up along with the sweat. The larger man beside him just relaxed, or tried to. There was a distinct bulge that had risen up between his legs that he was unable to relax away. His muscles still quivered and I realized why now. They quivered with restraint.

Remembering my first meeting with Gryphon, I suddenly blushed with an appalled "Oh, my God, I didn't mean to do that" kind of horror. I'd forgotten about aphidy, the innate, sexually attractive force between Monère men and their Queens. Some built-in thing that was supposed to help propagate the species.

Aphidy certainly hadn't been the force I had intended to use. Didn't know I could, really. God, I was lucky that the two men had chosen to behave themselves. That they hadn't jumped on me, overcome with lust. How embarrassing that would have been. Embarrassing enough as it was. Like flashing your underwear in public. My face flamed.

The larger man, with light shiny hair the color of sunbeams, spoke from where he stood. I couldn't really blame him for not coming nearer. "Welcome, Queen Mona Lisa, Warrior Lord Amber, Warrior Lord Gryphon, members of milady's court." His vowels were rounder, his consonants softer. "I am Bernard Fruge, one of the elders here. On behalf of our community, we welcome you."

Two representatives to greet us. I was happy with that. Didn't like a big fuss. And remembering my mother, Mona Sera's little group back in New York, the community that Bernard spoke of probably numbered no more than twenty. We'd probably bump into them sooner or later.

I delicately cleared my throat, unsure of protocol. But surely you couldn't go too far wrong with simple politeness and courtesy. Right? How hard could this Queen thing be? "Thank you, Mr. Fruge."

"Bernard, please, madame."

Madame? Wasn't that French? Made me wonder if a Full Blood Monère could be French.

The little man standing beside Bernard cautiously took a small step forward. Throwing back his shoulders, which had inadvertently hunched, he puffed out his chest like a little pigeon. "Allow me to introduce myself as well. I am Horace, the former steward here. I will be staying a short while to introduce you to your many holdings before returning to my Queen, Mona Louisa."

My eyes narrowed as I felt a subtle tension gather behind me in my men. I wasn't entirely sure, but I think he just insulted me by not addressing me by my title. One thing for sure, though. He was Mona Louisa's man. Therefore, our enemy.

I returned Horace's insult by not addressing him in turn. "Is that normal protocol, Amber?"

A long silence and then Amber said, "I am . . . ah, not entirely sure, milady."

Oops. I figured Amber would know, being one of the oldest. One hundred and seven years old. I figured wrong.

It was Aquila who rescued me. "Yes, milady. That is a normal courtesy extended a Queen when she takes over a new territory."

"Thank you, Aquila." I didn't bother thanking Horace.

Bernard smoothly stepped into the hostile silence. "If you will kindly direct us to your luggage, madame, we can be on our way."

For the next ten minutes all the men busied themselves loading our many trunks and various baggage into the back of two large SUVs, one dark green, the other spotless white.

"Tomas, Aquila, Rosemary. If you will please go with Horace," Gryphon instructed smoothly. Silently I approved the division. It kept Thaddeus, Jamie, and Tersa—the youngest, the most vulnerable—with us.

Reluctantly, Tomas and Aquila stepped into the dark green car, which had Steward Horace at the wheel. Looking as if she smelled something foul, Rosemary took a backseat also, leaving the front passenger seat conspicuously empty. Apparently they liked Horace as much as I did.

The largest among us, Amber took the roomy front passenger seat, dipping the white SUV down with his weight, while the rest of us piled into the two back rows, which were surprisingly spacious and comfortable. Bernard, who was driving and sitting closest to Amber, became visibly nervous. More, I think, as a reaction to Amber's sheer size and presence than to the fact that he was a Warrior Lord.

A glint caught my eye and made me focus more closely on the hands gripping the steering wheel. Bernard wore a simple gold ring on his left hand, fourth finger. A wedding band? Did the Monère marry?

"Cool. These are Suburbans, aren't they?" Jamie asked with youthful enthusiasm. Unlike most Monère, he liked to use American slang that he had picked up from watching television.

"Yes," Bernard confirmed, smiling at Jamie through the rearview mirror as he pulled out of the airport. That smile alone made me like him. Not all Monère were kind to Mixed Bloods. *Useless inferior mongrel mutts* was more their common thought and reaction. Although that wouldn't be quite the politic view to express before one's new Mixed Blood Queen. Not unless one wanted to commit suicide, that is. Still, I liked him for that smile.

"Suburbans are what the president and all the top government officials travel in," Jamie enthused.

Bernard seemed so normal, so human—they all do in the beginning—until he asked, "Which president?"

"Of the United States," my brother, Thaddeus, replied.

"Oh."

See, not so human after all.

THREE

We passed New Orleans and headed into the ... I wouldn't call it suburbs, exactly. More like pockets of civilization carved out among the wild. It was lovely, the farther away from the city we drove. Rich with lush green foliage, thick woods, rolling fields. Twenty-five miles later the smell and feel of water permeated the air more thickly. Nearby, the flowing Mississippi River murmured a gracious welcome as we pulled into a long, private driveway. Rounding a bend, Bernard glanced in the mirror back at me. "Welcome to Belle Vista, your new home."

It seemed there would be no shabby warehouses disguised as mansions here in Louisiana, like back in New York. No, sirree. Here was a blatant, in-your-face mansion. No hiding. No pretense. Soaring three stories tall, and so many columns ... over a dozen at first glance. Lots of columns. Lots of windows. Lots of grandeur.

An ancient towering oak draped with Spanish moss dramatically framed the building on the left. A rounded, pillared wing, the gentle sweep of a half-circle was visible to the right. Cast-iron balustrades gleamed darkly in the night. When I realized my mouth was agape, I gently shut it.

"Belle Vista is set on the rise of a twelve-foot arched foundation—what kept it dry when other homes flooded. It's a plantation home originally built in 1857," Bernard announced proudly as our vehicle rolled to a gentle stop.

Home didn't quite describe the immense structure.

We piled out of both cars, all of us captured by the sheer loveliness, the old, timeless grandeur of the magnificent edifice.

"It's beautiful," Tersa whispered, expressing the sentiment for us all.

"Greek revival," Thaddeus proclaimed, more technically. "Although it also has a definite Palladian influence."

Horace sniffed with surprise, looking even more weasel-like. "You are correct, young man."

"Fluted columns," Thaddeus muttered, "and my God, look at the amazing Corinthian capitals. The size of them. Hand-carved, I'll bet."

The step Thaddeus took toward the house was halted by my hand. "Wait," I said.

There were no other cars, which was why I'd missed it at first. Although hard to imagine how I could have missed it . . . the hundreds of countless heartbeats. Slow, slow heartbeats. Much slower than the human heart. "There's people inside." My voice flat, I looked sharply at Bernard and Horace.

Bernard dipped his head calmly. "*Your* people, my Queen."

My people? So many? My palms suddenly grew damp.

Amber and Gryphon stepped up on either side to flank me. Tomas and Aquila surrounded Rosemary and the children—although they weren't technically children. In fact, Tersa was actually older than I was, but that was how I thought of them. Chami automatically took the rear guard. All done without thought.

Bernard's eyes widened. "They are here to welcome you, milady." Milady, not madame. Using the more standard, formal Monère address to . . . what . . . calm the savage beast, I mean, Queen? My eyes probably did look a little wild.

"It's okay." I didn't know who I was reassuring, him or me. "Let's go meet them." I tried for a smile. Bernard didn't look too reassured by it. It was probably more of a grimace, but I couldn't help it. I was looking forward to this about as much as I would have liked having a rotting tooth drilled and scraped without Novocain.

Horace and Bernard ascended the wide, flat stone steps and opened the front oak-paneled double doors, moving slowly so as not to spook the wild beasts. They were half right, I thought as we followed them up the steps. We were definitely spooked.

My inner voice was shrieking: What? Were we crazy? The ten of us deliberately walking into a houseful of hundreds of Full Bloods? Maybe that's what being a Queen was . . . crazy. No other reason why a sane creature would deliberately put herself among such out-numbered odds.

The entry hall was large and airy, reaching all the way up to the roof. . . . Grand. A spiral staircase flowed majestically up and around invitingly to the second level. Veined marble tiles, rose white, gleamed spotlessly beneath our feet—had we wiped them before entering? I couldn't remember.

You didn't even need one of those big-ass overhanging crystal chandeliers to impress people, although there was one of those, too. Just the sheer size of the place, all that generous space—how could one place have so much damn space!—took one's breath away.

It was as if the steward read my mind. "Fifty-three thousand square feet. Many of the furnishings, paintings, tapestries, and rugs are originals imported from Europe," Horace informed us primly, his voice muted as though it would be a sacrilege to speak too loudly. "As is the marble, of course."

Of course.

I sniffed, not in a huffy way but because there was a distinct metallic tang in the air. "Is that . . . gold?"

Horace gestured to the walls. "Fourteen-karat gold-leaf wallpaper."

Was he for real? My nose said he was. Sheesh!

I followed him and Bernard in a near daze as they turned right, leading us down a wide, expansive hallway to another set of double doors, paneled cherry wood, these. With a flourish, Horace swung them open. "The Grand White Ballroom," he intoned.

Grand and white was right: White tiles. White marble mantels. A sea of white faces all staring at us.

I swallowed.

The collective power from that room crept over me like thick sticky invisible fingers pressing down over my skin, almost smothering. I felt the power within me start to instinctively react and strangled it back, kept it choked. Definitely not a good time or place to let my aphidy run loose. I don't think even Amber or Gryphon could save me if it did. Not against so many. Jesus, how many people were there?

"We number four hundred twenty-three, milady," Bernard answered. Again that annoying knack. I didn't like it that he and Horace seemed to know what I was thinking.

My heart skipped a beat when the sea of faces suddenly dipped down and turned back up en masse, like a fluid wave. They had bowed, I realized. Just bowing to me. A normal courtesy, I reassured myself over my loudly pounding heart. Although they were the ones suddenly looking scared.

"Milady," I heard Bernard say in an odd tone.

I turned to see him staring with appalled fascination at my hands. At the two sharp long knives I was gripping. I resheathed them calmly, casually, without a blink, as if it was a normal occurrence for Queens to unconsciously call their blades to hand—one of them a silver blade I had taken from their own former Queen's hand. I wondered if any of them recognized it, as I dipped my head, nodding to the crowd in return.

Bernard cleared his throat cautiously. "If you will . . . uh . . . step this way, Queen Mona Lisa." He indicated a large ornate chair set on a raised dais—a throne, really. "I will introduce your people to you." He said it like a question, and appeared quite relieved when I nodded and took a seat calmly at the throne. Amber stood on my left. Gryphon on my right. After a brief hesitation, the other seven members of my little group followed, standing several yards behind me, keeping our formation of protection intact. And watching our backs.

A small group, all fair blondes, was led forward by Bernard. Two women and one man. The women were presented first.

"Lady Margaret Fruge," Steward Horace loudly announced as a lovely woman with delicate features, her hair swept back neatly in an intricate coil, curtsied gracefully before me. It felt awkward enough just sitting there as she did that, with her head so near my feet. What she did next shot my feelings straight past awkward all the way to aghast. Kneeling, Margaret picked up the hem of my dress and kissed it. Now I knew why Queens wore long gowns. So their subjects could kiss the hem. Jesus fucking Christ!

She remained kneeling.

At an utter loss for words, I fluttered my fingers at her, indicating she should rise. Uncertain, she glanced sideways at Bernard, who nodded. She stood but kept her head bowed before me. My eyes flashed down to her hands and I saw that she wore a simple gold ring on her left hand as well.

"Your new Queen, Mona Lisa," intoned Horace.

Hesitantly, as if she was unsure of what to do next, now that I had disrupted their normal proceedings, Margaret curtsied low once more. "My Queen."

"Are you related to Bernard?" I asked.

Surprised, she looked up, bobbed her head, and quickly looked down once more. "His wife, milady."

"A pleasure to meet you, Lady Margaret." I gestured to my right, since it seemed as if Horace had no intention of introducing anyone. "This is Warrior Lord Gryphon." A hand sweep to my left. "Warrior Lord Amber."

"My lords." Another curtsy as she kept her eyes lowered. I wondered if her back hurt from all that scraping and bowing.

Margaret stepped back and the other woman moved forward and curtsied. Her hair was light and fair, like a sheath of wheat bleached by the sun, long and flowing. Her features were like Margaret's but a little sharper, bolder, the nose taller, the mouth fuller. The color of her eyes, I noted when she glanced briefly up at me, was an unusual shade of gray.

"Lady Francine Fruge" was Horace's crisp announcement.

She started to kneel.

"Just a curtsy is fine," I said firmly.

She stood.

"Queen Mona Lisa." There was a look of disapproval on Horace's sour face as he grudgingly continued his introduction. "Warrior Lord Gryphon and Warrior Lord Amber."

A second low curtsy from Francine. "My Queen. My Lords." Her gray eyes, I noted, lingered a little on Gryphon, eliciting mixed feelings in me. Mostly annoyance.

"Are you also a member of Bernard's household?" I asked. My guess was Margaret's sister, but with a Monère you could never tell. They all looked young. She could have been anywhere in age from twenty to two hundred—I think their hair started to gray after that—and anyone from great-granddaughter to great-grandmother. Safer just to ask how they were related rather than presume.

"His daughter, my Queen."

See.

My eyes sharpened upon her with interest. I'd never

seen a complete Monère family before. A whole unit—
father, mother, daughter . . . a precious child.

A man stepped forward next. His bearing was graceful
and confident and more than a touch arrogant. It might have
come from his looks. He was fair, like the others, with a
thick wave of sun-kissed hair, strikingly handsome like one
of the ancient Greek gods. Tall and moderately muscled,
with lovely moss-green eyes. But his was a mere beauty of
the world, a cold surface perfection. Something to admire
from afar, like a figure on a coin, or a cold marble statue.
Gryphon's beauty was otherworldly, like that of a fallen angel's, unmatchable, with a drowning sensuality that made
you want to touch him, stroke him, to breathe his essence
deep into your body and wrap yourself in his sweetness.

"Dontaine Fruge." Something about the way Horace announced him proclaimed him special.

My eyes narrowed as I sensed him, the quiet thrum of his
power. He was strong, much more so than Bernard. Perhaps
the confidence wasn't just in his looks then, I thought, as
Horace went through his spiel.

Dontaine swept a courtly bow. "My Queen." Kneeling,
he pressed a kiss to the back of my hand. Other men had
kissed my hand before when acknowledging me, so I
couldn't protest, though I wanted to. Because Dontaine did
it differently. His lips caressed my skin with conscious,
provocative heat that deepened the green of his eyes to a
dark fiery jade. And he didn't just touch me with his flesh.
He touched me with his power, a taste of it. A different
kind of power than any I had ever encountered. An electric
strumming that danced like little shocking jolts upon me.
Pleasurable, for the moment, but with the dark promise of
pain if it continued.

I removed my hand and he drew back.

"Another Fruge?" I asked coolly.

"Margaret is my mother."

Interesting how he'd answered that.

"And Bernard?"

"My mother's second husband."

"Your stepfather, then."

"Yes, my Queen."

So Margaret had borne two Full Blood children. A precious girl and a powerful warrior. They were a prized family, no doubt favored by their former Queen, Mona Louisa, with their fair coloring so like her own. Dontaine had clearly held her favor, I intuitively knew. Why, then, had Mona Louisa left them here for me?

Dontaine turned his head to my left, looking behind me, and inclined his head respectfully. "Warrior Lord Amber." But when he shifted his gaze to my right, there was some knowledge, some subtle difference in those cat-green eyes. "Warrior Lord Gryphon, a pleasure to see you once again."

"Dontaine," Gryphon replied, his voice bland, and I knew without looking that his body and face were as inscrutable as his tone.

They knew each other. My brow creased as I pondered that. Dontaine had not been with Mona Louisa at High Court. And then it came to me. Mona Louisa had brought Gryphon here to her home when he had bartered his body to her in return for protection for me. Had she paraded Gryphon here before her people, her new pet? Her new toy to play with before he died from his silver poisoning? Had she shackled a jeweled collar about his throat and held the leash in her hands, the way she had displayed him at High Court? The answer *yes* whispered to me with certainty.

Oh, baby. No wonder you looked so sad.

FOUR

THE REST OF the introductions flowed forward like fast streaming water, filling the vessel of my mind with a general feel for the whole, but slipping away if I grasped for much detail. Like individual names, for instance. They were a glittering throng, dressed in their best to meet and greet their new Queen, the women sweeping the floor with their gowns like antebellum beauties, the men dashing and neat in their formal wear. They fit into the grand ballroom like naturally extended props because the fashion could have been set back a couple of decades or even a century. Sashes accented men's waists. Bow ties, neckties, even knotted cravats topped off crisp white shirts. In general, there were many more men than women, as seemed to be the norm among the Monère. But there were at least twenty women here; the whole number I had expected to rule. By the count of their women alone—those rare, precious women—this must have been considered quite a prosperous territory, even though it was still recovering from the ravages of Hurricane Katrina.

With the ceremony completed, refreshments were served and we were expected to mingle. I was never good at mingling. I grabbed Gryphon and slipped out onto a balcony, closing the French doors behind us. The cool night welcomed us with an airy embrace, a breeze rifling through our hair, over our faces, kissing our skin with refreshing grace.

"Gryphon, are you all right?" My question was like the night itself. Soft, natural. A whisper of sound. I touched the side of his face and Gryphon brought his hand up to cover mine, as if he would keep it against him always. Turning, he pressed a gentle kiss into my palm.

"I am well," he said quietly.

"You were here before."

"Yes."

"You met these people."

"Some of them."

"Did you . . ." I hesitated. "Did they . . ."

A breeze rustled the leaves, swaying some of the giant trees in the distance.

"Do I need to kill anyone here?" I asked abruptly.

Gryphon laughed but it was a sad sound that made you want to weep instead of smile.

"No, my heart." He called me that but it was the other way around. Gryphon was my heart. My reason for being here. "No one. Mona Louisa was selfish. She desired the gift of walking under the sun only for herself first before any others. I shared no one else's bed here but hers."

Gryphon was able to venture out without impunity into the light of day now, a rare ability for a cold-blooded Monère. Not many things could kill the Monère but the sun was one of them. Stick them under the hot rays and it fried them, literally. One hour and they would be lobster-red and panting. Four hours and they were covered in sores and great boils, their skin sloughing off. And they would die without a healer's aid. That's what my dear mother, Mona Sera, had done to Amber. A remembered shiver rippled over me at how Amber had looked when she had done that to him.

I had passed on my ability to Gryphon to withstand the sun when I had taken him as my lover. For the Monère, sex was much more than the slaking of lust—it was also a way to gain new powers and abilities. Another reason why promiscuity was the norm. Mona Louisa had tried to acquire that ability by sleeping with Gryphon in turn. I wonder if she had been successful, if the sun's heat was nothing but a mild kiss upon her skin now. I sincerely hoped not. I hoped that when she stepped out into daylight, it burned her fair skin to a dark red charring crisp.

Dropping my hand, Gryphon stepped back from me, leaving me feeling coldly bereft. His voice was a low, barren sound in the night. "When you took me back, even after knowing I had been in Mona Louisa's bed, I could not believe it, that you still wanted me, desired me. I considered it a miracle. A miracle that I cherished with all my heart. But I knew it could not last." His blue eyes drifted closed, his heavy lashes casting delicate shadows over his cheeks.

"There are things about me, about my past that I would have kept from you always, were I able to. But you can never outrun your past, even if you have wings," he said, with a small wry smile. In his other form, Gryphon was a falcon.

Then his smile dropped away. "There are people in there who know me. Know of my past. They would have found a way to whisper it into your ears. I have found that I do not wish to wait in agony, in unknowing torment. I will tell you myself and have done with it."

Faint light streamed out from inside the ballroom, allowing me to see those beautiful eyes weighed down with deep shadows. His voice dropped until it became a bare whisper of sound. "In other places, other courts, with other Queens, I have done things with women . . . with men. I've done things you could never begin to imagine. Done and had things done to me . . ." His voice shook with remembered pain, with remembered shame.

I reached up and kissed his trembling lips. To stop him, to take away his pain.

"Shhh. It's all right," I murmured, stroking the dark silk of his hair. "That's all behind you now."

Gryphon was only seventy-five years old. Considered young, especially to have acquired so much power. But even among the lovely Monère, where the plainest of us still drew a human's eyes, he was exceptionally beautiful. Many Queens would have welcomed him in their beds. Until he had become too powerful for them.

I knew that Gryphon had been part of a caste of what they called comfort men and comfort women. Mona Sera had used him to whore with humans in return for business deals and monetary concessions for what she wanted. But he was speaking of times and experiences even before Mona Sera. Quite frankly, I couldn't imagine what could be worse than being used as a whore for humans. Monère received no pleasure in mating with a human. I knew that fact personally. I had taken two human lovers to my bed before I learned of my Monère heritage and had gotten pain instead of pleasure. I'd thought I was frigid. As usual, it had been the sticky matter of bedding the wrong men. Or in my case, the wrong species. Finding Gryphon had been like stumbling upon an unexpected treasure when I had given up all hope.

"I love you," I said with soft fierceness. "I will always love you. Always want you. Nothing you say or do—what anyone says—can change that."

Uncertainly, Gryphon's hands came to rest lightly against my back. "Truly?" His forehead sank down to lean against mine, as if his head were too heavy for him to hold up. His rigid body softened against me and his harsh breath blew in soft puffs against my lips.

"Oh, Gryphon. You are my mate." I would tell him this over and over again until he finally believed me. What a sad pair we were. Both of us expecting the other to leave. "You are *my* heart. I will love you until the end of time."

His arms crushed me to him and he buried his face in my hair, murmuring my name. And I wished the crowd gone. I wished us alone so that we could touch each other, reassure each other, kiss each other. Not chaste kisses but hot, wet ones, our tongues merging, twining together even as we merged, and twined our bodies as one.

Loud voices from inside suddenly intruded upon our stolen solitude. We drew apart, looking at each other, and I watched as Gryphon drew composure down across his face like pulling on a smooth blank mask.

"It seems we are needed inside," he said.

I nodded. He opened the door and we stepped back into the room.

One nice thing, we didn't have to push our way through to the commotion in the center of the vast room. People stepped back, parting for us like the Red Sea, and then merging seamlessly back together again once we had passed.

Blond, handsome Dontaine was faced off against Amber. The air bristled and crackled with the energy and tension between the two men. Chami and Aquila and the rest of our little group stood in silent solidarity behind Amber. So much for mingling.

"What's going on here?" I demanded, stopping before the two of them.

"Dontaine has issued me a challenge," Amber said. His low angry rumble filled the room.

"A challenge?" I repeated. "For what?"

"For you," Gryphon said quietly. "Or rather for the right to you."

"What?" I wasn't sure I'd heard him correctly.

"I've issued Warrior Lord Amber a challenge to a Battle of Strength," Dontaine said, watching my face. "For my Queen's favor."

"How," I asked clearly and carefully, "can you hope to win my favor by fighting with one of my men?"

"I, too, am now one of your men, milady," Dontaine said.

Okay. Bad phrasing.

"Challenges are a traditional way for warriors to pit their strength one against the other in a permissible manner, abiding by rules," Gryphon quietly explained. "It is one way a strong male can rise above another."

"Like a cockfight?" I asked, lifting my brow.

Gryphon bowed his head. "Quite similar, yes."

"And the winner? Gets what?"

"The winner assumes his defeated opponent's rank if it is greater than his own."

"Don't tell me you can acquire the title of Warrior Lord that way." It was more than just a title and the nifty medallion necklace they wore. That was just window dressing for the power beneath it.

"No, milady, you are correct. Men cannot become Warrior Lords in that manner. If Dontaine defeats Amber, he would merely be acknowledged as the dominant male." Gryphon hesitated, and I was coming to learn it was never a good sign when he did that. "The overall winner, however. The one who defeats the Queen's champion, is usually taken to her bed."

"Is that a requirement?" I asked blandly. If it was, things were going to change pretty darn quickly around here.

"No. It is just what Queens usually do."

Silly women. Turned on by all the blood and macho violence, no doubt.

"Dontaine's not following the rules," Tomas said with quiet aggression. His voice also twanged with shimmers of the South, but it was a different flavor from the others here. "He has to start from the lowest in hierarchy and battle his way up. Not the reverse order."

Dontaine glared coolly at Tomas. "I shall be happy to do so. Do I start with you?"

Tomas bristled at the insult.

We didn't have a pecking order, really. And I'd hate to have to have an official one. But, yes. Amber pretty much was at the top.

"No need," Amber said. "If you are foolish enough to issue me a challenge, I am more than happy to accept it."

What was Amber doing? And here I was, just about to forbid it. Only if I did that now, I'd be going against Amber, challenging him, setting it up so that one or the other of us would have to back down. Mentally, I threw my hands up in the air. Amber was a big boy. As a Warrior Lord, he was essentially my equal. I had no right to tell him what to do. Even though I badly wanted to.

Almost as one, first Dontaine then Amber turned and strode to the balcony from where Gryphon and I had just come. With a graceful leap, they jumped over the railing to land blithely on the grass twelve feet below. Like water pushed by a strong current, the people streamed outside, some following Amber and Dontaine's path, jumping down lightly like cats, others going out the front door. Still others flowed out a side entrance. Everyone seemed to know where to go. Eager excitement filled the air as hundreds of people merged into the forest and disappeared like pale moths suddenly swallowed up by the night. Picking up my skirts, I hurried after them with Gryphon at my side, tracking the men by sight and sound.

"Why is Amber doing this?" I whispered, my tone low and furious, angry that I couldn't do anything about this.

"It is inevitable that challenge be given," Gryphon murmured beside me. "It is the normal course of events when taking over a territory, the strong men jockeying for position and rank. It is better that Amber meets the challenge now rather than one of the others. One decisive defeat may stop other challenges from arising."

We came to a clearing. Amber and Dontaine were removing their jackets and shirts, and a ring of spectators had already gathered around them. Bernard had his arms around his wife and daughter. Worry marred the smooth line of Margaret's brow but excitement glittered in Francine's fey gray eyes. The moonlight cast deep shadows over her sharp features, throwing an almost wolfish cast suddenly to her mien.

We were just coming off a full moon. The waning moon cast an almost perfect circle of light around the clearing, glowing with pale light upon Dontaine's rippling muscles. He was tall and well built. But Amber stood a head taller; Dontaine didn't even come close to matching Amber's weight and sheer massive bulk. God, was Dontaine crazy? How could he hope to win?

"One thing I want made clear, Dontaine." My voice sang out into the clear eager night. "You will not come to my bed this way."

He looked at me, a question in his eyes.

Oh, hell. Anger was making me stupid. The way I'd phrased it made it sound as if he had a chance when he truly didn't. Maybe it was time for some plain speaking.

"Frankly, you will not come to my bed in any way. Not any of you, other than those who I have already chosen, Lord Amber and Lord Gryphon." Announcing that I had two lovers didn't cause a single Monère to blink. I, however, couldn't help blushing. My human upbringing was showing.

Dontaine kicked off his shoes, peeled off his socks, and cast a cocky grin my way. "I would hope to change your mind, milady."

"Trust me. This is not the way to do it."

Amber unbuckled his sword, handed it to Aquila, and stepped out of his shoes. "What shall it be, Dontaine?" Amber growled.

"Two-legged form. Upright," Dontaine answered. "I'll even let you keep your dagger, Lord Amber. Non-silver."

Generous of him, but not as much as allowing a silver dagger would have been. Wounds inflicted by a non-silver weapon healed almost magically fast, while wounds made with silver healed human slow.

"Challenger sets the rules," Aquila murmured to me from my left. The others had joined us.

"That doesn't seem fair," I muttered.

Aquila shrugged. "The defender is presumed to be stronger."

Amber drew the dagger Dontaine had allowed him. Light glimmered off the knife's edge and the sharpness, the lethalness of the blade, made me shiver. "They're not allowed to kill each other. Right?"

Silence.

I turned to look squarely, demandingly, at Aquila.

"It happens at times, though rarely," Aquila admitted.

I suddenly found it hard to breathe. "What?"

"Where's your dagger, Dontaine?" Amber asked, drawing my attention back to the inner circle.

"I shall not be needing one," Dontaine replied, and a sudden wash of hot energy filled the air. It was similar to what he had done when he had kissed my hand. But more. Much more. Waves of incandescent energy started pouring out from him, and Dontaine's image suddenly wavered slightly, as if a pebble had been cast into a pool of water and was rippling the clear, unblemished surface of his skin. It was like the wind blowing over a field of grass. Like a trick of light that made you want to rub your eyes and make sure that what you were seeing was real. That the sight of bones snapping, stretching, and reshaping was reality. That the image of nerves, tendons, and muscles all glistening wetly was not an unpleasant dream. That the fur suddenly flowing over his skin, and the snout that was slowly distorting Dontaine's face with an obscene crackling of shifting bone was not something in a nightmare.

Dontaine's beautifully tailored dress slacks were beautiful no more as he grew taller and yet taller, the sucking wet sound of muscles and flesh and ligaments stretching and popping, realigning, making me nauseous. The sturdy cloth ripped with a sharp sound and the tattered hems of his pants came up to his calves like little boy's britches, much too small. The top button had popped off and the lower seams had split right up the sides. The zipper, though, was still holding valiantly, sturdy thing.

I'd seen others change into their animal form before. It had been quick, beautiful, and natural. A shimmer of energy and light and it was complete. This was nothing like that. This change was slow, painful, and obscene. A stretching out, slowing down of the process, arresting it in an unnatural state. And the result was monstrous.

The creature—for that was what it was—threw back his head and howled. Pure liquid joy. Something wild freed. A wolf on the hunt, only he wasn't a true wolf. It was as if Dontaine had arrested the transformation halfway to completion so that he stood even taller than Amber, massive in height and weight. Half beast, half human. I'd seen something similar once before, but that had been down in Hell. This . . . this *thing* that lurched before me was covered with fur, truly more beast than man. He wasn't quite as big, as bad, as ugly as the alternate form the demon dead took, but it was close.

Dontaine's hands abruptly shot out to the side and spasmed briefly. Great hooking claws popped out from the tips of his fingers, making my heart stop.

"Dear God," I breathed. "What is that?"

"Half Change," Gryphon said quietly. "A rare ability."

I remember embracing my beast. I had done so for the very first time a few days ago, loosing the tiger within me that I had caged all my life. I had called it forth to save my brother and when I changed, I had broken free of the demon

chains that had bound me. Chains that I could not break free
of in my human form. We were stronger in our animal form.
And I had a terrible feeling Dontaine was harnessing that
greater power in his Half Change state.

With a roar, Amber rushed him. They sprang in the air,
flew at each other and met with a stunning, reverberating
impact that had to have been felt by everyone there. They
thudded to the ground, shaking the earth, lifting dust into
the air, rolling, grunting, growling, claws raking, dagger
flashing. Blood flowed like thick black liquid under the silvery moonshine and screams of pain rent the night, both
Amber's and whatever Dontaine had become.

"Stop it! Make them stop," I said, clutching Gryphon
wildly, my eyes on those terrible claws, remembering vividly
how with one swipe of claws like that, a demon's head had
rolled onto the ground, severed from his body. That was one
of the ways to kill a Monère, taking out the head or heart.

"Challenge has been given and accepted." Gryphon's
eyes, dark in the night, watched the battle without emotion.
"I cannot stop it now."

"He's stronger than Amber, isn't he, in that form?"

"Yes."

"But that's not fair."

"They abide by the rules set."

I wanted to scream. "Can Amber do that?" I asked.
"Change halfway?"

"No."

Gryphon might have lied to me in the past, even slept
with another. But he'd done so to save my life. In his own
way, he was honorable; true blue like the color of his eyes.
He followed the rules. I turned to another beside me who
was less honorable. One who did not follow the rules set by
others.

"Help me," I said to Chami, my chameleon. My assassin.

"What would you have me do, milady?" Chami asked quietly. Before I could speak, he lifted me and carried me swiftly

back several yards as Amber and the beast—it was hard to think of him as Dontaine—tumbled mere feet away from us.

This close I could see Amber's heavy, bunched-up muscles straining as the wolf man slammed him down into the ground. Both of Amber's wrists were trapped in his grip, pinned, the dagger useless in Amber's right hand. The creature's claws were contained, busy restraining Amber, but he still had another weapon that Amber did not have, not in his human form. The wolf beast snarled, his lips curling back. Blood and other fluids glistened on his wicked, sharp fangs. He lunged with those deadly teeth for Amber's throat and my scream of horror ripped through the air.

With a massive effort, Amber twisted to one side and those sharp, ripping teeth missed, just grazing his skin, leaving a sharp line of blood like a liquid necklace to pool around his thick neck. Another bunching of his muscles, a heavy grunt, and Amber lifted Dontaine just enough to get his feet between them. With a sudden heave from both arms and legs, Amber tossed him off and was on his feet, magically fast. He crouched and sprang after Dontaine.

I gripped Chami's hand urgently. "Help me stop them."

"Do you wish me to kill Dontaine?"

I blinked. "No, I don't want anyone dead. I want to stop them *before* someone dies."

Chami hesitated. "If you are going to break a rule, it should be done cleanly, completely."

"I don't want you to kill Dontaine, Chami."

He looked at me, his narrow face tight and troubled. "Milady, I do not know how to stop him without killing him."

I blinked my eyes and it was as if I suddenly saw clearly what was before me, like a blind man regaining his vision. Wiry, slender Chami stood before me, a fragile looking creature compared to the monster I was asking him to face. Chami's strength lay in his stealth, in his ability to creep upon his victim undetected. His strength was in killing his prey unseen, not in fighting.

I backed away from Chami as I realized that he would not be able to help me either. Whirling, I turned and ran into the clearing, toward the combatants.

Behind me I heard Gryphon yell, "Mona Lisa, no!"

"Stop!" I shouted as I ran to the grappling opponents, a struggling mass of fur and flesh twisting on the ground. "I command you both to stop!"

Writhing and thrashing, the two locked combatants twisted and rolled over me, knocking me to the ground. I felt the heavy crushing weight of them briefly, endlessly, then they were off me and I was gasping. Turning my head, I looked up into Dontaine's eyes. Disoriented, I noticed his eyes were still the same shape, like a human's. But what looked out from within them was not human. His jade green eyes had melted to the color of glittering honey, with that odd clarity that animals have, as if you could see clear through them. Wolf eyes. Amber lay pinned beneath him, both of them an arm's-length away from me.

"Stop it! Both of you!" I cried in a harsh, breathless whisper. It was desperately lacking in forcefulness as a command, but I was trying to regain the air that had just been squished out of me.

"I will be acknowledged Master of Arms?" Dontaine growled. His voice was deeper, rougher, like it took great effort to force a human voice through that harsh animal snout.

"Yes," I instantly agreed.

"That is not all I desire," Dontaine rumbled, his voice painfully deep. This close, the brush of his power was different, odd, more electric. His beast's power washed over me and made me gasp, made me writhe. It beat upon me and was almost pleasurable; it contained that edge of pain that threatened, that made it sweet. It called to something within me. Something that wanted to rise up and meet it.

It took all of my effort to concentrate on Dontaine's words, his meaning. He was saying that he wished to be my lover. And I understood then why Gryphon had left me to go to Mona Louisa's bed. What did sleeping with an-other matter? As long as the one you loved still lived and breathed.

"I will take you to my bed once," I said to that half-human, half-animal face.

"No!" Amber roared, and that one word tore through him like a cougar's scream. He gave a sudden, powerful shove and the two of them rolled away from me, wrestling, grap-pling once more, illustrating the sad truth that it takes two people in agreement to maintain peace, and only one to start a fight or continue it.

Hands snatched me up in an almost painful grip, drag-ging me back safely to the crowd of onlookers. I turned to see Gryphon, his eyes blazing down at me. "What are you doing?" he demanded harshly, no longer calm, far from de-tached.

"I'm trying to stop them," I replied shortly. "Almost did."

Gryphon's eyes swirled with fear and anger but the rough screams, the piercing cries, the growls and grunts of rage—animal, human; no difference—drew our attention back to the center. Amber and Dontaine had separated. Both had sprung to their feet. Both were bleeding and battered. And both were fiercely determined to win. They came together in a blinding rush and Dontaine's claws swiped down in a tight slashing arc, ripping with ease through Amber's chest and shoulders.

Amber stood there, unguarded, and let Dontaine rip into him for an unbelievable moment. Then reaching up with an almost casual grace, Amber grabbed Dontaine's unprotected neck with his right hand, dug in assuredly, and ripped Don-taine's throat out. A thick chunk of meat and cartilage spilled from Amber's hand onto the ground as if in slow mo-tion. There was a moment of stunned silence, of stillness. And then came a slow gushing of blood, a dark spurting of fluids. Dontaine fell onto this back, writhing, twisting, his chest heaving, struggling to take in air and unable to do so.

He gurgled, emitting wet guttural sounds as if he were drowning in the wash of his own blood and fluids, lying there on the ground helpless.

"Oh, my God!" I broke from Gryphon and threw myself down beside Dontaine. His odd brown eyes, like clear honey, looked frantically up at me. I reached a tentative hand out toward the raw gaping maw of his throat, but stopped short of touching it. The glistening bones of his white spine gleamed visibly. I turned helplessly to look up at Amber. He stood over his fallen opponent's head, gazing impassively down.

"Is he dying?" I asked. It was hard to believe otherwise, looking at Dontaine desperately gasping like a landed fish for air. I knew that to kill a Monère you had to take his head or heart or poison him with silver or the sun. But surely this much strategic damage would kill him, too.

"No. This will not kill him," Amber said. "He will be uncomfortable until he heals and is able to breathe once more, but he will not die." The calmness of his deepened voice contrasted wildly with his eyes. Eyes that had turned feral yellow. Eyes that were screaming inside with the aggression of his beast, triggered from the recent battle.

My hand lowered hesitantly like a fluttering butterfly, undecided where to land. I finally touched Dontaine's shoulder, feeling thick fur brush coarsely against the smoothness of my palm. The creature reached up as if to grip my hand. Then remembering his own claws, he dug his hands into the ground instead, sinking the long sharp nails deep into the dirt, forcing that part of him, at least, to lie still while the rest of him spasmed and shook. His chest bucked and heaved, trying to draw in breath. But how could you breathe when your windpipe was torn out?

I felt Dontaine quiver under my hand. As I touched him, his power zinged into me and my palm started to tingle. Nothing unusual with that. I was a healer and I wanted to heal him. But then my whole body started to tingle, to pulse, and that was not usual. The smell of blood and the scent of raw meat filled my senses, blinding me until it was all I could see, smell, taste. I could almost roll the coppery sweet tang of blood on the back of my tongue and taste the salty sweetness of warm tender meat in my mouth. My skin began to itch, to burn, to heat. And the cloth rubbing against my skin suddenly seemed unnatural, unwanted.

"Her eyes," I heard a woman gasp.

"She's changing," Amber said. "Dontaine's beast is triggering her own."

It took a moment before I understood what he had said. I was starting to lose myself. "No," I growled. My voice was rougher, deeper, as if I had swallowed gravel and it was rubbing against my throat. I lifted my eyes up to Amber and shook my head, fighting it. "No."

Gryphon spoke quietly to Amber, gazing down at me. "Take her, watch over her."

"No," I gasped, fighting desperately not to rip my clothes off and free my itchy, prickly skin.

Amber scooped me into his arms like a little child and ran from the clearing, away from all the people, the curious watching eyes. He loped into the woods, away from all that raw pungent meat. But the smell of blood still rode thick in the air, right beside me, up against me.

I turned my head and like a magnet, my eyes were drawn to the blood seeping down Amber's chest, his slashing wounds looking like dark lines of melted chocolate in the night. But chocolate could never taste this good, this rich, this alluring. Like an irresistible summons, it drew me. And I answered its call, lowering my mouth, letting my tongue press deep inside, digging into the fresh wound as I lapped up the sweet liquid elixir of his life. Amber groaned in painful pleasure, his breath coming heavily, his slow heart thudding loudly. We were deep in the forest now.

"What will it be, Mona Lisa? Sex or meat? We can change and hunt. Or we can fuck."

Dimly, I realized those were the only two ways to channel my beast's energy. It was there just below the skin, a waiting tension, like water ready to spill over the brim, just barely contained. And fresh from battle, with bloodlust singing in his veins, Amber needed the release, too. He was giving me the choice. And he was warning me. He'd said fuck instead of make love. That was what it would be if I chose that option in both of our heightened, aggressive states.

But it wasn't really a choice. Changing into my beast scared me spitless because the beast, once loosened, took me over completely. I lost all sense of self and just became the animal with its need to kill and eat blood and meat, to tear into flesh and sate its hunger. They told me it would get better. That as I changed more, I would gradually be able to control my beast better. That I would be able to retain my sense of self. Control it. But I had run from it my entire life, suppressed it, scared of losing my precious, necessary control. I couldn't face it yet. Not yet.

"Sex. I choose sex." His eyes gleamed brightly as I drew his head down to me and pressed my mouth hard against his. He let me slide down from his arms onto my feet as his tongue swept inside, tasting his own blood on my lips. He growled and lifted me up, pressing my hips hard against the solid thick ridge of him that had risen up. I made a hungry mewling sound and rocked my pelvis against him in hard pleasure-seeking surges. He pushed me away before I could wrap my legs around him, and unbuckled my belt with two rough pulls. It clanged to the ground with the weight of my daggers.

"Lift your arms," he commanded. I did so and he swept my gown from me. All that covered me now was ivory lace panties, a fragile barrier. Amber cupped a big hand there between my legs, his thick fingers pressing against my moist lips.

"You're wet," he said.

My breath caught as with a rough twist, a sharp pull, he

ripped the cloth away. And then I was completely naked. Amber pushed down his pants, stepped out of them, eyes blazing, and I let my eyes feast upon him.

How magnificent he was. My vision was sharper, clearer somehow and I saw things in the minutest detail. His yellow eyes glowed in the dark, a bright feral gleam. I could see every separate striation in his irises; they were liquid pools of swirling amber. His brown hair flowed in thick waves, wild and untamed, each strand clear and distinct to my eye. Ribbons of blood decorated him like trophies from his battle. He stood before me like a giant monolith, his shoulders so wide that they would block out the moon when he lifted himself over me and covered me. His arms bulged with a thickness that was greater than my thighs. The flat plane of his stomach narrowed down to slender hips, and his abdomen rippled with living ridges and valleys, dipping and flowing. His legs were like two strong columns, beautifully carved, bulky sinew and muscle. And between them rose his sex, heavy and proud. A rampant rod that was in perfect balance to the whole size of him in thickness and in length. He was a big man, all over, his strength great. And I suddenly couldn't swallow. We'd made love before, never fucked. But it wasn't fear that dried my mouth. It was hunger.

I moved to flow against him, but Amber stopped me. With his broad hands against my shoulders, he spun me around. But instead of drawing me back against him, I felt his teeth press against the back of my neck. He nipped me. Hard enough, pleasurable enough to have it actually hurt. He'd always treated me with the gentlest of care before. Startled, I looked back at him and met those gleaming yellow eyes. His cougar eyes. They glowed eerily in the dark; alien, other. He was bent down, crouched over me, and I became sharply aware of the sheer size of him, of how much bigger he was than I. The solid mass of him, the heavier weight, his greater overpowering strength. He was a natural predator and the

sharp blade of fear prickled my skin, pleasant and not, raising goose bumps upon my shivering flesh. My nipples tightened and drew to pebble hardness. His pupils expanded,
widened, almost swallowing up his irises and his nostrils
flared wide, as if he had smelled the tang of fear mixed with
my arousal, and found it intoxicating.

A low rumble started deep in his chest and my heart
fluttered in the cage of my chest like a captive bird.

"Run," he growled.

I stared back up at him with wide eyes, fear and desire
twin captives within me, merged and inseparable.

"Run!" he repeated, his voice gravel rough, barely rec-
ognizable.

I turned and ran, my senses quivering with that odd
heightened alertness, my strength boundless. He gave me a
few seconds head start then came after me. I didn't hear
anything, just felt the heavy waves of his power pounding
behind me, closing in. Just before he touched me, I veered
sharply to the right. I laughed tauntingly as he overshot me,
then laughed again, a teasing invitation as I looked over my
shoulder.

"Catch me if you can," I challenged in a low, husky voice.

He turned abruptly and came after me again, a silent
shadow, white teeth gleaming in a wicked grin, his feral eyes
dancing with the joy of the hunt. I screamed as he pounced
and darted to my left. He was big but I was quicker. I feinted
and darted, his hands gliding over me, missing me, and grasping air. Touch then go. Pounce and evade. Fleeing, chasing.
Dangerous foreplay that somehow felt natural to the cat
within me, a wild courtship that heated me to liquid softness so that my musky scent wafted behind me, an invisible
trail to tease his nostrils, driving him even more aggres-
sively forward.

I feinted to the right. He grabbed my arm and I turned
and raked him with my nails. I snarled, teeth snapping at his
hand and he released me and I was free once more, laughter

trailing tantalizingly behind me. I faked left, darted right, and glanced back to see him right behind me, eyes intent, a great, silent stalking shadow.

He leaped and tackled me. His massive weight hit me hard, rolling us both to the ground. I scrambled to my knees and tried to crawl out from underneath him, my heart pounding, my eyes gleaming with excitement, but he captured me, one hand clamping my waist with an iron grip. One twist and my hair was wrapped tightly around his right hand, trapping me, holding me still with rough firmness. His teeth sank into the back of my neck, not breaking skin, but almost. The delicious promise was there in the edge of his sharp teeth, the threatening pressure, the warning growl, the forceful shake. All of it came together like proper ingredients thrown serendipitously together.

Submission clicked in me like a switch thrown and I stilled, shuddering, no longer wanting to run from him. Purring, I arched up and pressed back against those delicious teeth, my hands braced on the ground. His restraining hand relaxed, opened, and left my waist. A flat palm smoothed down my buttocks. I pushed my eager bottom back against him with an inviting wriggle. Gasped as his fingers slipped down my back crevice, lightly passing over a hole he shouldn't have touched and continuing forward, seeking and finding and sinking into my wetness with two big fingers. I groaned, panting, as I was stretched and opened. I felt his chest rumble against my back, a trembling vibration that passed through me and caused me to tighten around his thick fingers. Then they were gone, those stretching invaders, pulled out from me despite my body's greedy, grasping clutch.

"No!" I cried.

His teeth released me and he shifted, aligning his body behind me, both hands gripping my hips.

"Brace yourself," Amber grated. Then with one wild plunge, he crammed himself into me, pushing ruthlessly through my folds, forcing me to accept him. All of him. It was too much.

I screamed, bucking. His teeth clamped down on my shoulder, a sharp stinging bite, and again it was like a magic switch being thrown. I subsided beneath him, quivering, and he released my shoulder and pulled out of me at the same time.

"Take me," he muttered and plunged back in, sinking deep, cramming me full once more, making me cry out. Stunning me with a brilliant rainbow wash of sensation that was almost too much, so that I couldn't tell if it was pleasure or pain. Or both.

I moaned as he pulled out nearly all the way, a sucking, sliding sensation that washed another rough wave of incredible pleasure through me. I felt every last vein and ridge of his full shaft brush across my screamingly sensitive, quivering nerve endings on the way out. I felt like an accordion. But instead of air, I was being pumped and filled with pleasure. Explosive pleasure coming in. Hot devastating pleasure pulling back out.

Gathering himself, Amber speared into me again with a heavy grunt, with the full force of his hips and back behind the thrust, forcing a sharp stabbing pleasure on me that was almost beyond bearing.

"All of me," he grated hoarsely.

God, I was full. So full. So unbearably full.

"Take me, take me," he chanted, sliding out, surging back in. A fast desperate rhythm. Full force. No holding back. Pounding into me, making me cry out with twisting delight, making me writhe with exquisite agony. Light exploded from me, shining from within me. Shooting from us both. We glowed from deep within where the light of our mother moon dwelled within us. We were but vessels holding the shafting radiance sent down from the moon until its release. And it came spilling from us, flooding the dark night with dazzling brilliance, with incandescent joy.

Amber pulled back and plunged into me with pounding force, again and again, as fast as he could go, as if he would force himself out the other side of me. It was a steady, unthinking, forceful drive to the finish, naked of all restraint. An unvarnished taking.

One final, ramming thrust that drove deep, deep inside of me, farther than I knew it was possible to go, farther than I thought it possible that I could take or accommodate, and then I was screaming, coming in a violent, convulsive, seizing release that felt as if it would rip me apart as I pulsed and pulsed in blinding, agonizing ecstasy.

I felt Amber clench his teeth and groan harshly, gutturally, as he came, too, ejaculating in a series of great shuddering spurts that seemed to go on and on, flooding his hot seed within me as I clenched and quivered and shook about him. I sucked air into my lungs, shaking, still shimmering though the light was fading, giving a final sweet moan as I felt him pull his heavy length out of me. My arms gave out completely and I collapsed to the ground, unable to move, the cool earth pressed against my cheek.

I felt him fall heavily to lie beside me and listened to our panting breaths for a moment. Then Amber moved and rolled me onto my back. Braced on his elbow, he loomed over me, looked down at me, a little hesitant. His eyes were back to his normal aquamarine. His beast, his bloodlust, was gone. So was mine.

His body was whole, smooth. All the gashes and tears and claw marks were healed, even though I hadn't touched him with my hands. Those handy appendages had been buried in the dirt, too busy holding me up as he pounded into me. Apparently all I had needed was just skin-to-skin contact to heal him.

My shoulder twanged where he had sunk his teeth into me and bit me. He'd broken skin. I could smell my blood in the air, and it hadn't healed. Why? Was it because I hadn't wanted it to? Bite marks from a lover were a compliment. A form of highest praise among the Monère, a sign that you were a most sensuous, pleasing lover. Had I been able to control what healed and what didn't? I testingly moved my shoulder and winced.

"Are you all right?" Amber asked.

All right. What mild words. I laughed and winced again. "I think so."

"Did I hurt you?" A soft question.

"No." I shook my head, smiled. "Although you almost killed me . . . with pleasure."

He crouched between my legs and spread them, gazing intently at where we had merged. It was silly to feel shy after what we'd just done, but I couldn't help it. He was *looking* at me. *Down there.* I felt the force of his attention there almost like a palpable exam. My hands came down instinctively to cover myself.

"Amber . . ."

"Shhh. Let me see with my own eyes that I did not truly hurt you." With soft insistence he moved my hands away and I let him, squeezing my eyes shut, feeling him gently spread my swollen folds.

Just that careful touch sent sharp sensations zinging through my oversensitive nerves and I gave a little whimper. "Amber, please. Enough."

Something soft touched me between my legs, and I opened my eyes to see him lifting his head. He'd kissed me. His fingers released me and his eyes lifted to meet mine as he crouched between my legs. I froze, and the sharp awareness that I was a woman and he was a man, that my body was made to receive his, passed between us.

He shifted back to my side and pulled me into his arms, lifting me so that I sprawled on top of him, his heart thumping in slow steady beats against me, his large splayed hands caressing my back. Possessive fingers brushed over the bite mark at my shoulder.

"You used your full strength, didn't you? You never did

before," I murmured against his chest. He'd always been so careful with me, so very careful, slowly and diligently working himself in until his full length was rooted deep inside me, and then keeping to an easy, gentle rhythm.

I'd known he'd held back. I just hadn't known how much.

"I did not know before that your other form was a tiger. You are even larger than I am in my cougar form. Just as strong, if not stronger than me," Amber said, and he sounded pleased. "Your eyes had changed. Your beast had partially emerged, giving you some of its power. I knew you would be able to take my full strength. And just once I did not want to hold back."

He was so big, he no doubt had had to be careful his entire life, to always be in control. This was probably the first time in his life that he'd let himself fully go during sex, that he hadn't had to taper his great strength. And he was right. I had taken his full strength—and it had been an incredible amount—and I had survived it whole, unharmed. Of course, I hadn't thought I would during the time. But I had. And I was suddenly glad I'd been able to. How hard it must be, to have to control yourself always while your partner lost herself completely in her rapture. To have to always reign in your strength, never let it go. To never loosen your control. That was the true joy of sex—letting go of your every inhibition and casting free from your moorings completely, surrendering to the unthinking heat and feel of it. How hard that must have been—to get a taste of pleasure but never truly taste the full bounty just within reach.

"I'm glad," I said, sighing, running my hand over his damp chest, petting him. "I'm glad you took your pleasure fully. You returned it in much greater fold."

"Mona Lisa." He breathed my name and hugged me to him like something precious.

I knew that my eyes had changed back to their normal brown. That my beast was gone. "My eyes," I said. "What color were they?"

"Green," Amber answered. "Pale green."

I froze as I felt the beast within me stir, lift up its head, and look at me with pale, shimmering eyes. *Soon*, it promised. *I'll be free soon.* Closing its eyes, it returned to its slumber.

I shivered, goose bumps spreading over me as if a ghost had walked over my grave. Pushing myself up, I looked around for my dress and finding it, pulled it on.

"We should get back to the others." Not that I was eager to, with all those people back there. They would know what had transpired between us the moment they smelled us. That was the problem with such acute senses . . . you couldn't hide anything from them.

Amber donned his pants, held his big hand out to me. I took it.

Fingers intertwined, our scents intermingled, we headed back.

FIVE

A SHOWER WAS what I wanted. But it didn't look as if I would get it right away. The people—*my* people now—had cleared out of the house. Nice. Fewer eyes and noses to witness their new Queen's inglorious return. But the few witnesses there were—my little group, and among them, my young, impressionable brother—were bad enough. Horace, the little weaselly steward, hovered anxiously in the background, apart from the others.

"What is he still doing here?" I asked. My hostile tone widened Horace's little eyes.

"He was not sure if you wished him to show you the rest of the house," Gryphon said. "I told him that you would not be interested in a tour once you returned, but he insisted upon waiting. He said he did not wish to risk offending you."

More like he wanted to find out what had happened in the forest so that he could report this to his Queen. He was Mona Louisa's spy as far as I was concerned, soon to return to her. I did not want him here.

"Lord Gryphon is right, Steward Horace. No tour to-night. I'll see you tomorrow."

"Very well, milady." Horace bowed his head, his eyes flickering from Amber's healed chest to me and back.

"Aquila, if you will please drive Horace to where he is staying," Gryphon said, telling me two things. One, that Horace wasn't staying in the house. Good. The other was that Gryphon didn't trust him either or he wouldn't have bothered to have Aquila escort him off the premises. All the other Monère had apparently walked, flown or what-ever, back to their homes. So could have Horace.

The steward obediently followed Aquila out the door. Car doors opened and shut. An engine started and pulled away from the house.

"Are you injured?" Thaddeus asked softly.

My eyes softened when I looked at his young, concerned face. He was sixteen, but looked much younger, thin and lanky, several inches shorter than my five foot eight. "I'm fine. Amber took care of me. But we both need to shower. Does anyone know where our rooms are?"

"Your suite is on the second floor in the west wing," Gryphon said. "But before you ascend, could you first look in upon Dontaine?"

"Dontaine's here?" I said with surprise. I hadn't bothered scanning the house with Gryphon, Chami, and the others here. I knew they would have ensured that the house was se-cure.

Gryphon shrugged. "There are no other healers. The one healer they had departed with Mona Louisa."

I wanted to close my eyes and rub my temples to ease the headache I knew was coming my way. Jesus H. Christ. Over four hundred people, my people, and no healer other than me. I was a registered nurse, sure. And had recently tapped into my healing power, true. Problem was, my abil-ity was limited. Very limited. I could only heal by having sex with the person. And I refused to do that with every person that got hurt. Getting a healer would be a top priority. I wondered how one went about getting one. But until then, it looked as if I was it.

I sighed. "Show me."

"Let me see to the others first," Gryphon murmured. He conferred briefly with Rosemary about settling the others upstairs. "The north wing," he told her.

"Can we pick our own rooms?" Thaddeus asked eagerly, looking to Gryphon first, then to me. Jamie and even Tersa's eyes brightened with interest.

I shrugged when Gryphon glanced my way.

"It seems that you may," Gryphon said.

Thaddeus whooped with joy.

"I have first dibs," Jamie yelled, loping up the stairs.

"Whoever calls it first," Thaddeus shouted back.

There was a clattering as the children rushed up the steps en masse, Rosemary behind them. Tomas followed with an indulgent grin. Chami trailed behind them, shooting a troubled look my way. Amber remained down below with Gryphon and me.

"Dontaine is in the guest room downstairs," Gryphon said. He seemed to know his way. Good thing. One could easily get lost in this vast space. Or one could just follow the rapid whistling air.

I heard Dontaine before I saw him. And smelled him, or rather, smelled his blood. Dontaine lay on his side on a bed, blood staining the sheets, the carpet, even the walls nearby. His eyes were open, green gems darkened with pain and anxiety. He'd changed back to his human form, I saw to my relief. Much easier to bear than that monstrous Half Form I had braced myself for. He was just a man now, injured, alone, his chest laboring for that little bit of air that whistled through his open trachea.

In the hour that had passed, the torn flesh around his throat had already started to heal. Enough fleshy tissue had regenerated so that his spine no longer gleamed through like a macabre illustration of living anatomy. Lying on his side as he was, blood and other fluids dripped down onto the floor from his wound instead of pooling there and hindering his airflow, but still there was a gurgling quality to the breaths he took. A bloody wash of fluids splattered out in a wide bursting spray as Dontaine went into a coughing, choking fit.

I rushed to his side, not able to do much but hold onto his shoulders and support him until the body-shaking paroxysm passed.

"Why is no one with him?" I asked, my voice harsh.

"He is an injured male. Who would you have had me tend him?" Gryphon asked.

"Anyone. He's hardly dangerous the way he is."

"On the contrary," Gryphon corrected me. "He is even more dangerous in this condition. Weakened, feeling vulnerable."

"Surely his family, at least, could have stayed with him."

"Lady Margaret and Francine wished to. I did not allow it," Gryphon returned coolly. "They had the option of taking him or leaving him here for you. They elected to leave him."

"If he's so dangerous, why are you letting me tend him?"

"You, milady, he will not harm." But both he and Amber were watching Dontaine quite carefully.

I blew out an exasperated breath and concentrated on Dontaine. "God, I don't know what his family expects me to do for him. What *you* expect me to do for him. Not much I can, really. But we can at least start with basics. I need a basin of water, towels—lots of them—clean linen, and some clean pants for him."

No one moved.

"We cannot get infections," Amber said in his deep, rumbling voice.

"I know that." It took an effort not to shout, to keep my voice calm and reasonable. "But if nothing else, he will feel better once he is cleaned."

They just looked at me. I glared back at them.

"Oh, for heaven's sake." I blew out a breath, grabbed ahold of my patience, and said more softly, "Gryphon, please. You seem to know your way around the house best. Amber will stay with me and see that I am fine."

Gryphon lowered his eyes to Dontaine and the two of them locked gazes for a long moment, with only the wet whistling of air breaking the silence. Then Gryphon inclined his head. "As my lady wishes." He glided out of the room.

I spied an adjoining bathroom and found one small hand towel and two thick bath towels in there. There were no cups, but there was a decorative ceramic soap dish. I ran the hand towel under cool water in the sink, wrung it out, and carried everything into the other room.

Going around the bed, I approached Dontaine from the front where he could see me, mindful of his uneasy state of mind. He stared at me, watchful, his expression as bland as he could make it. That same blankness of expression that I had first seen in Amber's face when he had looked at his Queen, Mona Sera. It was a look that said *I'll take whatever punishment you mete out and not cry.* I hated that look.

"It's okay, I'm not going to hurt you," I softly reassured Dontaine. "I'm just going to wash the dirt and blood off you. I'll be as gentle as I can."

I sacrificed one fluffy towel, laying it over the bloody, wet floor by the edge of the bed. I positioned the soap dish to catch the blood trickling down from his throat, and knelt before him. Then hesitated, damp washcloth in hand.

Touching Dontaine when he'd been coughing and choking had been instinctive. Touching him now, as he looked up at me with his carefully blank eyes, was different, harder. I had never treated a patient that I had agreed to take to my bed before. The awareness of those spoken words was suddenly there between us, heavy in the air, the realization that we could have been sharing a bed even now. That I could have been covered with Dontaine's scent instead of Amber's. Of course, Dontaine had lost and I no longer had to sleep with him. But it was still very hard to bring myself to deliberately touch him as he watched me.

I brought the wet cloth gently to his face and brushed it over his forehead. At that first touch, Dontaine's eyes closed, and the tension gripping him eased, freeing me of my tension as well. He was relaxed and still as I smoothed the cool cloth over his cheek, down his jaw. His eyes opened, and I felt his gaze touching me as I wiped his shoulder, moved down his long arm, and cleaned each finger. He kept his gaze fixed upon me, the harsh sound of his breath whistling in and out of that hole in his throat as I gently washed him.

"I do have some healing ability," I said to Dontaine softly, apologetically, "but it's not something I have much control over." I felt those green eyes shift to Amber. Knew that he noted Amber's healed state. Knew that he could smell our commingled scents, and once more yearned for that shower. I felt his glance return to me, and felt the question hover in the air as if it had been asked aloud. *Why couldn't I heal him like I had healed Amber?*

I didn't bother to answer it.

"I'm sorry," I said instead. And I was. But he wasn't dying. He was healing miraculously fast on his own. I was not going to fuck him.

But the pain from his wounds . . . that I could do something about. Putting down the cloth, I laid one palm over the deep slash that began at his shoulder. My other palm came to rest where the wound ripped across his bicep. Amber's dagger had not been silver, so instead of gaping wide, the flesh had already pulled together, beginning to knit, fill in. Amazing.

Sometimes you forget how intimate touching someone really is. It requires closeness, your skin against theirs, feeling the softness of their flesh, the suppleness of their muscles, the little downy hairs covering the surface. It was even more intimate when they looked at you, and you looked at them. He was cooperating. I had no need to capture him with my eyes, hold him in my thrall. I doubted I even could; he wasn't human. I kept my eyes fixed instead on my hands.

A bare flexing of will, summoning a part of me that was always there, like my beast. But this power I welcomed, was unafraid of. And it came to my call, awakening from the core of me, flooding me with a cool rush beginning from my heart and spilling down my arms, into my hands. Those pearly moles, the Goddess's Tears, embedded in the hearts of my palms, tingled and heated. Like a knowing, living thing, the power seeped under Dontaine's skin, assessing the damage, and removing the pain.

When it was done, I lifted my hands, feeling his intent gaze hard upon me. Folding back the dirty washcloth to reveal a clean side, I began washing Dontaine's other arm, reaching across him. "I cannot heal you, but I can ease some of your pain," I said, my eyes on the washcloth as it moved over him.

I felt Dontaine's attention leave me, focus behind me, and when I turned, I saw that Gryphon had returned. He set the supplies he had brought on top of the bureau.

"Where's Amber?" I asked.

"He left."

"Why did he do that?"

"Dontaine will be able to rest easier if Amber is not here," Gryphon said, turning to pick up a basin he had brought. A natural move, but one that allowed him not to meet my eyes. Gryphon went into the bathroom, filled the basin with water, and set it by my side, his presence breaking the tense awareness between Dontaine and I. Gratefully, I rinsed the bloody cloth in the basin, wrung it dry, and began cleaning Dontaine's chest, moving the cloth carefully over the injured areas, pressing my warm, tingling palm over his wounds.

It wasn't until I reached Dontaine's abdomen that I grew uncomfortable once more. A distinct bulge had risen, impossible to ignore. He couldn't help it, I told myself. It was the natural reaction to being so close to a Queen, to being touched by her. But still . . . my hands fluttered and my eyes didn't seem to know where to look.

Gryphon didn't help when he murmured, "Let me help you remove his pants." He stepped forward.

Beneath my hand, Dontaine's relaxed muscles sprang alive, bunched and ready, almost vibrating with tension. His lips drew back in a silent snarl and his hands—powerful hands that had remained still and quiescent while I had cared for him—lifted, fingers curled like claws in clear warning.

Gryphon stilled and backed away slowly. "It seems that you must do so."

I wanted to say Dontaine actually didn't need to be changed, after all. But that would have been too cowardly and too obvious after I had made such an issue of cleaning him, and having Gryphon fetch clean clothes for him.

"Let me wash his back first," I said instead, grateful to move on to a less provocative area of his body. I rinsed the washcloth again in the basin, then hesitated. It didn't seem a good idea to move behind Dontaine where he would not be able to see me. Lifting up from my knees, I sat on the edge of the bed in the little vee of mattress space where Dontaine's stomach curved around. I had to lean in close, almost pressing against Dontaine's chest to reach his back. It was an awkward position, but it worked. I quickly, carefully, washed his back, skimmed my tingling palm over the gashes and stab wounds, and looked down to see how he was faring. A mistake. The heat in his eyes, the look on his face, had me shifting unconsciously back. Another mistake. Just that small movement and something hard and happy was pressed up against my hip. I'd forgotten how close to him I'd been. Almost sitting in his lap.

Dontaine's right hand slowly reached out. I watched it like a mesmerized rabbit watched a weaving cobra before it struck. Watched it come closer and closer until he finally touched me, his hand coming to rest fully, heavily on my hip, his fingers splayed. He was injured, weak. But his touch was not that of a patient thanking his nurse. His touch was questioning, questing, almost a claiming. Asking permission to move up . . . or down.

I drew in a sharp breath and my eyes shot to his, held his, as my left hand slowly came up to cover his hand and to remove it from me. I slid off the mattress, back down to my knees, and put that dangerous, roaming hand gently on the space I had just vacated.

Forget being obvious or cowardly. No way was I taking off his pants.

I cleared my throat. "His pants are fine. I'm . . . uh, just going to change his sheets." Mentally I cringed when my voice came out lower and huskier than usual.

"Are you sure?" Gryphon asked. It sounded like he was smiling at me but I didn't look up to see if he truly was.

I nodded, not looking at either of them. Men. Nothing but trouble. Even when you were trying to help them.

I gathered the clean linen Gryphon had brought in. "Dontaine, I'm going to go behind you now to loosen and roll up the bed sheet."

Again that silent warning snarl.

"All right. Maybe not," I said, trying to work out the logistics in my mind. "Then I'm going to have to kneel on the mattress in front of you and bend over you to loosen the dirty sheet and secure the clean sheet."

No snarl. Apparently that was fine with him. Dontaine scooted back to make more room for me, a clear invitation.

"I'll roll both the dirty sheet and the clean sheet behind you. You'll have to lift yourself up, and I'll roll them both underneath you to this side." Staring hard at him, I said, "No hanky-panky while I do this."

Dontaine's teeth flashed in a wolfish grin. Obviously he was feeling better. His breathing still whistled, but it was easier, less desperate. And I wasn't sure, but I think the

wound in his throat had filled in even more. If I stared and
kept my eyes fixed on it, I wouldn't see the healing. But
look away and then look back minutes later, and you could
see a small difference. It was like a flower slowly unfurl-
ing. The minute actions themselves were invisible. But you
could note the progress.

I knelt in front of him, my weight sinking into the mattress so that Dontaine rolled against me. But he was behav-
ing himself. He kept his hands off me. I leaned over him,
tugged the sheet loose, rolled it up, and secured the new
sheet as best as I could, all the while sharply aware of Dontaine's bare skin, his bare body, pressed up against my
legs. "Lift up," I said. He did, shifting easily. I eased off
the mattress, and rolled the bundle beneath him, stripping
off the stained sheet and tucking in the new one. "There.
All done," I said, stepping back.

"Are you?" Gryphon murmured.

"Yes, this is as much as I can do for him. I can't heal
him."

"Can you not?"

I turned and stared hard at Gryphon. "Not without fucking him." And my tone clearly said I was not going to do
that.

"How do you know?" Gryphon asked.

Actually, it was a good question.

"Healing power is within you," Gryphon said.

"You mean, just touch him and try to heal him?"

"That is the way other healers do so. Have you never
tried to before?"

I shook my head. Not since tapping into my new healing power. I had failed in the past and presumed it would be
the same now.

"Why not try now?" Gryphon asked, oh so reasonably.

"Why not, indeed?" It would be a wonderful ability to
have, to be able to heal someone without having to get naked
and intimate with the person I wanted to heal. My thoughts

flew sadly to Beldar, my mother's warrior, the last man I had healed. Though I had not taken him into my body, I had been intimate with him. And it had hurt something within me to have known him so, and not be able to claim him. To have to give him back.

"All right," I said, making up my mind. "Let's give it a try after I finish up here first." I emptied the bloody contents of the soap dish into the basin of water, dumped the dirty water in the sink, and returned to place the empty basin beneath Dontaine by the edge of the bed to catch any dripping blood. On my hands and knees, I used the dirty sheets to mop up the rest of the floor. I looked up to see both of them staring at me.

"What?" I asked.

"It is . . . most unusual to see a Queen cleaning the floor," Gryphon replied, his eyes wide and surprised.

I shrugged. "Someone has to. I do toilets and bathtubs as well."

"A woman of many talents," Gryphon murmured huskily. With but the tiniest inflection and a look in those crystal blue eyes, a picture of soft sheets, bare skin, tangled limbs, and heated sighs filled your mind, enveloping you in sensuality. That was Gryphon's talent, his power.

"Getting me in the mood before the laying on of hands?" I asked, my voice trembling slightly.

"It cannot hurt."

"It worked. I'm more than ready."

"Are you?" Gryphon asked.

I nodded, tore my eyes away from Gryphon, and walked to Dontaine, deliberately laying both of my hands on him. One on his chest, one on his shoulder, covering two wounds. Concentrating, I called up that power within me once again. It came, spilling down my hands in an effortless shimmer, a tingling force. I let it sink down into the torn flesh of his shoulder, trail down to the very base of his injuries. And as the power seeped through him, I thought of his skin whole, unblemished. Closing my eyes, I pictured it in my mind, torn flesh knitting together. *Heal!* I thought. *Heal.*

My palms tingled, heated. And then stopped.

I opened my eyes and looked down. His wounds were still there. I made a soft sound of disappointment and let my hands drop away. "I can't do it."

"Let me help you," Gryphon said. Slowly he eased up behind me. Dontaine watched him with wary green eyes but did nothing else.

"Sex opens you to your healing power," Gryphon murmured softly. "Use that. Open yourself to it, do not try to shut it out. Touch him." He guided my hands back to Dontaine.

"Stroke his chest. Feel his skin, how soft it is." Gryphon's voice was like a delicate purr in my ear, as tantalizing as the supple flesh beneath my hands.

"You are aware of him, of his body. Do not fight it. Let it wash over you. Smell his scent, his body's musk as it readies itself for you." Gryphon guided my hands lower to brush over the tense ridges of Dontaine's abdomen. Then even lower until I brushed over the thick bulge of his arousal.

For one second, I was tempted to linger over Dontaine, to trace the dimensions of that lovely erection. To squeeze him and feel the fullness and heaviness of him in my hand. Dimly, I realized that wasn't normal. That wasn't me. And that realization was enough to break the spell and jerk me back, breathing heavily.

I backed away from both of them, my eyes wide on Gryphon's face with startled comprehension. "You're seducing me for him. You sent Amber from this room deliberately with this purpose in mind. You *want* me to sleep with Dontaine. Why?"

Gryphon didn't even bother to try to deny it. "He has a great gift," he said with simple reason.

"And that is reason enough to throw me to his bed?"

"Do you remember what you made me swear when I was dying? When I had resigned myself to death?" Gryphon asked me in a low tone. "You made me promise to fight, to live so that I can serve you."

Gryphon spread his hands open in a speaking gesture. "I am serving you. We have enemies. They will not stop coming after you. And Dontaine has a rare ability, a great gift. If he passes it to you, you will be even stronger, even harder to kill."

"You *know* how hard it is for me to face my beast," I whispered. "That change . . . a Half Form like that . . . the possibility that I could become something monstrous like that . . ." I laughed harshly. "Oh, Gryphon, you do not know me well. That is the strongest argument to keep me from Dontaine's bed."

I shook my head, backing away. "I will never sleep with him. Ever."

Whirling, I ran from the room.

Six

I**T WAS TIMES** like this when I realized how different we were. No matter how much I loved Gryphon, and he loved me, we were different. I was part human, and I clung to my humanity with both hands, wrapping it around me like a comfortable, familiar blanket in this new and frightening world. I kept expecting Gryphon to be more human, and Gryphon kept expecting me to be more Monère.

I found my room by opening my senses until I could hear Thaddeus, Jamie, and Tersa, faster heartbeats than the others. I veered left from them toward the west wing. There were two other doors in that wing, across from each other, but I was guessing my room was the one at the very end. The big-ass room was larger than my entire apartment had been back in Manhattan. Airy, spacious, opulent like the rest of the house, with its own sitting room. High ceiling, big bed with red silk sheets, and plush carpeting were my fast impressions as I swung into the bathroom connected by an open archway. The bathroom was just as big as my living room had been.

I stripped off the gown, left it on the floor, and stepped into the lavish shower. It was more spacious than a bathtub even, with clear walls and door. Didn't matter. No one to see me. More important to turn on the shower, step under it, and let the tears finally flow. Cool water ran and I cried silently, letting the water wash over me, rinsing off the dirt and blood, wishing it was that easy to rinse away the hurt and pain I felt.

We are not humans, Gryphon had told me. Even after all they had done, all I had seen them do, all I had done, unbelievable non-human things . . . still I hadn't really understood him until he did something like this. Want me to sleep with another man just to possibly acquire his gift.

It hurt.

I didn't understand how Gryphon could do that. Not just be passively okay with it but actively try to seduce me into it because he had known it was not something I would have done myself.

I am serving you, Gryphon had said. The sad thing was that he honestly believed that. It was a time-honored Monèrian Queen tradition. Sleeping with men, then casting them aside when they became too powerful. And the men slept with their Queens because they were drawn to them, and because they wished to acquire more power to survive, to advance. A dangerous tightrope that many of them fell off of. Because what did Queens do to men who became too powerful for them to control? They killed them. Another time-honored Monèrian Queen tradition. Like a black widow spider, killing the males she mated with.

I am serving you.

Gryphon was keeping to the promise to which I had made him swear when I was afraid of losing him after I had only just found him. A promise I had selfishly wrenched from him because I did not want to be alone again. I'd made him promise to fight to live. He was fulfilling that promise.

Only . . . oh, baby, serve me another way. Not like this. Not like this.

When I was clean, when the tears finally stopped and my breathing finally evened, I turned off the water and toweled off. Big fluffy towels to go with the big fluffy room. I was alone and thankful for it.

I'd been alone all my life. Physically, the last three years. Emotionally, almost all my life. Ever since Helen, the human mother who had adopted me and loved me as her own, died when I was six and I entered my first foster home. In the long years that followed, I'd grown used to that solitude. The last couple of weeks, I'd gone from just taking care of myself, to taking care of nine others. And now finding I had to expand that to over four hundred more. God! The pressure, the responsibility, was almost smothering. Deliberately, I slowed my breathing. Wouldn't do to hyperventilate.

I felt dawn like a gentle promise, advancing slowly, inexorably. Pressing against the horizon, creeping ever closer. Someone had unpacked everything and put all my stuff away. I fumbled through the drawers until I found the big T-shirt I slept in. Old, worn, comfortable, and familiar. I had a sudden sharp need for things comfortable and familiar. With the soft cotton pressed against my skin like a faithful friend, I crawled between the sheets, tired and heartsore, and welcomed the unthinking bliss of sleep.

～⚬～

A WOLF HOWLED at the crack of dawn. Not a rooster. A rooster would have been preferred. Nasty though it would have been, a *cock-a-doodle-do* wouldn't have shot me out of bed with the hair on the back of my neck standing on end.

It came again, a long, jarring mournful howl.

Shit!

I threw open a couple of drawers—didn't know where

everything was. I finally found a pair of jeans, slid into them and into my shoes in almost one continuous motion, and ran out the door. Other doors opened. I met Gryphon and Amber, still dressed, at the end of the corridor. I caught a glimpse of Chami, Tomas, and Thaddeus, who looked as if they had thrown on clothes as quickly as I had.

Down the corridor, Tersa poked her tousled head out. "What is that?"

"Good question," I said, looking at Gryphon. "Is that Dontaine?"

"No." There was an odd look on Gryphon's face, almost as if he knew what it was but didn't wish to tell me.

Another eerie howl floated up the stairs. I ran after it, chasing it like an ethereal specter down the spiraling steps, the others behind me.

"Wait," Amber called out behind me. "Let us go first."

I ignored him, bypassing the last twenty steps by leaping over the carved wooden balustrade and landing lightly on my feet. I dashed down the hallway, opening my senses. There. I passed through the kitchen, the laundry room, and came to a closed door. A sniffling sound came from behind it, and a heartbeat. Not a slow, slow one like Amber's or Gryphon's, whose hearts beat no more than thirty times a minute. A moderately slow one like mine, like Thaddeus's. Fifty beats per minute. And it wasn't fur I smelled. Not an animal. A human.

The door was locked.

"Open the door," I said softly to whoever was behind it.

The sniffling stopped, but the door remained locked. The rest of the gang came pounding up behind me.

"No, do not open it, Mona Lisa," Gryphon said.

For some reason, I did not want to listen to Gryphon tonight. In fact, I felt a strong urge to kick open the damn door just because he'd told me not to. And looking at me, I think Gryphon somehow knew what I was feeling. He held up a ring of keys.

"Open it," I said flatly and stepped aside. See, reasonable. It wasn't smart to ruin one's own property if you didn't need to.

Gryphon inserted a key. He knew exactly which one, I noted. He opened the door and I stepped inside. I didn't need lights to see in the dark. We were creatures of the night. Darkness was our home. I saw as clearly as if sunlight had flooded the room.

A boy was locked up, shackled in silver manacles against the wall. I could tell it was a boy because he was shirtless. All he wore was a pair of ragged pants that made Dontaine's ruined pair look pristine. Dirt, mud, stains, and bruises covered him. His hair was long and matted, hanging about his face in dreadlocks. Not a fashion statement but the real thing caused by dirt and tangled, unwashed hair. The boy's eyes gleamed like shiny wild things from behind his straggles of hair. Yellow teeth were bared and a growl rumbled from his throat.

He was Thaddeus's height but so different from my brother. Thaddeus had the thinness, the lankiness of a young boy about to sprout. This poor creature's thinness was the thinness of hunger, of starvation. His rib bones pushed out, while the skin covering them seemed to be trying to suck them back in, dipping so painfully inward into a belly that wasn't just flat and hollow, it was concave. But he was strong. Every bit of flesh he had was lean, developed muscle. The wiry strength of his body, even more than his clothing, and his hair, bespoke his wild state. He looked to be even younger than Thaddeus. Fourteen, maybe. And he'd been crying, alone in the dark.

"He's a Mixed Breed," I said. My senses told me that. And not just half. More. Possibly three-quarters of his blood was Monère. Like me. Like Thaddeus.

Someone flipped the switch and fluorescent light lit the room.

A sharp gasp. Then Tersa whispered, "Oh, dear Goddess."

I kept my attention fixed on the boy. "Can you understand me?" I asked softly.

No reply. Just that warning rumble.

"It's okay. We're not going to hurt you," I soothed.

When I turned to Gryphon, my voice wasn't as gentle. "What the fuck is this?"

Gryphon had on his impassive face, the one that told you nothing. "A present Mona Louisa left behind."

"How long has he been here, locked up like this?"

"Horace did not say," Gryphon said quietly.

"Two days." It was Dontaine's raspy voice. He'd pushed through or maybe everyone had just stepped back and let him through. He'd healed enough to close his windpipe but not cover it. The little bones and cartilage of his trachea were clearly visible, moving as he talked. He didn't drip blood, but it glistened there. Wet meat. "He existed in the bayou. She had him captured two days ago. Left him for you."

No need to ask why. The message was clear. *This is what Mixed Bloods are to us.*

"Was he causing trouble?" I asked.

Dontaine shook his head slightly, making the loose flesh move around his trachea. It was even worse than watching him talk.

"He is a wild thing," Dontaine said.

"I kinda got that when he howled," I said.

"Grew up in the swamps. But no, he was not killing cattle or raiding human livestock."

"Would they have killed him if he was?" I asked.

"Yes."

I didn't want to ask, to know, if they had killed others like this boy. Nothing here to take my rage out on if they had. Mona Louisa was gone. Although maybe the boy's mother was still here.

"One of the women here had him." I said it as a fact, not a question.

"Sweet Mother, is that what you do with Mixed Breed children here? Leave them in the swamps?" It was Rosemary who voiced that angry question. Rosemary, a Monère woman who had loved and raised her Mixed Blood children, keeping them with her instead of abandoning them to the humans. Or abandoning them in the swamp. Jesus.

"Some women. Not all," Dontaine replied. "Mona Louisa did not care what they did with them."

"God," I whispered. I turned to Gryphon. "You knew he was here. And you left him here. Like this."

"I would have told you, after Dontaine. But you were upset. I thought that you had been through enough already tonight."

"Not upset enough to leave this boy here like this." Gryphon knew my body intimately, but I wondered if he knew me at all. "Release him. Where's the key?"

Gryphon shifted along the ring until he came to a smaller key, shorter than the rest. "If you will leave, I will free him."

"No fucking way."

He sighed, a faint sound of anger, of unhappiness. But he wasn't the only one angry and unhappy here.

"It will be easier for the boy with less people here," he said.

I had to agree with Gryphon about that. I turned around and scanned the faces present. Amber was too big, too intimidating. Of all the men there, slender Chami looked the least threatening. Funny how deceptive looks can be.

"Chami, you stay. Everyone else leave."

"Mona Lisa . . ." Amber said.

Even quiet Tomas was protesting. "I don't think that's—"

I held up my hand. "I'm staying. A woman will be less threatening to him. Everyone else out, now. That's an order."

Obedience to a Queen was deeply ingrained, it seemed. They shut their mouths and left.

I turned to Gryphon. "You, too."

Something indecipherable rippled across that cool mask

of his for a fleeting moment. Silently, he pushed the key into my hand and left. And the ache in my chest grew heavier.

"No killing, Chami. Just restrain him if you need to. But don't hurt him."

Chami nodded his understanding.

The door opened and Tersa slipped in. Her eyes glistened and her face was damp, as if she'd brushed away tears. Quiet, gentle Tersa no longer looked so gentle. Her eyes shone fiercely and she looked like she wanted to strangle someone—a heartless pure blood mother, perhaps. "Let me help."

"No," I told Tersa softly.

"I am the smallest. The least threatening."

Tersa was even smaller than the boy. And so much more delicate that the thought of letting her anywhere near him chased my heart into my throat to beat there like a trapped, frightened thing. "No."

Tersa looked at me. Tersa, a girl who had hardly spoken aloud since she had been raped. A girl who had been careful to avoid close proximity to any man other than her brother.

"He's like us. He could have been me or Jamie," she said. "See, he's stopped growling. He's looking at me curiously."

I turned and saw that what she said was true. The boy was sniffing the air, his nostrils flared, his eyes intently focused on a person even smaller than himself. Intent and curious, as if she was an unknown entity. A girl.

"Please," Tersa said, "let me try."

It was the hardest thing to put that key in her hand. "If I say stop, you stop, and back up slowly from Wild Boy, here. Understand?"

Tersa nodded. But it was an absentminded gesture, as if her attention were already focused on the boy she approached with care. "I'm Tersa. Tersa," she repeated, putting a hand on her chest, indicating her person. "I'm going to free you from those nasty chains. I won't hurt you," she murmured, coming close to him.

He was staring at her intently, his eyes an unusual light gray, almost silvery in color—keen pale eyes peeking through a tangle of hair. His nostrils flared wide like a wild animal scenting for danger.

Tersa was close enough now so that all it would take would be one lunge forward and he could rip into her with his teeth. I wanted badly to snatch her back to safety. But any sudden movement now might trigger the very violence I wanted to avoid. It was hard, so hard just to stand there and let her put herself in danger like that.

She talked to him like he understood her, her voice a constant soothing murmur telling him she wanted to help him, that all of us wanted to help, as she inserted the key. It didn't matter what she said, what the actual words were. The tone, the gentle way she said it was the real message. *I'm not going to hurt you. I want to help you.*

Slowly, carefully, gently, Tersa freed him from the first manacle, opening it and sliding it off. The loud sound of heavy metal clunking as it fell back against the wall was jarring in the tenseness. The boy shot Chami and me a quick piercing glance, assuring himself that we were still far enough away from him, that we hadn't moved, then returned his attention back to Tersa. He watched her as she crossed in front of him over to the other side and opened his other manacle. It clanked with a heavy thud against the wall, and he was free. His body was tense, quivering, ready to spring away. But he didn't move, even though his body clearly wanted to. He just stood there looking at Tersa, less than a foot between them, his head tilted just the slightest bit, as if the soft lilting words were as fascinating to him as the smallness of her person.

"I'm going to give you my hand," Tersa said in her soft, soothing murmur, like water flowing gently down a stream. Slowly, she lifted one hand, held it out to him. "Take my hand and we'll leave this room. We'll leave this horrible place. Walk right out of here together."

Moving as slowly as she had, the boy crouched down and brought his face closer to that small outstretched hand, sniffing it, inhaling Tersa's scent. She stood completely still as he edged closer. Her gentle flow of words dried up and stopped as he brought his face close to her arms, sniffed, and moved to her chest, her stomach, down the skirt of the dress she wore.

Tersa took a deep breath in, let it out. Held still under his keen inspection of her. Finally, he was done, moving back a little.

"See, harmless," Tersa said softly. She reached her hand once more out to him. "Give me your hand." She tapped her open palm twice as she said the word *hand* and pointed to his hand. She had his full attention, at least, if not his comprehension. I held my breath as Tersa slowly reached out that short distance and touched his hand. He quivered but otherwise didn't move as Tersa gently took his hand in hers.

"See, it doesn't hurt," she murmured and smiled for the very first time. It transformed her face into something beautiful and the boy gazed at her, mesmerized.

She took a little step toward the door and tugged on his hand. "Come on. Let's get out of here." He took a little step as well, allowing her to pull him forward.

"I'm going to open the door," I said quietly. "Chami, go on out. I'll follow you."

Chami didn't argue with me, good man. The door closed behind us then opened a moment later. Tersa came out leading the cautious, tense Wild Boy by the hand. His eyes darted around, taking everything in. His nostrils flared.

The delicious aroma of cooking meat filled the hallway, like an invisible beckoning hand. I sent a silent thanks to wonderful, smart, kindhearted Rosemary as we followed the scent out to the kitchen. Rosemary had cleared out the rest of the people so that the kitchen was empty but for her.

"It's a bit on the raw side, but I don't think he'll mind," Rosemary said, setting down a plate of steak on the round kitchen table. A glass of water and cutlery sat neatly on the side, a butter knife instead of the usual sharp steak knife, thank you, God.

Tersa led Wild Boy to the table, taking an empty seat. His eyes flickering from the meat to us, he sank hesitantly into the chair next to her. Chami, Rosemary, and I stayed back, giving them plenty of space.

"Go ahead," Tersa said, gesturing to the food. "Eat."

He lowered his head, sniffed it curiously, and sat back up. He didn't touch it, though he was obviously starved.

"Tersa," I said. "Cut a small piece for yourself. Chew and swallow it. Show him that it's safe to eat."

Wild Boy watched intently as Tersa used the knife and fork to cut off a tiny portion. "See," she said, after swallowing it. "Delicious."

He didn't bother with the fork and knife. He just picked up the meat with both hands and took a huge tearing bite out of it, wary eyes fixed on us as he chewed hungrily. He gulped it down, barely taking time to chew, like a wild animal afraid that its food could be taken away from him at any moment.

Rosemary took a deep breath and I saw the shine of tears in her eyes.

Tersa picked up the glass of water, took a drink, and held it out to him. "Water."

Awkwardly, he cupped the glass in his greasy hands, sniffed, and cautiously tipped the glass into his mouth, tasted, and swallowed. Satisfied it was nothing but water, he opened wide and poured the contents down his throat. Part of it trickled down his chin. It was heartbreakingly obvious everything was new to him, including cooked meat.

"Should I make him more food?" Rosemary asked, speaking softly.

"No," I answered. "Too much food and he might throw up. That's enough for now. Let it settle in his stomach."

"Then if he's all through eating, a bath is what he should be having next," Rosemary declared.

Tersa nodded in vehement agreement with her mother. "Absolutely."

The idea of trying to give Wild Boy here a bath boggled my mind. Although, with Tersa, he'd been remarkably cooperative so far. Well, can't tell unless you try.

We ended up using Dontaine's bathroom, the closest to us. The smell of blood in the room, on the mattress, along the walls, brought all of Wild Boy's senses quivering to the fore. He growled deep in his throat at the sight of Dontaine and watched carefully as the taller man slowly circled wide around him and left, ceding the room to us.

My presence and Chami's didn't seem to bother him. He seemed willing to tolerate us. But Tersa was the only one he allowed close to him, warning us off with a low growl if we ventured too close.

Rosemary left to rustle up some clothing. "And towels," I told her. "Lots and lots of towels." I ran the water in the tub, tepid temperature, reasoning that it would be what was most familiar to him. Hot water against his skin for the first time in his life was something I'd leave for a later adventure.

The sound of running water drew the boy to the bathroom and he looked about the room in fascination. Unfortunately, the tub filled all too quickly. Now we were left with the hardest part, the quandary of how to get Wild Boy into the tub without him going ballistic on us.

"Any ideas?" I said to Tersa.

She shrugged. "I'll get into the tub first to show him what to do, like with eating." Kicking off her shoes, she stepped, dress and all, into the tub and sat down. Her skirt billowed up in front of her like a wet balloon. She pushed it down until all the material was submerged.

"Water," she said, swirling her hand in the tub. I passed her a washcloth and she dipped it into the water, lathered it up with soap, and starting scrubbing her hands. "Wash."

Wild Boy watched her with fascinated intent. His eyes narrowed, then grew round as Tersa lay back, submerging her hair. Sitting back up, she poured shampoo into her hand and proceeded to lather up her long mane.

"Wash hair," she said. Leaning back, she submersed her hair once more, keeping her face above the water. Sitting up, she squeezed the water out of her long tresses. I passed her a towel, and she stepped out of the tub. Water splashed and dripped down, making a total mess of the floor. No help for it.

"Your turn," Tersa said, pointing her hand at him. "Wash." She took his hand and led him, if not eagerly, then at least unresistingly to the tub. The bathroom was big enough so that I could keep a good distance away. The tub, thankfully, was also positioned so that he had a good visual of the bathroom and the bedroom beyond where Chami had stayed.

Wild Boy stepped into the tub and sat down. Voilà. Mission accomplished with hardly a splash. He was an intelligent creature and we had shown him what we wanted him to do.

Tersa knelt down at the side of the tub, facing him, and started to soap up the washcloth. She started with his hands. Dip, rinse, and his hands came out of the water clean, his tanned skin looking almost startling white against the rest of his unwashed self. He looked at his cleaned skin with as much shock and absorption as we did.

The water was already a swirling brown. By the time Tersa had scrubbed his chest, back, and legs, it was a muddy dark chocolate. He seemed fascinated with the slippery soap, playing with it as she washed him down.

"Wash hair," Tersa said, pointing to the top of his head. She pantomimed laying her head back. Wild Boy let the soap slip from his hands into the water. With a quick checking glance around the room, pinpointing our locations—we hadn't moved—he focused his eyes back on Tersa, and in an act requiring so much trust on his part, he leaned back until his hair was beneath the water, leaving his throat open and vulnerable. With a surge he sat back up, splashing water on Tersa. She gave a startled little shriek and laughed. She actually laughed. It was a happy sound and he smiled at her. She smiled back.

Shampooing his hair was the hardest part. Tersa ended up using almost half the bottle, making him dip back down several times to rinse.

"I wish we could use conditioner," Tersa murmured, "and rinse him off with clean water." The tub was the consistency of muddy soup by now.

"Next time," I said, handing her an armful of towels that Rosemary had brought in, and a clean shirt and pants that I recognized as Thaddeus's. Wild Boy watched my approach and retreat with alert eyes but no growl.

"We've pushed our luck and his patience enough," I murmured. "Let's dry him off."

Getting him dressed was another pantomime play. Once he understood that Tersa wanted him to take off his pants, he dropped them without a shred of modesty. Tersa calmly averted her eyes and handed him first the jeans, and then the oxford shirt. The latter she had to help button up when he didn't seem familiar with the process. A brilliant choice, that shirt. His sight was never blocked as it would have been had they pulled a T-shirt over his head. And no underwear or socks. Just the two basic articles of clothing.

We left his hair to dry naturally. The whine of a blowdryer would have been beyond bearing for all our nerves, I think.

The hard part actually came when Tersa moved to change out of her wet dress. Rosemary had brought her a change of clothes, leaving them on the bed. Chami stepped outside to give her privacy. Wild Boy, though, didn't like it when Tersa tried to shut the bathroom door, closing him in. He growled and pushed the door open. Neither did he like it when Tersa stepped into the bathroom herself and started to close the door, leaving him out in the bedroom. Another warning growl. We finally ended up with me holding two towels in front of her while she changed, leaving the discarded dress a sopping heap on the floor. I scooped up the dripping bundle and stuck it in the bathtub, wiped the soaked bathroom tiled floor with the damp towels, and left everything in the bathtub for someone else to clean up later.

"What now?" Tersa asked, blinking sleepy eyes. Dawn had risen an hour ago and the sun was a low ball in the sky. No way of seeing it: The inside shutters had been closed over the windows and thick black-lined velvet curtains were drawn over them. But I could feel it with sharp awareness with a knowing part of me.

A Mixed Blood, Tersa wasn't affected by the sun as the others were, their bodies growing weary and leaden, sleep pressing like a heavy blanket upon them. When she yawned, it was simply because her body had adjusted to the cycle. Awake at night. Asleep during the day. Now it was time to sleep.

I gestured to the bed. "Think he'll sleep here?"

"Not alone," she replied.

It was hard to think. Like her, my body had become accustomed to the nightly hours we kept. And it had been a long night for me. For all of us. I forced my sluggish mind to think. I didn't like leaving Tersa alone with Wild Boy.

Should I have Chami stay down here with them? No, scratch that. Accustomed though Wild Boy seemed to him, Tersa wouldn't be comfortable sleeping in the other man's presence. That left me. But after all I'd been through tonight, I needed some time alone to think, to shore up my battered heart, to push back my fears and hurt.

Rosemary saved me by poking her head through the door. "I'll stay here with them, milady."

I nodded. As I stumbled out of the room, Rosemary slipped in, the door closing softly behind her. Chami stood up from where he'd been sitting with his back against the wall. He moved without his usual grace and quickness, the only visible sign that he was feeling the soporific effects of the sun.

"Where's Dontaine?" I asked.

"I sent him upstairs. He's bunking with me tonight."

"Good choice." Dontaine may have been wounded, but he was healing fast. He was a stranger and powerful. Formerly Mona Louisa's, maybe still hers. Chami would keep an eye on him.

"Thanks, Chami, for everything tonight." I trudged down the hallway, heading, I hoped, for the spiral staircase that would lead me to my bedroom. "You were great."

"You thank me?"

Something in his voice made me stop and turn around.

Chami wore an almost incredulous look. "When I failed you?"

I frowned. "You were perfect with Wild Boy there. Quiet, non-threatening."

He gave a low, harsh laugh. "I did nothing."

"Doing nothing was exactly what I needed you to do. How do you see that as failing me?"

"I did not help you stop Dontaine from fighting Amber when you asked me for my aid."

Ah. The challenge. It seemed so long ago now. I'd forgotten about it. Chami obviously hadn't. I sighed, gathered my wits about me. "That was my fault. I should not have asked you."

Chami flinched as if I'd struck him.

"I meant that I should have known better. Killing is what you do best, and I did not want Dontaine killed."

"Yes, killing is what I do best," Chami confirmed quietly, his lean face inscrutable. *Chameleon.* He was still: Not the way humans are still, but completely immobile in the way reptiles are. Utterly. So that you aren't sure for a moment if they are real, living and breathing, or just a stuffed replica.

"I used to hate doing that," he said, speaking softly, without passion, without inflection. "Ending someone's life without any warning, without any chance. Whether they deserved to die or not. Very uneven odds with my ability to remain unseen. Few detected me. Sliding my knife into them was so easy that it felt like I was cheating. I used to hate it when other Queens prized me for that talent, and expected me to serve them in that manner." He gave a humorless laugh. "I didn't know how I had grown to depend upon that skill until I failed you. Twice now."

"Are we back to Kadeen again?" Kadeen had been the demon dead who had snatched me. "You and Amber almost died trying to stop him. You did not fail me. If anyone failed, it was me. I failed to protect you."

"It is not a Queen's duty—"

"It's a Queen's duty to care for her men."

"Not by physically fighting."

"Why not?"

"That is not what we expect of our Queens," Chami said gently.

"Chami," I said, equally gently, "in case you haven't noticed, I'm not like other Queens."

He laughed. A real laugh this time. "I could not fail to notice that."

I smiled, feeling a small glow of pleasure. Each rare laugh from my men felt like winning a prize. "You served me well just now, being there in case I needed you. But not being in the way. You serve me well by being a mentor to the younger ones, by teaching them how to use a dagger, how to protect themselves. By distracting them from me when you see that I'm uncomfortable. By being thoughtful." I cupped his lean cheek tenderly. "You don't have to kill anyone to serve me, Chami. You can serve me best by looking after my brother, keeping him safe."

His hand came up to cover mine, press it against his face. "That I can vow to do with all my heart. Thaddeus is very special to us all."

"Thank you. You have a wonderful way with the kids, you know. They look up to you." Only because my hand was against his skin did I feel the slight warmth. I lowered my hand to see if what I suspected was true.

"Chami, are you blushing?"

He didn't seem to know what to say. I took pity on the poor fellow. "Now, if you really, really want to serve me, you can help me find my way to that damn staircase so I can climb up to my room and crawl into bed."

"As my lady wishes."

We found the staircase and he headed off to his room while I headed in the opposite direction toward mine. But when I rounded the corridor, I knew that sweet blissful sleep was still a ways off. Gryphon sat in front of my door. Obviously waiting for me. Obviously wanting to talk to me.

"May I speak with you?" he asked.

Sometimes I hate being right.

My footsteps grew even heavier. Wanting to talk to your lover first without wanting to jump her bones was never a good sign. My heart pounded with dread, with what I feared most. He was going to leave me.

Gryphon rose to his feet as I nodded. Without a word, I opened my door, walked in, and felt him enter behind me, a soft presence. A sitting room next to one's bedroom was a good idea, actually. I sat on the plush sofa. Gryphon took a seat across from me, not next to me. Another bad, bad sign.

Unconsciously, I rubbed my chest, trying to ease the achy feeling there beneath my breastbone as I looked at Gryphon. My first love. He was as beautiful to me now as when I had first seen him—the ebony black fall of his hair

like a shiny cascade of darkness about him. The pearl
white glow of his skin like flawless porcelain. His hauntingly lovely eyes, crystal blue and clear. That beautiful, full
lush mouth, red like a river of passion, as tempting as Eve's
apple. The first time we'd met, the moment my eyes had
fallen upon him, something elemental inside of me had
recognized him—mate—and had reached out to him.

"You no longer desire me," Gryphon said, breaking the
silence.

I let my hand drop from my chest when I became aware
that I was rubbing it. "No, I desire you still. I will always
desire you."

His lovely eyes were sad, so sad, a liquid pool of unhappiness. "You say that and yet you sit there, far apart from
me. You cannot bear to touch me after I told you what I had
been."

I was suddenly confused. He'd been the one to sit apart
from me. Hadn't he? "What are you talking about?"

"You are angry with me. Disgusted with me tonight, after I told you how others had used me."

"I was angry with you because you put my hand on another man's groin."

He shook his head, eyes downcast. "You say that is the
reason, but that is not the true reason." And incredibly, he
seemed to believe that.

"Gryphon, what you did before, what others did to you,
does not matter to me. It's you, us now, that matters. I'm
angry with you because you threw me at another man. Because you left a poor boy alone, shackled like an animal,
when you could have freed him much sooner."

"I did not know what to do with the boy. And when you
ran from me and from Dontaine . . ." He looked up and
something like hope glimmered in his eyes. "Is it really as
you say?"

"Having my lover wanting me to sleep with another
man is not a small thing to me, Gryphon."

"We are Monère, Mona Lisa. We are not human."

"You keep saying that. But I *am* part human."

"If I could acquire gifts as easily as you, I would sleep with Dontaine myself in the hopes of passing it to you," he said quietly. And, dear Mother of God, he really meant it.

"But other Queens," he continued, "other men, do not gain gifts and powers as you seem to. Sandoor and his band of rogues. They had a Queen who they bedded for over ten years, and they did not gain much power from the matings or the Baskings. But one time with you"—he turned his palms up in a graceful gesture—"and Amber and I can walk in the sun. You can see with my falcon's clarity of vision, and have gained some of Amber's great strength."

"Terrific. So I'm even more of a freak than I thought, like a sexual vampire who sucks up gifts instead of blood."

"You give generously as well as acquire."

I smiled bitterly. "Puts a whole new spin on being a generous and giving lover."

Gryphon ignored my sarcasm. "I believe what you say is true. You give more when you make love."

"And maybe I do that because I don't sleep with every man that walks by me, even those thrown at me," I said gently.

That quieted Gryphon for a moment. Gave him something to ponder. "Perhaps that is the case," he said finally.

"I only want you and Amber."

He looked at me with solemn eyes. "Amber, I can see why. But me—"

"How can you doubt that when every woman who looks at you desires you?"

His eyes turned hard and scornful. "They desire only my body, my flesh."

"I'm guilty as well. I desire your body. You have a beautiful body," I said softly.

His eyes grew heavy-lidded. One look from those slumberous eyes and I suddenly burned.

"You are different," Gryphon said, his voice a low husky timbre that sent a silvery shiver like an invisible hand sweeping down my spine. "You desire not only my body but my heart. My very soul."

"Do I have your heart?" I asked.

"It beats only for you."

"Oh, Gryphon." I reached for him and was suddenly in his arms, held tight. "I thought you were leaving me," I whispered against his neck.

"I thought you wished me gone."

"Never. No matter how mad you make me. Don't leave me. Don't ever leave me again."

"No," he promised, carrying me into the bedroom, his heart beating strong against me. "No, I won't."

He set me down beside the bed and swiftly removed my clothes. And as he undressed me, the anger and the fear suddenly changed into something else. Into something hot and possessive and tender. I brushed my fingers across the back of his nape and felt the soft feathery down hidden there like a secret pleasure. The scent of him, that faint, fresh, clean scent that was just him filled my lungs. Gryphon.

I'd be able to pick him out from a hundred other men blindfolded just from that unique fragrance. He smelled like the wind, like the night, like soft fluffy feathers and gentle kisses, sweet passion.

Other women had wanted him, had possessed him, had used him. But now he was mine and I wanted to wash away their old scents, rub off their long faded touch, their greedy, grasping imprints. Smudged fingerprints on the window of his soul.

He'd pleased so many. But had they pleased him? Had they tried to find his pleasure, his desire?

I pushed away from Gryphon. "Let me," I said, my voice a low soft whisper as he reached for me. "No, don't touch me." I captured his eyes, captured his hands, and lowered them down to his side. "Let me please you."

He looked into the promise of my eyes and shivered.

"Let me undress you," I breathed.

Both of us watched as I lifted one hand and brought it to the first button on his shirt. One infinitesimal moment stretched long before I finally touched it, and his breath caught as if I had touched other things. Leisurely I circled one finger around the smooth rim of that button. His muscles tightened. I looked up into his eyes and smiled. Unhurriedly, I pushed the button through the hole, skimmed my finger lightly down to the next hole. Slowly, I unveiled him, a beautiful hidden masterpiece, unwrapping him bit by bit like the sweet present he was. He was a breathtaking symmetry of flowing grace, of strength and power, a gentle river of muscles and tendons, bone and flesh, perfect in its creation. A worthy, worthy gift.

His shirt fell to the floor and I watched the gentle rise and fall of his chest with complete absorption, full appreciation. He was like God's first creation. Broad, graceful shoulders, the gentle swell of smooth chest, honey-colored nipples that I suddenly ached to taste. I knew them to be as delicious as they looked, sweet to the tongue, pleasing and responsive to the hand. Heat flooded me and the flesh between my legs grew throbbingly soft and full. Aching. But I held myself still, not touching him. Not yet. Not yet.

His eyes were darker now, the pupils expanded, racing to the very rim, his irises completely swallowed up. Holding his gaze, I sank to my knees before him, ran my eyes like a tactile caress down the long length of him, letting them feast over what I would not allow myself to touch just yet. Letting them drop lower. My breathing quickened and his stomach ridged as I reached out my hand and laid it there, barely there on top of his pants, and gave a slow, one-fingered caress over the top edge of the cloth, my fingers brushing the silky hair dusting his abdomen and trailing tantalizingly down below the pants, but not touching skin. Another leisurely sweep around and around the rim of the

single button on his pants. Just below that little button lay a
larger, longer, throbbing thing. I felt my breath puff against
my hand and caress his flesh.

He shuddered. I trembled.

"Mona Lisa." His voice was a bare rasp.

"Shhh," I gently whispered.

Slowly, oh, so slowly, I pushed that button through its
hole, and carefully holding the zipper, touching nothing
else, I lowered it. The harsh metallic rasp of it coming down
tightened my nipples, brushing like fingers of sound over
my swollen secret parts. Kneeling like a supplicant before
him, my naked breasts a gentle sway away from touching
him, from rubbing against his legs, I pushed down his pants,
revealing him whole, bare, and beautiful.

No underwear. What a lovely surprise.

I gave a hum of pleasure, of appreciation as I looked my
fill. He bobbed before me in standing glory, darkly flushed,
wonderfully engorged, his full veins traversing the surface
like dark satiny ropes. A drop of pearl-white fluid trembled
at the very tip. My tongue flicked out, licking my lips, but
only my quickened breath touched him, caressed him. His
hands clenched. I looked up and up at him, and smiled as if
I had swallowed his cream.

"Dear Goddess," Gryphon breathed. "Mona Lisa, you're
killing me."

"I haven't even started." It was a dark promise.

Crouching down, dropping to my hands, I crawled
slowly, sinuously around him and rose on my knees behind
him, my breath a soft puff on his back. And then lower. My
hands came to rest on his hips, and at that first contact of
skin to skin, Gryphon inhaled a shaky breath. Exhaled
sharply as I slid my hands around him in front, like two
slithering serpents wrapping around him. Forgot to breathe
when they twined around the base of his tree and slid up
his long, hard, sprouting length.

One thumb smoothed over his weeping head, dipping

into the wet prize, smoothing it over his sensitive crown. His buttocks tightened and flexed. Irresistible. I didn't even try to resist. One hand went south unerringly to cup his lower sac. The other hand wrapped around him in a squeezingly tight grip, pumped down and back up his sturdy pole. He sucked in another breath and quivered as my thumb smoothed over the crown, smearing more liquid pre-come over the plump head as I swept over the top. All by feel alone. I didn't need my eyes to see what I was doing. I knew him intimately.

On the downward stroke, holding his shaft tight and fisted hard, I squeezed his balls with firm, gentle pressure. Giving into temptation, I sank my teeth into the tantalizing fullness of his left buttock cheek, just below the teasing dimple near the base of his spine. He gave a low hoarse cry as my teeth sank in, breaking skin, tasting his blood, tasting him. Sweet, salty. Gryphon. Like the nectar of life.

He cried as I pumped his hard, swollen shaft again, as I lifted and squeezed his hard balls together up against the base of him, as I swirled over his head with sliding, gliding, lubricating friction, giving a passing, pinching caress with forefinger and thumb just below his under ridge where the nerves collected in a rich sensating bundle.

His hands came down to grip my arms. Not to stop me, but to hold himself as his knees buckled. I caught him, lifted him easily in my arms, and laid him down on the red silk bed sheets like a divine pale offering. His eyes were dazed and wide, his gaze fastened upon my lips, on the drop of blood dotting the right corner of my mouth. He watched, breathing fast, as my pink tongue came out and licked that crimson drop into my mouth, tasting him again with sultry appreciation.

"You taste like life," I said. "Like moonlight itself."

I crawled over him and crouched down, lowering my mouth to his. "Taste yourself," I whispered and kissed him. A soft press of my lips against his. A promising lick, a rasping of tongue. His mouth parted and I delicately entered.

Our tongues swirled, danced, mated. And then he was in my mouth, thrusting, thrusting, his tongue moving in and out in an act as old as time immemorial, making me gasp, making me burn. Making my honey flow, wetting me, and filling the air with its sweet musky scent, with our scent. Blood and sex. A potent combination.

I pulled back, panting. Licked my lips and tasted him, blood and saliva. But it was another fluid I was suddenly hungry for.

"Let me touch you," he pleaded.

I looked up at him. Let him see my wicked grin. "No, it's just you this time. You. Let me please you, let me please you." Bending low, I slithered over him, slithered down him, touching him with just my nipples. I rubbed my tight raspberry points over his peaked nubs, circled them together, pleasing us both, and ran them in twin lines of fire down his hard chest, his ridged abdomen, past his hips. I parted his legs, spread them with my knees, slid down into the space I had created. The springy hair of his groin was like a tickling kiss on my chest, his hard smooth length like a pulsing satin rod, soft and hard against my cheek. I rubbed my face against him, rolled him over my jaw, against my neck, inhaling him, drinking in the smooth incomparable feel of him, teasing us both until I could wait no more and I turned my face and took him into the hot wet cavern of my mouth. He slid in with a sigh, with a groan. With a tightening of his entire body and an inner clenching of mine.

"Dear Goddess. Sweet Goddess," he gasped and lifted his hips, arching into me, pushing deeper into the greedy wet suction of my mouth. I pulled back, up, up, to the very tip and tasted him, swirling my tongue over him, over that blind weeping eye, another rich essence of him. And I hummed my satisfaction.

With my eyes closed, I felt him begin that wondrous dance of light. A drawing of the inner life up into the outer being. My eyes opened and watched the beautiful subtle glow start to take him, to sweep across the pure alabaster of his skin with a cool white blush, growing more and more brilliant. To seep into his very skin, become part of it. Change him from a creature of the night into a creature of glorious light, his skin glowing, radiating from him in shafts of light that filled the room. He was unearthly beautiful in his pleasure. And his pleasure became mine, and that inner light began its eager dance within me. My skin changed, softened, glowed, and it was as if our very flesh softened, dissolved, became no more. We melded into one another where we touched, skin against skin, and then it was just light touching light, becoming one.

I filled my mouth with him, sinking down so that my lips almost touched his base, almost enveloped him whole, my lips tight around him. My right hand reached down between us, dipping down to borrow some of my own liquid honey, rising back up to squeeze his balls because I could not resist their hanging temptation, then moving farther behind, up and back, until my questing slick finger found and circled his tightly puckered anal hole.

My other hand squeezed his left ass cheek, finding where I had branded him and bit him, and I circled that tender broken skin. He trembled beneath me, in my mouth. I stroked up and out, my lips tight, grazing his veiny surface with my teeth as I swept up his pole, my tongue circling him. Finding him at the top, my tongue swept over that blind tender slit that oozed the sweet essence of him.

I pierced him with my tongue, that little hole. Penetrated him with my finger at his other, forbidden hole. And probed him with yet another finger, digging into the broken skin where I had bitten him, abrading raw, tender flesh.

He cried out sharply, sweetly, and convulsed around my finger and in my mouth. And feeling his hot jetting stream filling me, tasting him, feeling him slide down my throat as his sphincter spasmed strongly around my forefinger like a tight little mouth, gripping me, oh, so sweetly, his wet blood from where I had branded him slicking my other fingertip . . .

The taste, the feel, the flooding of me with his essence brought me to my own release, an almost gentle wave of pulsing, quiet convulsing. And while my body still quivered, I found myself hauled up his, his heart thudding against mine. I wrapped my arms around him, held him tight as the last of the light was absorbed back into us and we were two separate beings once more, two separate skins.

"Mine," I whispered fiercely against his neck. "You are mine."

"Yes, I am yours. Body, heart, and soul," he breathed, a soughing surrender, holding me tightly to him, soft bemused wonderment in his voice. "And you are mine."

SEVEN

THE KNOCKING ON the door was loud and intrusive. The sun was still up, high in the sky, shining fiercely. I felt as if I'd barely closed my eyes. Gryphon stirred beside me. Knocking was way better than just barging in, but still . . . this had better be good.

"They're gone, milady. Tersa and the boy." It was Rosemary. She spoke urgently but quietly through the door. No need to shout, I heard her clearly.

I found my clothes scattered on the floor. Gryphon was dressed before I was. He opened the door as I secured the daggers around my waist, and Rosemary slipped in.

"I'm sorry, milord, milady. But I've searched the entire house. They're not here. And your brother, Thaddeus, is also not in his room."

My brother still often rose in the afternoon while the others slept, not quite adjusted yet to our reverse schedule. I could almost see what had happened: Tersa discovering Wild Boy gone back to his home—the forest, Thaddeus the only one up and about; both of them going out to search for him. Tersa and Thaddeus out there alone! Aw, fuck.

I threw open the door to find Amber in the hallway, fully dressed, his hair tousled from slumber but his eyes alert. Maybe throwing on clothes was like going to the bathroom for men; they just did it quicker than women. He'd obviously heard Rosemary.

"The others?" I asked Amber.

"Sleeping. It would be hard to rouse them."

"Wake up Chami," I instructed Rosemary. "Tell him what's happened. Have him guard the others here." It was the best I could think of for now.

I ran down the stairs, Amber and Gryphon behind me. "How did they leave the house?" I asked.

"A window was open in the dining room," Rosemary answered, coming down the stairs with a surprisingly light tread for her girth and stature. You'd expect someone with that heavy build to thump. "I closed it."

"Lock up behind us." I went out the front door.

The burning sun was directly overhead, causing both Amber and I to squint. Sunlight didn't fry us, but our eyes were sensitive to the bright light. I had a pair of sunglasses somewhere up in my room. God knows where they were hiding. No time to waste scrounging around for them. A pity. Already my eyes were starting to water.

I scanned completely around me but found nothing in the near vicinity. Nothing human, that is. Plenty of wildlife out there. I turned to find Amber scenting the air, his nostrils wide and flaring, eyes bright amber yellow.

Gryphon had undressed completely, his clothes neatly folded on the ground. Gee, maybe it wasn't a girl-guy thing. Maybe they just had more practice than I did. A shimmer of energy, sparkles of light, and Gryphon was soaring in the air, wings spread more than ten feet long, a giant, graceful snow-white gyrfalcon. A few beats of his gray-tipped wings and he was high in the sky, circling above us.

"They went north," Amber said, sprinting across the lawn, darting into the woods. I followed behind him, jumping over rocks and fallen tree trunks, ducking branches, brushing past bushes. I moved with natural grace and speed, but nothing like Amber. He flowed like water flowed in a river, naturally, skimming through the brush without disturbing a single leaf. He moved as if he knew where every rock, every tree, every branch was. He moved with a fluidity and swiftness that came from tapping into his beast, from utilizing his cat senses. And watching him, following him, slower, less sure, I wished that I could do as he did.

I caught brief glimpses through the trees of Gryphon winging overhead in a silent, graceful, effortless glide. And though my senses were less keen than Amber's or Gryphon's in their animal form, I could smell the brackish smell of still water, of decaying leaves. The ground beneath us grew wetter and softer. They'd gone into the marsh land, the bayou. There were nasty things that lived out there. Things that could eat you. What the fuck were they thinking?

I heard them now in the far distance.

"Wild Boy," Tersa called.

Then my brother's young tenor. "Wiley, buddy, where are you?"

Wiley?

Above us, the falcon gave a piercing shriek.

"Tersa, Thaddeus!" I shouted, still running, leaping, following Amber almost blindly as he headed toward the voices, feeling a tide of relief welling within me at finding them.

"Mona Lisa?" Thaddeus called out with surprise.

Then came a sound that abruptly changed relief into a quick flash of terror—a loud splash. A startled scream.

"Tersa!" Thaddeus shouted.

And then a second softer splash, more controlled, from the other end of the bayou, like a large predator entering the water, hunting its prey.

"Get her out of the water!" I threw myself forward without regard for quiet or stealth or whatever path may or may not be before me. I cleared my own path, leaping over things when I could, crashing through shoulder-high weeds and thickets when it was the shortest route, my heart pounding, drowning out all other sounds until I heard nothing but my panting, my running feet. My fear.

A scream splintered the air as I broke through to the edge of the bayou, and the sight that filled my eyes stopped my breath, the only reason I knew it was Tersa screaming and not I.

A dripping Thaddeus stood valiantly in front of a soaked, bedraggled Tersa where he had obviously dragged her a few feet up the bank. But getting out of the water had not guaranteed safety. My brother faced a hungry alligator, intent on its kill. Only it wasn't just an alligator, it was a damn leviathan. The creature's full length was hard to ascertain as its tail was still in the water. But it definitely stretched longer than my brother's five and a half feet. Maybe three times longer, three times heavier.

Most animals of nature have some redeeming beauty, but not so this creature. It was truly ugly, a bowlegged, stumpy, flat thing with a long powerful body that slither-crawled just above the ground. It's rock-armored hide had lumps and bumps jutting out of its surface like sharp, hideous growths. Like a thing of monstrous evil, a reality much worse than what you dreamed of in your nightmares. Its cold, flat light eyes were the only things that looked alive, although alive was a generous description. Looking into those cold gleaming eyes, you knew they possessed no mercy, no joy, no emotion other than hunger and the need to sate that hunger . . . cold, cunning, and calculating. Like my mother's eyes.

Thaddeus's power flickered in the air, appearing and disappearing like an invisible beat in rhythm to Tersa's screams. He wielded his right fiberglass cast like a shield before him. He'd broken his arm in the car crash that had ended his parent's life but had spared his. The cast was no longer pristine white but a muddy gray from his dunk in the bayou's dark chocolate waters.

Thaddeus leaped back as those yard-long jaws lunged forward incredibly fast, snapping shut bare inches from his ankles. A freaking too-near miss. But instead of retreating, Thaddeus stepped forward, swinging his cast like a club, cracking it against the flat snout and sending the gator's head flinging back. Unfortunately, the blow must have been swung during one of Thaddeus's off-power flickers; the power he packed behind the blow was nothing more than human strength. The low and heavy reptilian body stayed anchored, gripping the land. The head came swinging right back, those deadly jaws yawning open once more and suddenly time seemed to slow down. It was as if the very air had thickened and grown sluggish. I had all the time to see Amber leaping for Thaddeus and Tersa. All the time to see that he wasn't going to make it, not in time. Not before that monstrous jaw closed around my brother's leg. All the time to weep and realize that there was nothing I could do.

I watched with a horror that filled and engulfed me like an overpowering wave as those teeth came closer and closer, and knew what the creature felt: a hunger for meat, a thirst for blood.

A piercing shriek ripped away the sluggishness, and motion sped back to the normal passage of time. What happened next was so surreally fast, it was hard to follow with mere eyes. A large falcon—Gryphon—dove with incredible speed and force in a breath-taking swoop, like a hundred-pound bullet hurtling down from the sky, unrestrained. The alligator's snakelike eyes rolled upward, sighting the new threat. Those tender eyes snapped shut just barely in time, a fraction of a moment before the swooping predator struck, raking sharp talons over the gator's craggy face, the protective eyelids, but missing the eyes, the only vulnerable spot on its armored surface.

The force and momentum of the giant falcon's rush, the brush of its wings, flung Thaddeus back into Amber's arms and barreled the nightmarish creature away, tumbling it back into the water.

Just barely in time, the bird pulled up, out of its death-defying dive, coming so close to the ground that dirt spewed into the air from where the talons scraped the bank. But as soon as the falcon pulled away, the alligator returned to its pursuit. It was right back there on the grassy bank as Amber swooped up Tersa with his other arm. For a bulky, hideous thing, it moved incredibly fast. But then, so did I. Only I wasn't on the bank, actually. I was in the water up to my thighs, behind the prehistoric beast, gripping its tail, yanking its swift rush to an abrupt, teeth-jarring stop.

I felt like I was holding a jagged rock. A rock that moved. A rock that had enormous force. Before I could flip the damn monster away from me, the tension in that long, long tail slackened.

Uh, oh.

With a striking blur almost Monère fast, it reversed and lunged for me. Sharp pain tore like hot searing iron through my meaty calf, and the sharp tang of blood rose into the air, dulled by the water, but unmistakable. My blood. *Oh, shit* was all I had time to think. Then with one easy toss from that strong jaw, I sailed in the air for a long brief moment and hit the water again, only deeper, sinking in the center of the bayou, water past my head. I bobbed back up and gasped for air.

Like a creature from hell, like a beast from a time long forgotten, the alligator sank into the water until nothing was seen but those cold, calculating eyes, rippling the water behind it in silent eddies with the powerful sway of its heavy tail, moving with a chilling speed in the water—oddly

graceful, when it had lumbered so awkwardly on land—
coming swiftly at me. *For* me.

Oh, God! Oh, God!

I started to swim, but water was not my natural terrain.
None of my foster homes had ever found incentive to fork
over money for swimming lessons. The best I could do was
a graceless doggy paddle. And with only three limbs. My
right leg was sort of numb and useless at the moment from
where the alligator had bit me. My swimming, if you were
kind enough to call it that, just wasn't going to do the job. I
heard—felt—the submersed creature gaining behind me
and turned to face it. I definitely wasn't going to out–doggy
paddle it; may as well meet it.

Then it sank completely.

Oh, double fuck!

A body sprang and sailed in the air like a flying monkey,
too small to be Amber, landing in an almost splashless
dive, knifing perfectly into the water near where the gator
had decided to play peek-a-boo-I'll-bite-you. They broke
the water almost immediately, the two of them intertwined,
thrashing.

It was Wild Boy—Wiley—wrapped around the alligator's pale belly with his monkey legs, an arm around the
partially opened toothy jaw, the other arm flashing up and
down, stabbing a pitifully small-looking knife into the
beast's underbelly. They disappeared beneath the water
again and I started paddling toward them.

The alligator was either going to munch on Wiley soon
or drown him, damn it!

"Mona Lisa!"

I turned my head to where Amber called to me and saw
him pointing up in the sky. I felt rather than saw the powerful presence swooping down.

"No!" I managed to get out before incredibly sharp,
painful talons sank into my back, digging deep into my
flesh. I was yanked out of the water, lifted into the air, then

dropped safely onto the bank. The falcon climbed the sky once more, gaining altitude for another dive. But would it do any good? It was hard to time an airborne strike with two thrashing figures popping in and out of the water at unpredictable intervals.

"Mona Lisa!" Thaddeus shouted, running toward me from the brush, Tersa beside him.

"Where's Amber?" I gasped, mostly from the pain. Take your choice now, talon-punctured back or teeth-ripped calf.

Tersa pointed behind me, at the bayou.

I whirled around. Amber was swimming rapidly to the center, and he looked like he knew what he was doing. But there was nothing else. Just rippling water. Then the boy-wrapped alligator broke the surface again. One big stroke and Amber was there, one hand wrapping around the tip of that long snout, slamming the jaw shut with almost casual ease, the other holding one of the creature's stumpy front legs. The animal thrashed and twisted, twirling all of them in the water, but not with ease as it had with Wolf Boy Wiley. It moved in the water with great difficulty, as if weighed down by a massive boulder, which I suppose Amber was.

"Go!" Amber yelled at Wiley, gesturing him away.

Wide-eyed, without hesitation, the boy did so, swimming for the shore with rapid, graceful strokes. Gee, did everyone know how to swim but me?

Tersa ran to meet him. "Wiley!"

When the boy was close enough to the embankment, Amber turned, and with a massive heave, sent the alligator sailing in the air, over the shoulder-high grass, soaring an impressive thirty feet at least before it slammed into a giant cypress tree with a resounding *thunk*. It sank down like a cut anchor, disappearing from sight but not sound. Unfortunately, from the breaking twigs and rustling leaves, the damn thing was still alive. But it was heading away from us, ceding the battle. Smart thing.

Wiley was out of the water, grinning at Tersa, practically

wagging his tail, happy and pleased with her lavish attention. But as soon as Amber came out of the water, the boy loped off into the woods.

"No, Wiley. Come back!" Tersa called after him.

"Let him go back to his home in the forest," I told her kindly. "His heart belongs in the wilderness. He'll come to us when he's ready. He knows where we are."

"Dear Lord, Mona Lisa," Thaddeus said, looking down at my leg. From his tone, it didn't sound good.

Reluctantly, I looked down, too. I'd been delaying that joyful chore until now. Okay—torn flesh, dripping blood. No big deal, I told myself as sounds around me muffled and my vision spotted. And I fainted.

~⌇⌇~

I CAME BACK to as we were climbing the steps to Belle Vista. Jeez, naming a house, can you imagine that. Though actually it was Amber climbing. I was being carried like a sack of wet potatoes in his arms.

Gryphon came rushing down the steps, dressed, I noted. All the others streamed down like graceful waves behind him—Chami, Tomas, Aquila, Rosemary, Jamie. Even Dontaine, who still seemed to be here. Dusk was falling and everyone was awake. Too bad. It would have been much nicer to creep in unnoticed. Other curious faces I did not recognize peeped out from the front door; house staff, I gathered.

"Dear sweet Mother of Light!" Rosemary exclaimed, catching sight of us. I inwardly winced. A ragged lot we must all look, with me most ragged of them all. "What happened?" she asked.

"Nothing," I reassured her. "We're all okay." No thanks to me.

"You are most definitely *not* okay," said Chami with some heat.

"It's nothing," I said.

"I am glad to see that you are awake," Amber rumbled. His deep, unhappy voice reverberated in his chest, passing through to me as he pushed into the house. "The nothing you speak of rendered you unconscious for the better part of an hour."

"Oh, that," I said, shrinking with embarrassment. "I just fainted when I saw what a mess my leg was."

"I thought you were a nurse," Jamie said, as I was laid gently down.

"Not on the couch!" I screamed as I saw the beautiful, now ruined, antique couch. Of course I was ignored. With a mental shrug, I relaxed my aching body onto the soft cushions, damage already done and all.

"We have to redecorate anyway," said Tersa in a quiet voice.

"Tersa, did you just make a joke?" I asked.

"Oh, milady!" She burst into sobs that made me cringe. Give me blood and gore any day. Tears horrified me. I didn't know what to do in the face of them other than say: *I give up. You win.*

"It is my fault that you were injured," Tersa cried.

"It was an alligator that took a chomp out of me, not you," I said, helpless before the teary onslaught.

"An alligator!" Tomas exclaimed with soft horror.

"I'm okay."

"You fainted," accused Aquila. Even good ole laid back Aquila was going to jab at me. I desperately wanted the peace and quiet of my bedroom. Unfortunately I couldn't get up and walk. The numbness had worn out and it was hurting like hell now.

"I fainted at the sight of all that blood and gore," I said.

"But you're a nurse!" Jamie protested again.

"Thank you, I heard you the first time." I shrugged. "It was other people's blood, other people's ripped, torn flesh. Never mine before." Everyone just stared at me. "So sue me."

My brother, the voice of reason, spoke up calmly. "We need to take you to the hospital."

"No!" I yelped. "No hospital. I'll have healed too much in the three or four hours they'll make me wait before they see me."

"So you heal quickly?" Gryphon asked. *Like us,* was the unspoken question. Like Dontaine. His throat was whole now, the skin perfect and unmarred, like magic.

"I don't know," I answered truthfully. "I was never injured before."

"Never?" Gryphon said with amazement.

"Not to this extent. Just little scrapes and bruises. I've always been faster and stronger than other humans." I shrugged again and winced, forcefully reminded once again of the fact that it wasn't just my leg that was injured.

"I had a charmed childhood." As far as injuries went. The rest of it, not so charmed.

Gryphon eased me forward to gaze at my back. He ran a finger lightly over where his sharp talons had punctured my skin. "I regret that I had to hurt you," he said with quiet sorrow, his rich blue eyes clouded over with remorse.

I laid a hand over his. "Hey, much better than being alligator meat."

"If you're not sure how quickly you heal, you should go the ER, have them stitch this up," Thaddeus said persistently.

"How bad is 'this'?" I asked, swallowing. "Do you think it's healed any?"

"I can't tell," my ever-truthful brother replied. "Too much blood."

Okay. Don't look, don't look. Or I'd be doing another swan dive.

"No hospital," I insisted stubbornly. Thaddeus looked like he was going to usurp my decision and the others frankly looked inclined to support his little revolt. I zeroed in on my likeliest ally. "Rosemary, take me up to my room, please. Help me get cleaned up."

"Well, that certainly cannot hurt your wound," she muttered sarcastically. Okay . . . maybe she was inclined to support the revolt as well.

Thankfully I felt her big arms wrap around me and carefully lift me up. It felt a little weird being carried up a winding staircase by a woman. Crap, how many stairs could a house, mansion, whatever, have?

Rosemary, bless her stout heart, brought me straight into the shower. It was more than big enough to hold two people, and for once I was thankful for all that luxurious space. We left my muddy clothes on the shower floor, dripping dark brown rivulets toward the drain. I felt like a baby as she toweled me dry and slipped the comfortable T-shirt that I slept in over my head, but I didn't complain, only sighed in relief as she laid me on the bed and propped a folded fluffy towel under my leg.

"How does it look?" I asked her.

"Like something big took a bite out of you."

"Not helpful," I muttered. No help for it. Bracing myself, I cautiously looked down at my leg. I wasn't entirely sure—my first look had been in a fainting swoon, after all—but I think it was a little better. Or maybe that was just because it had been cleaned up. It wasn't bleeding much, just oozing sullenly, and throbbing like an abscessed tooth ready to spew out its rotten pus and decay.

I swallowed, took a shallow breath, and looked away. Rosemary pressed a clean washcloth to my leg. The poor towels. Between Dontaine and I, we would have a bunch of them to replace.

The *thump thump thump* of whirling blades grew loud and deafening in my sensitive ears before I mentally turned the volume down. "What's happening?" I asked Rosemary. She'd gone to the window, peering out.

"It's a helicopter."

I know that, I wanted to say, but kept my sarcasm tightly clamped and unspoken. It wouldn't help, and she'd been only kind and helpful to me.

The wind from the whirring blades through the open window blew back Rosemary's hair, and the curtains fluttered as the helicopter landed.

"What's a helicopter doing here?" I asked.

Before she had time to answer, the noisy aircraft had lifted from the ground, flying away, and the answer to my question hurried up the stairs and walked into my room.

"Halcyon?" I said, gawking at the golden-skinned man who had just entered. He was a slim man of average height and average build. An elegant man with expensive and exquisite taste. He wore his usual ivory silk shirt—he had a closetful of them. I know, I saw them. But instead of the diamond cuff links, black onyx rimmed with gold peeked in tasteful display from his cuffs today. Narrow tailored black pants and dashing knee-high black kid boots completed the outfit. With his somber expression and aloof air of reserve, he looked like a nobleman from an era a couple of centuries gone by. It was what I'd first noticed about him when we had met—that reserve, that apartness from others, that . . . loneliness.

No one would guess at first glance that he was the High Prince of Hell. That he was one of the demon dead, something that even the Monère feared. The demon dead were what the Monère became when they died, those with strong enough psychic power to make the transition to Hell and sustain a physical presence there. There was nothing unusual about Halcyon that one could sense but for his golden skin and those long nails that graced his fingertips, sharp as knives.

"Mona Lisa." His voice was as cultured, as elegant, as the man himself. The worry I saw in his face, however, was foreign. Worry was not something you usually saw in his face. Worry was usually in the other guy's face.

"What are you doing here?" I asked, pulling the bed-sheet up high, suddenly, terribly conscious that the last time I'd seen him, he had brought me to a dripping climax from a bite alone, sipping my blood. *A small taste of me as I taste you.*

I became vividly aware that I wasn't wearing a bra, not that I really needed one, lightly built as I was, but it was a shield of sorts between my nipples and the revealing sheet. Even worse, I was highly conscious of the fact that I wasn't wearing any underwear. Not a state you wanted to be in before a man who didn't even need to touch you to really touch you.

Another person slipped into the room. "Healer Janelle," I said like a numb nut, "what are you doing here?"

She wore her usual maroon gown that denoted her gift and her status. Janelle was the High Council's resident healer back in Minnesota.

I know. What's in Minnesota, right? It's a place with acres and acres of pristine land and untouched forests, right near the border of Canada. Perfect really for Monère head-quarters.

Hey, it'd worked so far.

"Gryphon called us and told us that you were injured and that there was no healer available to you here." She came to the bed, *tut-tutting* as she saw my leg. Turning to the others, she said, "If you will give me a moment alone, please, with my patient."

It took a lot of guts to kick the High Prince of Hell out of a room, and to do so politely. Halcyon nodded and gra-ciously stepped outside, Rosemary behind him. I un-clutched my flimsy sheet and relaxed. Janelle, watching me, just quirked her brow.

"It's, uh, nice of Halcyon to escort you here," I said. "To see that you arrived safely."

"It was not my safety that was his primary concern," Janelle replied dryly.

Okay.

"Have you tried to heal yourself?" she asked.

The thought of healing myself had, in fact, occurred to me. I'd actually been expecting Gryphon to walk in instead of Halcyon. But somehow, being all torn up and gory and throbbing with pain that really, really hurt, didn't quite put you in the mood for sex, at least when I was the one hurt. See, real limitations here with my healing gift.

I shook my head.

"Would you like to try?" Janelle asked. "Or would you rather I save the lesson for later and heal you first?"

I looked up and searched her eyes. They were as kind and as clear as always. No hidden innuendo, no sign that she was suggesting we engage in a bout of lesbian sex. Was she?

"I, um, can't seem to heal myself without being intimate with others."

She blinked. "I see. Have you ever tried healing without sex?" *She* had no problems using the three-letter *s-e-x* word, obviously. Though it was odd as hell hearing *sex* coming out of her serene mouth.

Thoughts of Gryphon guiding my hand down to cover Dontaine's stiff groin flashed through my mind. I pushed it away. "Yes, and I wasn't able to," I replied.

"You were able to take away pain with touch, if I remember correctly."

I nodded.

"Would you like to try at least that?" she asked.

That I had no problem trying, and wanted to kick myself for not thinking of it first. I took a deep breath and laid my hands over my torn-up leg; didn't even have to look to do that. I concentrated, went deep within myself, and pulled up . . . "Nothing," I said frowning. "It's not coming."

"Never mind, child. Forgive an old teacher. It is hard for one to concentrate when one is in such pain." Janelle laid her hands gently upon my leg, barely touching. Just the pleasant sensation of her touch for a moment, then I felt a soft surge of power, a steady humming that at first covered my skin, easing the pain, and then sank down like gentle warmth deeper into the flesh, melting, knitting, making whole. It wasn't a fast process like the explosive healing burst of power that came with my orgasmic release. It was a slow, steady streaming of gentle power. I felt a warmth, a tiny vibration in my flesh as she worked, oh, so patiently, her hands relaxed and still, her face serene and kind as a healer should be. Just being in her presence was an easing balm. Only the faint moisture that dewed her lip and dampened her brow betrayed the effort it cost her.

She removed her hands and my flesh was whole, my skin unmarred. A residual warmth remained for a moment in my healed tissues like a lingering essence of her, then it was gone.

"I wish I could do that," I said with wonder in my voice.

The healer smiled. "I will teach you. Now, where else are you hurt?"

EIGHT

THE SURPRISES WEREN'T over yet, I found, when I walked downstairs a short time later and felt a distinctive presence before I saw her.

"Mona Carlisse," I exclaimed. I'd rescued her from a band of outlaw rogues, the same ones that had captured me. Beside her sat her daughter, a little girl with gold spun hair and sea blue eyes so like Amber, her half brother, who had settled his large presence in the far corner by a windowsill.

"And Casio. What a pleasure it is to see you again," I said, smiling. The neat and clean and beautiful child looked so different from the wild creature I'd first met in the forest.

Mona Carlisse stood up nervously and bent her head in greeting. "Mona Lisa. Forgive us for coming uninvited."

"Not at all. You are always welcome here."

Some of the stiffness left her at my warm greeting and she introduced the two men who had also stood when she had risen. "These are my guards. Miguel . . ."

He was a dark-haired, mustached man, trim and dapper, about my height, not much taller than his Queen. Though his soft dark eyes shone with warmth, and his mouth curved with easy charm, I sensed some tenseness, some constraint in him as he bowed.

"And this is Gerald."

The other guard, more serious in mien, also bowed in greeting. There was an uneasiness in him as well. He was taller, with sand-colored hair and watchful hazel eyes, broad-shouldered but slender. From the feel of his presence, I would have pegged him as the younger of the two, but I could have been wrong. Age did not always correspond with strength, I'd found.

"It is actually I who brought them along," Healer Janelle said. "It was too good an opportunity to allow to pass. I wanted Casio present, if I was to spend time teaching you the healing arts. I wished to use the opportunity to begin instructing her as well."

"Casio?" I said.

"She has the gift within her for healing, I discovered," Janelle said.

"How wonderful." I smiled at Casio, then wrinkled my nose at the shy child. "Although you will probably learn quicker than I."

Casio hid her face against her mother's side, but not before I caught a glimpse of a smile.

Tomas and Dontaine were also in the room. "Tomas, where are the others?" I asked.

"As you were indisposed, Lord Gryphon, Chami, Aquila, and Thaddeus accompanied Steward Horace on a tour of your holdings, after which the good steward will be leaving."

I nodded my approval. Sooner seen, sooner gone. "Thaddeus went with them?"

"More the other way around," Tomas answered, his sweet plain face twisting wryly. "The others are accompanying Thaddeus and Aquila. Those two seem the most comfortable with matters of business."

Another area in which age did not correspond with expertise. Thaddeus, though young of age, was not tender. He seemed more confident in the affairs of commerce than I.

"Did Jamie and Tersa also go with them?" I asked.

Tomas glanced briefly at Halcyon, sitting alone in a chair, a flickering gaze that danced quickly away. "They are helping their mother in the kitchen."

I frowned, wondering if they were uncomfortable in the presence of strangers, then let the thought go as Dontaine stepped forward and knelt before me. Tall, fair, and dazzlingly handsome, he was a forceful presence, especially when compared to Mona Carlisse's two guards—much more striking in looks and strength. "My Queen. I wished to thank you for your care before I took my leave," Dontaine said.

"I did nothing," I said, speaking the unfortunate truth. "You healed yourself."

"You were . . . kind when you need not be." A hint of sadness lurked in his moss-green eyes. Gone was the cockiness, the eager challenge. He was dimmed a bit without it, somehow. I hadn't realized what a large part of him that confident arrogance had been, or that I would miss it now that it was gone. He stood and turned to go.

Mona Carlisse's presence reminded me of what I had once advised her about men. Sometimes you just had to trust them. You would know soon enough whether your judgment had been correct.

I called his name. "Dontaine."

He stopped and faced me once more.

"What position did you hold? As a guard," I clarified quickly when I realized it could be taken in another manner. Like in Mona Louisa's bed.

"I was second-in-command to the Master of Arms."

"And the Master of Arms? Where is he?"

"He departed with Mona Louisa," Dontaine replied.

"I see." A quiet pause. "Then I would ask that you take up the vacated position."

"Me?" He looked to Amber, dazzled, confused. "But I lost the challenge."

"You did not need to challenge for the position. I would have likely made the appointment in light of your experience, had I known."

"But I lost," Dontaine repeated like a broken record stuck in a groove.

I sighed and turned to the man who had defeated him. "Amber, do you wish to be Master of Arms?"

"No. I have the position I desire." Amber's eyes heated and warmed, making me blush. Making it clear that the position he held and was so very pleased with was in my bed.

"See?" I said, turning my attention back to Dontaine. "I'm going to give you enough rope to either hang yourself or prove yourself to me. You have the position on a tentative two-month trial period. You know the needs of this territory and the men here. Organize them as you will, but out of courtesy, I would appreciate it if you kept Lords Amber and Gryphon and me appraised of all matters." My eyes narrowed. "I want things changed, Dontaine. No more fights or challenges, understand? All advancement will be made upon merit of strength, on experience and skill. You are going to set new rules and implement the changes. I cannot afford to waste any more time having my men fighting amongst themselves, especially when we're short a healer. Are you up to the challenge?" Mentally I rolled my eyes as I heard myself. I couldn't believe I was starting to talk like a Queen.

Dontaine snapped to attention, his eyes sparkling with wonderment and a return of his eager, passionate spirit. Cocky confidence rang once more in his voice. "Yes, my Queen."

"Good," I said, happy to see some of his natural irritating manner restored. "We'll see how comfortable the fit is to us both two months from now."

"Yes, milady . . . and thank you." He bowed low and left.

My first new act as Queen. I searched out Amber's eyes and was rewarded with his approval.

"It is a good decision," he said quietly.

"God, I hope so." I really, really hoped so.

༄

ROSEMARY HAD TAKEN over the role of chatelaine of the entire house, not just of the kitchen, God bless her capable soul. Under her guidance, the mess we'd made in the downstairs guestroom had been miraculously cleaned up. Fresh air wafted in through the open French windows and the sweet perfume of roses drifted up from the sprawling English gardens below. Dontaine's blood had been washed from the walls and scrubbed from the carpet. I'd have to ask Rosemary how she had accomplished that amazing feat. She'd obviously had more years of experience cleaning up blood than I had. I was just more experienced in spilling it.

"Will this be okay?" I asked Halcyon, gesturing to the room. Rosemary had suggested that Prince Halcyon stay down here. Janelle, Mona Carlisse, and her small entourage took up the remaining guest rooms upstairs. Full house now.

"This will be fine," Halcyon said. He'd been unusually quiet and reserved. We were the only ones in the room, although I was sure Amber was keeping an ear open and tuned to all that we said. But at least Amber had the courtesy to give us a semblance of privacy. Had Gryphon been here, we would not have been alone. The one single person in the world who seemed to trigger Gryphon's jealousy was Prince Halcyon. All other men, he seemed eager enough to throw me at or on, as long as they had a smidgeon of talent they could pass on.

"I'm sorry the room is so small," I said inadequately, stuffing my hands in my jeans. "But at least it has a private bath."

"This more than suits my needs," Halcyon assured me, as polite as I was, making me wonder what we were doing, dancing around like this. We weren't usually like this, tiptoeing around each other.

"I am glad you are better. May I see your leg?" he asked, kneeling before me in a fluid movement.

At my clumsy nod, he carefully lifted the denim cloth, baring my right calf. He behaved himself, no invisible caressing hands or such, but I felt his gaze running like an actual weight over my healed skin. Somehow, baring that small inconsequential bit of my leg felt as if I were exposing other, more private parts of my body to him.

"Does it still hurt?" Halcyon asked softly.

"No." Gently I stepped back out of his reach, and the denim slid down to cover me once again. "Uh, thanks for bringing Healer Janelle here so quickly."

"I am happy to be of service." He stood gracefully, his dark brown eyes unreadable. "Perhaps now that you are well, I should go."

"You hate the room," I said, distressed.

He gave a tiny hint of a smile. It flickered for a moment like a shy moth then disappeared. "No, but you seem nervous of me." His voice lowered, roughened. "You have no need to fear me, ever."

"Oh." I closed the distance between us and took his hand in mine. "Never think that. I'm not afraid, just a little embarrassed." I gave a short laugh. "Hardly dressed upstairs and naked the last time you saw me."

I brought his dear hand to my cheek, felt the brief caress of his palm and the lightest touch of his sharp nails against my skin before he turned his hand over and brushed me with the back of it, turning those lethal nails aside.

"I'm glad you came," I said fervently. "I am always, always glad to see you."

"Ah, Mona Lisa." He carefully drew his hand away.

"Stay for a while, if you can."

He searched my eyes, deeply, intently, before saying, "I can."

I smiled. "Good. Then do. Is there anything else I can get you? That you need?"

He studied me for a long moment then shook his head.

"We'll talk more later, after I get Mona Carlisse and her people settled." With that promise, I left.

He was such a lonely man, I thought sadly. And that loneliness was seen most sharply when he was among others, lonesome in a crowd. There was an invisible wall between him and the rest, a wall of fear, a shield of caution. Separated by his differences. I'd met him in a sun-dappled meadow before I knew what he was. I knew him only by the fruit of his actions alone there in the wilderness with him, unprotected. And his actions had been those of a gentleman, kind and concerned, that of a friend. I'd teased him and held his arm before I knew that those deadly nails, when lengthened in his other form, could slice off a man's head with one easy stroke, that the demon dead could take the form of a beast far more fearsome than Dontaine's Half Change.

My elegant demon prince. He'd saved me, brought me back from Hell, and told me that he loved me. And I had asked him to find another to love, for both our sakes. Were I less scrupulous, less stringent in my morals, he and I would be lovers as well. Although perhaps it was less morals and more fear that kept me from reaching out to him. Fear of losing the precious love I had only just found with Gryphon and with Amber. It was hard enough bridging the differences between us without throwing a new friction into the mix. I sighed. I'd gone a lifetime without love and now an abundance of it threatened me.

There was no aphidy, no chemical pull between the demon prince and me. Just a short wealth of trials and experiences that had bonded us. Pure emotions. I fell for the heartbreak of his agony. Suffering drew me. Some inbred instinct in me wanted to ease it gone, caress it away.

In truth, had it been Halcyon that Gryphon was throwing me at, I may not have resisted.

⁘

"ANOTHER STRONG WARRIOR yet you add to your fold," Mona Carlisse greeted me upon my return to the elegant parlor. She shook her head disbelievingly. "How fearless you are." And then more quietly so that I had to strain to hear her, "You shame me."

"Whoa." It took me a moment to realize what she was talking about. "Do you mean Dontaine?"

"Yes." Mona Carlisse was conspicuously alone in the room. "I hope you do not mind. I sent the others away."

"Why?"

"I wished to speak with you alone."

I lowered myself onto the oversized armchair across from her. "How can I help you?" I asked softly.

Tears glistened for a moment in Mona Carlisse's pretty eyes before she veiled them with her long lashes. "Is it so obvious then, that I need help?"

I chose my words carefully. "Forgive me. Your hands betray your distress."

She looked down at her clenched fists, opening them. Her nails had dug half crescents into her palms. She gave a brittle laugh, and self-consciously relaxed her fingers.

"Are you well?" I asked gently. She was a beautiful woman, this Queen that I had somehow befriended. The only decent one I'd met so far.

There were other things that I had noticed about her but did not mention. Other things that had also hinted of trouble. Her hair, for one thing. Its length was coiled back in an elegant knot, revealing the purity of her large brown eyes and delicate oval face. It was an attractive arrangement, but Monère Queens usually wore their hair long and loose, flaunting their beauty, their availability, their power. Mona Carlisse had worn her hair bound back like this when I had first met her, held captive by a band of rogues led by Amber's outlaw father. Sandoor had faked both his and his Queen's death, so that no one had known Mona Carlisse was still alive. She'd been at their mercy for ten long years and they had showed her none. It was an experience bound to leave ugly scars. It actually spoke greatly of her strength that she had emerged from the ordeal with her sanity intact.

"No, I am not well." Mona Carlisse angrily wiped away a tear that had spilled over. "I had returned to speak with Healer Janelle, but she cannot help me because . . ."

"Because it is not your body that is injured," I finished quietly for her.

"No," she said sadly. "What ails me, she knows not how to repair."

Were it any other woman, I'd have taken her in my arms and soothed her like a child. But the presence of a Queen was abrasive to another Queen. Prickles of hot awareness was already a low stinging buzz against my skin just sitting this close to her. Distance, a lot of it, was a more natural order of things between two alpha gals. Nature's design to help propagate our species—disperse wide and rule. So on and so forth, and all that other crap.

Mona Carlisse's wounds were not on the surface. They were deeper, darker . . . her heart injured, her trust betrayed. Serious injuries. And yet, her spirit had not been broken. Frankly, she needed to see a shrink. But somehow, I doubted the Monère had anything like that available. For one thing, they hadn't evolved enough for something that . . . unnecessary; that's how they would see it. A doctor for the mind was a luxurious matter, really, not something the brutal Monère society would have advanced to yet. It was a harsh culture. If you were that weak and fragile, you died, simple as that.

"Do you have any psychiatrists in your . . . I mean, our society?" I asked.

"What is that you speak of?"

Mentally, I groaned. Times like this, I hated being right. "Do you have any counselors, priestesses or wise women you can speak with?"

"No one," she said, looking at me intently. "No one but you."

Great. I pitied her. Fixing things was not one of my talents. Destroying things or people that threatened me or mine . . . that came far more naturally to me.

Yeah, yeah . . . I was a nurse and I'd had some basic training in psychology. But I'd never taken any advanced counseling courses. Those hadn't been offered to mere nurses. But it seemed that I was all she had. Poor thing.

"How can I help you?" I asked again. Maybe if I asked enough times, she'd finally tell me.

Her brown eyes dropped back down to her hands. They had tensed again. She spread them deliberately, fanning them flat on her lap. When she spoke, it was so softly that I had to strain forward to hear her. "I cannot bear to be intimate with any of my men. I cannot stand to touch them or have them touch me."

Pity stirred in my breast. "It's only been a week since you've reclaimed your rule." And her freedom.

She shook her head. "It only worsens with time, not eases. My people, my men, do not know how to treat me. I am so different from what I was before. So much less."

"All your people were returned to you?" They'd been scattered, absorbed into other territories when all had thought that she had died.

"Yes, but perhaps it was a mistake to call them back to me. They all remember me as I was, and are disturbed greatly, unsettled by what I have become."

"And what have you become?" I asked gently.

"It takes a great deal of arrogance, of natural fearlessness to be a Queen. To rule a people."

"Does it?" I said, my tone sardonic. "And here I thought

it was just nasty personality traits that came from having too much power."

"We are raised such, for a reason," Mona Carlisse said somberly, looking at me with her wounded doe eyes. "Even you have it in natural abundance."

I winced. "I don't consider it one of my good points."

"It is an important part of what makes you a good Queen, Mona Lisa. And yet you temper it with kindness, with compassion. With love."

I winced again, more and more uncomfortable. Especially with the last word. Four-letter words were almost as bad as three-letter ones.

"I have spent a great deal of thought on the matter and have concluded that it is the combination of hardness and softness that draws your men to you, that binds them to you with a strength that is even stronger than demon chains." Mona Carlisse sighed, and it was a sad, lost sound. "I have no arrogance left in me. No confidence. And I am too afraid to risk kindness or love. Indeed, I live in constant fear and distrust."

"What are you afraid of?"

She smiled sadly. "That someone will betray me once more. Fake my death. Steal away with me as Sandoor had once done." Her knuckles whitened as her fists balled up once more. "I would truly rather die than put myself at the mercy of such men again. But I cannot rule this way, mistrusting my people, having them unsure of me."

She looked up and whispered, "And I fear what I am becoming. Miguel, my guard . . . he has grown stronger in my long absence." She laughed harshly, unhappily. "He possesses not even one half the power of your Dontaine. And yet, many times as I lay alone in my bed unable to sleep, I considered killing him before he became too great a threat to me." Her eyes were a luminous brown floating in a sea of welling tears as she said softly, "I loved him once."

"Oh, honey."

"I considered giving up my throne," she confessed in a quiet whisper, "but then what would I do? My people would be absorbed elsewhere as they were once before. But who then would protect me? You called me a good Queen and I was once, but with this killing dread in me, I fear that I may easily become the bloodiest Queen of them all." The horror of it was clear in her shaky voice.

I made myself take a deep, calming breath. "But you didn't kill him."

"What?"

"You said that you thought about killing him, but Miguel is still here, alive, by your side."

She nodded, hugged that fact to her in comfort. "I wish to reclaim that part of myself that I have lost. But I do not know how."

And she hoped that I did.

The solution was obvious to me, but I didn't think she would like it. But you know that saying: Nothing ventured, nothing gained. Trite but, oh, so true. "Choose one of your men. Take him to your bed once more."

Mona Carlisse just looked at me with those swimming eyes. "It was once a great joy to me. But that seems so long ago, a distant memory. Any pleasure I once felt in mating has long been pounded out of me."

I winced at her choice of words. It was unfortunately literal. The rogues had not been gentle with her.

"They used me like a whore and beat me when I did not glow beneath them. They not only raped my body, they raped my mind, turned it so that I had to make *myself* feel pleasure as they rutted over me. All I feel now is disgust and dread at the thought of being intimate once more with any man."

"You said under them."

"What?"

"You said that they forced you to submit your body, your

will, your pleasure to them. Why don't you turn it around, vent some of that anger and resentment that you have bottled within you?"

Mona Carlisse looked confused. "What are you suggesting?"

Good question. We'd see if the answer was as good.

N I N E

W<small>E WERE BACK</small> in what I thought of as the dungeon. It
wasn't, really. It wasn't even in the basement, probably
because houses in flood-prone Louisiana did not have
basements. The houses here in this wet state were actually
perched up on blocks of brick or stone.

The dungeon was just a room set back in the house, not far
different from the other rooms in the house. Only this room
had chains of silver manacles secured to the wall. There were
a few changes to it since last I saw it. It was clean for one
thing. And instead of Wolf Boy, those chains now contained
Gerald, the less powerful of Mona Carlisse's guards. One she
had never taken to her bed before. He was shackled in those
chains in his full naked glory, slender but well muscled.

If I was uncomfortable there was no one else to blame
but myself. It was my idea, after all.

No, we hadn't tackled Gerald to the ground, stripped
him of his clothes, and snapped those manacles around him.
He'd actually removed his clothes and willingly stepped

forward and allowed us to secure him in those strength-draining chains.

We, or more accurately, I, had explained to Gerald what we were hoping to do. He'd looked at Mona Carlisse, his Queen, with naked, yearning devotion shining in his lovely hazel eyes, and replied, "Yes, anything."

The brilliant idea was to have the man completely at Mona Carlisse's mercy, to put her in total control. To have *her* take *him*. Of course, I hadn't expected to be in the same room when she did it.

"I will not be able to do this thing without your presence," Mona Carlisse had told me.

"But don't you want some privacy?" I'd wailed.

Obviously not. "You make me feel safe," she said.

I had looked at her blankly.

"You stopped Amber from raping me when he was filled with bloodlust and barred inside that hut with us. You risked yourself instead."

Not quite the whole truth. "I did that not really to save you but for a more selfish reason. I didn't want Amber declared rogue for raping a Queen." I shrugged. "I was willing. It wouldn't have been rape."

"Nevertheless you saved me, and then again later, as we fled from there. I feel safe in your presence. I will not be able to do this thing that you ask of me otherwise."

And so I found myself stuck inside that little room, backed into the farthest corner, not knowing where to look after I had secured Gerald's shackles, placed the key down on the ground next to his feet, and backed away. Gerald didn't seem to mind. He was slender but well muscled, and down below, heavy and full. He stood there pointing at full mast, face serene. The chains had enough length so that he stood several feet out from the wall, a willing captive, arms and legs slightly spread, patiently waiting for whatever his Queen desired to do to him.

"You may not receive any pleasure or satisfaction. Much less power," Mona Carlisse had warned him.

"Anything you desire, my Queen," Gerald had replied in gentle understanding. "Even blood, even pain."

I don't know that I could have made such a promise knowing what she had gone through.

Mona Carlisse reluctantly walked to him now, still fully dressed, a folded black tie in her hands and uncertainty in her face. Gerald averted his eyes and lowered his head, as if he knew it would be easier for Mona Carlisse to tie the cloth around his head and blindfold him if he did not stare at her. He may not be the strongest of her men, but he was worthy of her.

She stepped back hastily as soon as she had knotted the cloth, her face pinched, her hands trembling, wary of being so close to a man, even one of her own. She stood there a moment, a shudder passing through her body, and I had a moment's thought that she would not be able to do this. But the inner, unbreakable core of strength beneath the soft, pretty surface that had kept her alive and enduring and sane for ten long years came to the fore then. Mona Carlisse let out a tremulous breath, squared her slender shoulders with determination and lifted a delicate hand. It stayed there, lifted, airborne, in uncertain promise before slowly, slowly, moving forward to touch Gerald's hair. His hair flowed just beyond shoulder length, loose in soft waves, released from its constricting tie, a rainbow of colors from rich brown to the palest yellow, like grains of mixed sand blended together, rippling with a healthy sheen.

The silky strands lifted and twined about Mona Carlisse's fingers with a bouncy life of their own as she caressed them, stroked them. She sighed and closed her eyes as she felt the fine, silken loveliness under her hand. Lifting her hand away, she brought her fingers to her own heavy coil. Pins dropped to the wood floor with little *pings* of sound, and her own hair loosened and unraveled, falling down and down, past her hips, a thick swath of extraordinary chestnut brown shot through with strands of gold.

And as her hair was freed, part of the tension that had gripped her unraveled as well, flowing from her, seeping away. Stepping past the chains, she moved to stand at Gerald's back. He stood calmly, unmoving, without tensing, though he must have sensed her closeness. Trust like that, devotion like that, was a bit scary. There was a lot of anger, a lot of bitterness and fear in Mona Carlisse. Even I did not know what she would do to him, beat him or fuck him. Either would make me hugely uncomfortable, but for his sake, I was hoping for the latter. Of course, she might not do anything at all, which would then entail another session like this all over again. How fun.

And yet not doing anything but just standing there, they made a beautiful picture. And an erotic one. Mona Carlisse's dark fall of hair and flowing black dress was a stark contrast to the naked loveliness of Gerald's pure white skin. She was fully dressed while he was nude and exposed, vulnerable in chains, wholly at her mercy. It was an intriguing study of black, silver, and white, a play of textures, colors, and light. Standing behind him, she looked the part of a black widow spider dangerously gazing at her captured prey, pondering whether to mate him or devour him. There was a terrible, stark beauty about the scene and, God help me, I was becoming aroused despite myself. I fought to look away but my gaze was drawn repeatedly back to the portrait of them.

Mona Carlisse's eyes captured mine. "Do you like what you see?" Her voice was darkly inviting.

I swallowed and nodded, knowing she could smell my arousal. I was unable to hide my body's reaction to her; no use trying to lie. "You are beautiful together," I whispered and looked away, embarrassed.

"No. Watch," she commanded, and I could not help but do as she bid. Mona Carlisse stepped closer behind Gerald so that she barely brushed him, her hands rising to touch his slender hips.

"You were beautiful together," Mona Carlisse said softly to me. "Amber and you, when you made love. You made what had become an ugly act for me beautiful once more."

Mesmerized, I watched. Her pale hands, framed by the blackness of her sleeves, drifted lightly over the flat plane of his stomach. Gerald tensed, then shuddered, his abdomen ridging as her hands glided upward over the gentle swell of his chest. Closing her eyes, giving a soft little sigh of pleasure, she embraced him, wrapping her arms completely around him and holding him tight, finding comfort. There was great pleasure to be had in just holding someone, of being held. Humans and Monère alike seemed to have that deeply ingrained need in them for the comfort of physical touch. I wondered how many years it had been since Mona Carlisse had been able to hold another man like this, of her own free will.

When she opened her eyes again and looked at me, wetness gleamed in the brown depths. She rubbed her cheek against Gerald's soft hair, hiding her face partly in the light, sand-colored fall. Then she stepped back.

She was done, I thought, and found myself pleased with the progress that she had made. And it was progress, her willingness to just touch a man, embrace him. But instead of walking away, she reached back. The rasp of a zipper sounded loud in the silence of the room and the weighty fall of cloth to the floor was an erotic whisper teasing all of our senses. She stepped out of her undergarments with a dainty step and I caught the flash of her milky whiteness behind him before I looked away. Looking at a naked man was one thing. Looking at a naked woman was quite another.

And yet . . . my gaze drifted back to watch her press herself fully against him from behind, to hear both their ragged release of breath at the brush of naked skin to naked skin, to almost feel the caress of her unbound breasts against his back, the curls of her silky thatch teasing his tight bottom. To see the pleasure sweep over her face as she absorbed the feel of unbound flesh against unbound flesh as she rubbed her entire body against him in a gentle swaying motion, sliding her hands over his bunched shoulders and down his bunched arms.

Mona Carlisse stepped out from behind Gerald, moving to his right, letting her hand delicately trace the muscles and tendons of that one strong forearm, smoothing her fingers over the silver shackle that bound him captive at the wrist. Silver was one of the Monères' weaknesses. They were sapped of their full strength once chained by silver.

She caressed the binding metal. Smiling at me, her eyes a glittering, shining blaze of brown, she angled Gerald to the side so that I could see them both in silhouette, so that she could still see me. Her loose and unbound hair flowed around her like a dark, rippling curtain, hiding one breast, revealing the lush fullness of the other, spilling down to curl just above her mysterious triangle of hair, drawing one's attention to the shadows there. With her dark, flaming eyes and that wicked, knowing smile, she looked like the original Eve. Only she wasn't trying to tempt Adam.

She moved to the front and touched Gerald like she owned him. She did with him as she pleased, and it pleased her to bury her hands in the fine richness of his hair, to nuzzle the tender line of his neck, seek out its secret hollows. To brush the vulnerable little bushes of hair peeping out beneath his outstretched arms, making him squirm in discomfort. To circle the brown flat nipples, peaking them to little points, making him squirm in pleasure. A finger traced over the seam of his lips, parting them, sinking a finger into his mouth and then pulling it out.

She was seeking out the most vulnerable parts of him, I realized. The crease of his elbows, his sensitive palms, the hollows of his knees, the softer, more tender skin of the inside of his thighs. And finally, there, where man was most defenseless. She cupped the tender sac of him in her hands, crouched before him, studying that part of him intently, his hairy bush almost brushing her cheeks, his risen sword pointing skyward, taut against his belly. Gerald trembled and I did not know if it was from passion or fear. A little of both, perhaps.

What would she do with that most vulnerable part of him?

Mona Carlisse rolled the little balls in her hands, tweaked some of the wiry hair, making Gerald jump, pulling a husky breath of laughter from her. She spilled her hands upward and grasped the fullness of him with both hands, firmly, not entirely gentle. He was of average size, not too big, not too small. Just right. One hand moved up, causing the loose, veiny outer skin to slip over his hardened shaft. Her other hand moved down, tracing down his length, seeking out and finding where he originated, to that little perineal swelling behind his scrotum from where he rooted. Having found what it had sought, the searching hand returned to its sister, snaking around his heavy shaft, pumping it fuller. An agile thumb slid up, smoothed around the crown, finding and spreading the drop of pearly essence that had leaked out from that weeping eye.

Mona Carlisse lifted her head and our eyes met and clung. Holding my gaze, she pulled his shaft down like a lever, stretching him level. Gerald pressed his lips tight at the sudden, abrupt move, holding back a cry. He trembled as he felt her hot breath fall upon his sensitive flesh. Groaned as she reached out with her long pink tongue and licked him, long strokes up like she was sipping melting ice cream. Held his breath as she pressed the plump length of his shaft against her opened mouth. As she dangerously grazed him, letting him feel the sharp edge of her teeth when she traced the length of him and swallowed him in, then released him from her red, red lips with a slurpy wet *pop*.

Mona Carlisse's arousal rose like heat in the air, a musky sweet scent to twine with Gerald's and mine. It excited her, having me watch them. It excited her having control like this.

She licked her lips with that pink tongue, her eyes glittering up at me. "Still like what you see?"

"It's a good show," I answered in a raspy whisper.

"It's going to get better." So promising, she stood up and lifted her pelvis over his levered-down length. Squeezing him between her legs, she rode him, sliding that stretched out shaft between the dewy cleft of her outer lips, so that it moved outside of her, not in her yet. I saw his staff disappearing between her legs and re-emerging, the veiny dorsal surface wet and glistening, christened with her juice. She slid off of him and he sprang back up to slap against his belly, making him flinch and catch his breath. She grasped him again, angled him back at a forty-five-degree angle, then straddled him once more. With her legs wrapped around him, she sank down, engulfing him into her, swallowing him whole into her body.

I closed my eyes, the image of his length impaling her, sliding into her, disappearing, eaten up by her, seared across my vision. The sound of her wetness as she moved upon him was slurpingly loud, calling forth my own juices. The sounds of his groans and her moans swelled my breasts, hardened my nipples.

"Watch," Mona Carlisse said softly and I opened my eyes, unable to do other than her bidding.

I watched her take her pleasure. I watched her ride Gerald with such vigor and force that he staggered backward under her uninhibited wildness, thrown off balance. His hands came up to grip her legs, support her, and the chains slackened with each step back that he took. He hit the wall hard, careening into it, then used the solid support to brace himself, his knees bent, his hips still, as she thrust herself upon him with fixed, ferocious intensity. Her slender white arms stretched up over her head like pillars of ivory, reaching for the chains anchored high above in the wall. A twist of her wrists and her hands wrapped those thick silver chains around her delicate flesh. With the hard metal biting into her palms, she lifted herself up, sliding herself almost off his shaft, and then dropped herself recklessly back down, plunging herself fully upon him with the force of her entire weight, crying out as she impaled herself upon his engorged length. Again and again she lifted herself up and dropped back down, sliding up off his glistening flesh, then slamming back down onto him, riding him so hard that I feared she would hurt herself, that she would hurt him. But his groans were of pleasure, not pain; her fervent cries not that of fear. She took him as if she was taking back a part of herself, with sobbing ferocity, with almost angry passion that was both beautiful and frightening to watch.

Brilliant light filled the room, coming free from their bodies—his bracingly still, hers bucking and heaving like a wild thing above him. The luminescence limned their bodies white and translucent, washing them in the beautiful color and dazzling brilliance of the moon's own rays, claiming them as her creatures, her creations—incandescent beings of light, their skin so radiant, so luminous that that was all they seemed . . . pure glorious light. Nothing but a wash of energy, stillness, and motion. Giving, receiving. Taking, giving. Surrendering, demanding. Claiming, reclaiming. Power flooded the room, and then she was shattering. And as the power of her release began to take her, she became shockingly still. So still, so frozen, as if she wished to feel fully the inner undulations of her secret convulsions, to savor abundantly the flooding heat of her claimed release. Tiny shivering spasms danced over her skin like ripples over a pond, fluttering over her closed eyelids as she shattered within.

With a harsh cry and one almost gentle thrust, as if he could not hold himself from that one small act after all his remarkably passive constraint, Gerald clenched his jaw and shuddered in his own groaning release.

Their panting breaths, my quickened breathing, sounded loud in the room as the light receded and returned back into them.

Mona Carlisse unwrapped the chains from her arms and tore the blindfold from Gerald. She cupped his face softly, and with him still buried deep within her, she kissed him gently. It was a tender act, more intimate than all that had just gone before.

"Thank you," she whispered against his mouth.

Gerald smiled, kissed her gently back. "My pleasure."

They both turned their heads and looked at me.

"Thank you," Mona Carlisse whispered to me.

"My pleasure as well." Opening the door, I quietly left them.

TEN

I MOVED DOWN the hallway with conscious care, feeling tense, overripe, as if all it would take would be the brush of another's skin against mine to set me alight. Need pulsed in me like a living thing, and my clothes were a sudden unwanted, unbearable abrasion. With each step, fabric brushed my erect nipples, pressed against my swollen secret lips. I was hungry to be filled. Aching to be taken.

I rounded a corner. From the darkness, a shadow detached itself and stepped forward. There'd been no heartbeat to warn me. No breath to hear. I halted.

"Mona Lisa." It was Halcyon, my golden-skinned Demon Prince. His eyes were the color of my favorite weakness, chocolate. I'd forgotten that chocolate could melt, that it could become hot and steamy, liquid with desire. That it could boil over with want. He held out one elegant hand to me and that inviting gesture spoke more clearly than words for him. *I know you need, I know you want. Let me fill you, let me please you. Let me love you.*

For one weak moment, I was tempted. His utter need

called out to me, it always had. But never had it drawn me more than now, when my body wanted him so. When filling his need would quench the ache within mine as well. So unbearably tempted . . .

But somehow I shook my head. "I'm sorry, I can't."

Never had I seen his eyes swirl with so much emotion. "Will there ever be a time when you think you can?" he asked softly.

"Halcyon," I said gently, trembling with the constraint I forced upon my willful body, "you cannot wait, hoping for that."

"Then why did you wish me to stay?"

Good question, when before I had asked him to stay away. No wonder he was confused. I was giving him mixed messages. I struggled to find the right words to express myself. But, dear God in heaven, it was so hard to do that when my body was literally throbbing in weeping need.

Words spilled out: Truth. "I'm selfish. I want to keep your friendship. You are very special and dear to me, Halcyon."

"More than a friend, but less than a lover."

"Yes." Then more softly, "I want us to be your family."

He looked at me, so still and quiet, though his eyes swirled with emotion. "You have a most generous heart."

"I am sorry I cannot offer you more." And I truly was.

"So am I." He looked at me with those chocolate eyes as I carefully eased past him, taking care that our bodies did not touch.

I took one shaky step away from him, then another.

"We both know I could just take you," he said quietly. "And that you would enjoy it."

"I know." And it wasn't just his superior strength. His mental powers were even greater. He had the ability to cloud my mind and lure me with the promised pleasure of his flesh. With a simple flexing of will, he could become so lushly sensual, making one crave for him. Fact or figment of my imagination, I did not know. The effect had been scarily real. With little effort, he could become the embodiment of pure carnal pleasure. Irresistible. And I'd had only a tiny taste of what he could do.

"But you are too honorable for that," I said.

"For now." It was a quiet, simple warning.

I backed up until I pressed against the wall. Tearing my eyes from his, I turned the corner and almost ran from my lonely Demon Prince.

And both of us knew that I did so only because he allowed me to.

∽

MY BREATH SHOOK as I reached the entrance hall. I leaped up the staircase with impassioned need and turned down the west wing, my senses already having found that which I sought. I stopped before the door half a corridor away from my own bedroom. The other room directly across it was empty. But not this one. Not this one.

The cool brass knob turned beneath my hand, and I entered, the heavy oak door shutting behind me.

The room was cool and dark, generous in size, spacious in feel like the rest of the house. A large bed dominated the room but my eyes were drawn to the windows. They were flung open to let in the night. Amber stood framed before them, looking out, his hands braced on the sill, his back to me, still as a statue under the moon's soft, glowing shine.

My swift feet were suddenly riveted to the floor at how he looked. Like a marble masterpiece chiseled by an old master, like an ancient god of war. Beautiful strength, brutish power. Only pants covered him. His feet were naked. The muscles of his bare back were tense, sharply defined, inviting one to trace each hollow dip and smooth rise. The deep swells of his arms were beckoning curves, and the tapering V of his waist drew one's attention and appreciation down to his tight, firm buttocks, hard as rock. But rock cannot be punctured by teeth. Rock did not taste sweet, did not bleed.

I wanted to mark him there with my teeth, with my love bite as I had marked Gryphon.

Amber turned slowly and faced me, and as enticing as the view from behind was, the front was even better. Even more interesting curves to explore here: the thick powerful mounds of his chest, the ridged flatness of his belly, the enticing fullness of his long, thick groin. His broad cheeks were slashed with color and his eyes burned amber-yellow, glittering, almost glowing. His nostrils flared wide as he scented me, scenting my need, scenting my arousal. His chest moved, drawing it deep into his lungs.

"Amber," I whispered and he came to me silently, with sure purpose and silent tread, unhurried. I waited for him, my heart pounding, my body yearning, unbearably tight. Aching. His big hands reached out to me and I almost cried with relief when he finally touched me . . . only to turn me sideways. I saw then what I hadn't seen when I first entered. A standing floor mirror, full-length and oval. But it wasn't the lovely cherry finish that I noticed. It was the image reflected back in its flawless mirrored surface. Us.

I wasn't one to spend much time gazing at myself. I knew what I looked like. Common brown eyes and straight brown hair so dark that it looked black. Not ugly. Not stunning. Pretty, if one were generous and I was helped kindly by makeup.

My body was just as common. A little on the tall side at five feet eight, slender but muscled, more athlete than centerfold. Far from lush. But it was a body that had served me well; I was happy with it. The only thing unusual about me was my eyes. They tilted up exotically at the ends. Almond eyes. Cat eyes. Other than that, I was just average, a simple fact I had long ago accepted and was comfortable with. My men were the beautiful ones.

I looked away from the mirror, started to turn back to Amber, but his large hand gently turned my face out again as he stepped forward, so that I was pressed with my back against his chest. "Watch," he rumbled in his deep welling voice, and a wave of trembling heat washed over me. I shivered with excitement, with embarrassment as I looked at him in the mirror. "You listened."

"And learned." The deep vibrations of the words rolled from the barrel of his chest into me, and plucked taut invisible strings of desire within me.

"You like to watch," he rumbled. "Watch us."

Though I was on the tall side for a woman, standing in front of Amber I seemed tiny, petite, my head coming only to his shoulders. He was a whole head taller than I, and so wide across that he seemed to encompass me. I looked delicate, fragile in his arms, my white skin somehow whiter, softer against the hardness of him. His brown hair was ashen silver under the moonshine, while mine was darkened to pure midnight blackness. We were a contrast of colors and textures.

As if cast under a spell, I watched as he lifted his large, broad hand and spread it across my upper chest, almost like a claiming, his fingerspan reaching from one shoulder to the other, sitting like a heavy solid weight upon me, loosening my knees and weakening my neck so that it fell back to loll helplessly against his shoulder. My eyes grew heavy-lidded, and yet I still watched, unable to tear my eyes away as he slowly unbuttoned my shirt, as he deliberately spread it open and slid it off me in a sensuous glide. I watched my chest lift and fall in quickened tempo, saw my breath catch as I felt him unhook my bra from behind and brush it down my arms, pushing it slowly down and down until it slipped free past my fingertips and fell to the floor with a white twin-cupped flutter. I closed my eyes against the sight of my naked breasts.

His hands lifted away.

"Watch." His rough command sent a trickle of wetness sliding down my leg. Only when I opened my eyes once more did he touch me again.

One big hand came to splay wide and open across my quivering belly. Deliberately, he pulled the button loose from my jeans, pulled down the zipper. A gentle push and the denim pooled about my feet. With his hands swallowing up my waist, he lifted me, freeing my feet, and with stunning ease carried me a few steps closer to the mirror. Languor made heavy my limbs and melting passion stunned me helpless in his hands, like a pliant doll with which he could do anything he pleased. I moaned at the thought, at the feeling of total surrender. His yellow glowing eyes burned me in the mirror, ravaged me fiercely with his restrained desire. One big hand slowly slid downward to my last remaining article of clothing. He cupped me lightly and fingered the wetness of the cotton crotch, making me tremble. Making me cry out as with one sharp, violent tug, he ripped it from me. I trembled helplessly in his arms, shocked and dazed.

"Put your arms around my neck," he growled roughly, his voice low and thick.

Biting my lip, I lifted my arms up above and behind me, wrapping them around his neck. I looked like a Christmas ornament dangling from his neck, and felt like one—on total display.

"Spread your legs."

Quivering, I jerkily obeyed, moving my feet wider apart, and trembled at what I saw in the mirror. I looked like a wanton stranger, naked and exposed while Amber stood large and powerful behind me, still wearing pants. Feet apart, arms lifted, my body was completely opened to him, to his body, his hands, his eyes. Shame twined with excitement, bedeviling, writhed like a living snake within me, making me shudder, making my small breasts swell even more, elongating my nipples, wetting my thighs with more rivulets of desire.

I could not bear to look at myself any longer. My eyes squeezed shut as I gasped in air.

"Open your eyes, sweetheart." Roughly tender, but still a command.

My eyes fluttered open.

"Watch me make you come," he whispered in a voice dark as midnight, coarse as gravel.

I almost exploded just hearing him say that. And then I did as one big callused finger touched me, found my swollen little pearl and stroked it. I lit up like a firecracker, spilling the room with light. Then I sparked and burst in air. I trembled and shuddered and cried as I exploded, and then cried again as I watched him sink that big finger into me. Watched the long length disappear up into my body as I twitched and jerked. I watched him—and felt him—slide that fat finger in and out of me, pumping me, prolonging my orgasm, milking my release to its very last convulsive drop.

I collapsed against him, stunned, amazed that Amber was doing this. Playing me like this. So easily, so confidently, so masterfully. And he wasn't done.

He slid his broad finger, covered with my juice, out of my grasping sheath and sucked the wetness of my pleasure into his mouth, his brilliant eyes a yellow blaze. "You taste like passion," he said, and I quivered and almost came again.

"Amber." It was a plea, a hoarse demand.

He stepped back and I gently swayed, barely able to stand on my own. Carefully, he eased down the zipper of his pants and freed his erection. It sprang out heavy, thick, and long, the engorged crown crimson with heated arousal, liquid excitement leaking from its tip. It looked happy in its freedom, bobbing in eagerness as he kicked out of his pants.

"Kneel down," he rasped harshly.

My heart, only just slowing, kicked into high gear again as I sank down onto my knees.

He positioned me so that I was turned sideways to the mirror, so that I could watch both of us in profile. "Brace your hands in front of you."

My eyes glued to his in the mirror as I bent forward and

braced myself on hands and knees before him like a supplicant, like a sacrifice, like prey he had chased and brought
down. He stood behind me for a long, long moment, a towering figure, both of us breathing hard. Then he knelt behind me, and that part of him that would enter me was tall
and upright, like a thick heavy pole jutting obliquely out
from his body.

"Watch," he growled.

Just that one word and like a conditioned animal, my
womb tightened, my sheath shivered, my nipples tingled,
and all the muscles of my body clenched.

"Open wider."

"Oh, God." I bit back a whimper and spread my knees
wider. Conversely, the opening of my legs made me feel
more empty, more hollow inside.

"Keep your eyes open. Watch us." With jaw clenched,
he guided himself to my dripping, shadowy cleft that was
achingly, throbbingly hungry once again.

I felt him push against my dewy nether lips, and in the
mirror, I saw him sink and push and grunt his way into me.
Invading me. In and in. Another thick inch. Then another.
Pull back, push in harder, with more force, fighting and
pushing his way inside me despite my wetness.

He felt massive. I felt full, lodged, wonderfully crammed.
He halted halfway in.

"No," I cried, straining back against him. "Don't stop."

"What do you want?"

"All of you."

He continued his slow, deep plunge. I groaned and panted
and pushed my hips back against him and gasped, "Yes . . .
more . . . oh, God! Oh, God! . . . Please, more . . ."

The light came like an exploding essence called out
from our bodies, so blindingly bright that I had to squint
my eyes to see. In the reflected glass, we looked like angels
aglow. Doing a most unangelic thing.

One heavy grunting thrust with his hips and he pushed all

the way in, nudging against my womb, and I went off again
in a second glorious release, crying out, gasping, spasming around him, squeezing him so tight that he groaned.
Feeling so weak and trembly that I collapsed onto my elbows, my cheek resting against the floor. When the waves
of passion finally eased to lap in gentle swells against the
shore of me, my lashes lifted once more and I saw his bright
amber eyes watching me in the mirror, his face tight, his
body tense, and I realized that he was still full and hard
within me.

"Watch," he said hoarsely as he began to move.

I gasped, shook my head, and cried out, knowing what
he wanted and knowing I could not take more. "No . . .
no . . ." My body twitched and jerked, reacting beyond my
control. I was too sensitive. It was too soon. Too much. I
sobbed and jerked forward to dislodge him, to break free of
his overwhelming fullness. He grabbed my hips, stopping
my escape, pulling me back with surging force against him,
sliding back in.

I shook my head wildly. "No, I can't." Tears trickled
down my cheeks.

Amber's arm clamped diagonally across the center of
my chest, lifting me up and back against him. The other
hand gripped my hip in an unbreakable iron grip, keeping
us together.

"Shhh," he crooned soothingly. "I won't move. Just let
me stay inside you."

I calmed at his promise, didn't fight him, but couldn't
stop trembling. My body was on overload, my swollen tissues quivering at the slightest movement. Even just the thick
unmoving presence of him deep within me, stretching my
screamingly sensitive nerve endings was only just barely tol-
erable. As long as he didn't move.

He held me like that, both of us on our knees, my back
pressed tight against his chest, my bottom snugged tight in
an unbreakable line against his groin as I knelt in the V of

his spread knees. His thighs were like massive tree trunks surrounding me, his arm a heavy restraining weight against my chest, caging me captive against him. I was impaled by him. Stretched by him.

When I had quieted, when I had stopped trembling, when my tenseness had eased and I tiredly relaxed back against him, letting him support my full weight, he nuzzled the top of my head with his chin. "You're beautiful," he murmured.

"No, I'm not."

"You are."

"Only in your eyes."

"Then see yourself through my eyes. I'm going to turn us," and with that warning, he shifted us slowly, carefully edging around until we faced the mirror once again. The move was surprisingly easy for him to accomplish, and no effort on my part. He just pressed me tight against him. His knees made two gentle surges that jangled my nerves so that I tensed, but not enough for me to fight him. It was the sight of us in the mirror that made me gasp.

He was like a pagan god of carnal desire, naked, gloriously powerful, holding a delicate maiden in his arms, surrounding her, almost encompassing her. She—I—looked so much smaller. Fragile and helpless in his massive arms, against that hard body that swelled with brutal strength, that bulged with muscles around her like a living, imprisoning tower of flesh. And yet she leaned back against him trustingly. And he held her, cradled her, restrained her tenderly, protectively in his arms, even as his eyes burned with the fierceness of desire, and sparked hotly with unspent passion. The contrast, the trust, was a beautiful image, innocent even. From the front, you couldn't see the hot, hard length of him buried snug within me. All you saw was the sleepy, sensual languor of my eyelids, the light rose color of passion—either spent or rising, in this case both— dusting my face, my neck, my chest. And I was beautiful like that, my lips red with passion, my eyelids drooping with sensual languor. My breasts slight, delicate, high and firm, accented by my narrow waist and the feminine flare of my hips. My dark brown nipples were jutting peaks, crying for attention. The hair between my legs was dark and enticing, moist from my passion.

Just the picture of us like that—spent passion, unspent passion, stirring passion all twirling, swirling around us—was like an invisible caress. Pleasure stirred within me once more, and the liquid heat of my renewed desire anointed him inside me. The knowledge of what was beyond that mirrored picture, what lay lodged thick and heavy and strumming within me like a dormant threat, was a subtle stimulation. The outer wetness of my triangle grew as I bathed him within, making him groan softly, pleasurably. Making him throb and jerk in involuntary upward surges within me, a stirring, quiescent beast.

"Watch us."

His words were like a hot pulse that quickened my womb, tightening me around him even more.

"Dear Goddess, you hold me so sweetly," he muttered, his chest rising and falling, lifting us both to his rhythm. He was like a giant sea of muscle surrounding me, within me. And I gave myself up to him. Floated in his pulsing hardness.

He growled deep in his chest, his brilliant feral eyes locked with mine as he sensed my acquiescence, the giving of myself to him wholly in whatever he wished to do.

But all that he wished to do was smooth his hands up the narrow flatness of my belly to rest just beneath my aching breasts, just barely touching the soft undersides with his thick fingers, his longs thumbs bracketing the sides of my breasts. And then stopping there, holding those big hands still, leaving my nipples straining, aching, quivering to be touched.

"Amber," I whispered, whimpered, my hands coming to

rest with hot need upon his wrists, my chest arching forward into his teasing, not quite cupping hands.

"What do you desire?" His breath was a hot stirring caress against my ear, making me shiver.

"Touch me."

"Where?"

A soft whimper of need. A gasped confession. "My nipples."

"They're beautiful, your nipples. So sensitive, so responsive." His voice was like dark, rough honey. "Ask me to touch your beautiful nipples."

I rolled my head back against him in denial, in embarrassment.

His forefingers moved in gentle strokes, teasing the underside of my breasts. Nice but not where I wanted those fingers.

"Say it," he whispered.

I shook my head but my want was too much. "Amber, please touch my . . . beautiful nipples." My face flamed. But as his hands moved up and his fingers brushed my aching nipples, embarrassment faded beneath the hot sway of passion.

"Watch how beautiful you are in my hands." And I did. I watched as he molded me, stroked me, gently squeezed and tugged on my nipples, elongating the dark rosy tips even as I felt him elongating within me. I felt the heavy beat of his heart against my back, felt a second echoing heartbeat within me. My tightly stretched secret flesh felt each quiver, each dewy drip of excitement that leaked from him, felt each lifting flex of his heavy pole.

I wriggled against him, letting him know that I would welcome his movement now. But he only squeezed my nipples hard, firmly. Rolled them with his rough fingertips. And continued to tug on the sensitive tips, pulling them out. Pulling them until they were almost obscenely long, jutting out like little pointy fingers.

"So beautiful," he murmured. "So incredibly responsive. Feel what I feel when I'm inside you."

His hands snaked down my belly, dipped gently between my stretched lips into my moist cavity with cramming fingers, feeling where we met, where he filled me. A few deep feathery caresses and then his hands left me and returned to my breasts.

With his first two fingers and thumbs creating little sheaths, with the moisture from my own vagina, he moved his fingers up and down the length of my stretched out nipples, tugging, pulling, squeezing the sensitive points, pumping the fuller areolae with a sliding movement. Squeezing then releasing.

"One more time," he rumbled like deep thunder. "Come for me."

He tugged with sudden fierce force and squeezed my nipples achingly hard. So hard that pain became sharp, almost unbearable pleasure, and I cried out and came, singing, zinging with passion like an instrument that he played at will. I convulsed deeply within, clamping tightly around his thick, throbbing pole, and like a silent mirroring echo, his fingers squeezed tightly, convulsively around my nipples. I convulsed and convulsed, waves of almost painful pleasure spreading hot and pervasive as a scorching wash of heat spilled through me. I came on a release harder, more violent, than the other two that had come before, feeling as if I was tearing apart inside, or trying to tear him apart. Trying to squeeze him dry, grind him flat. And the squeeze and press and pull on my nipples was a silent echo of what I did to him inside.

Amber groaned and shuddered and heaved as if I were hurting him, and maybe I was. His fingers were so tightly, ferociously clamped around my nipples. And I couldn't stop myself, couldn't control my inner muscles. Could only spasm and squeeze and clench him in my violent rolling climax until I freed his inner tears and he was crying within me, gushing within me hotly in a fountain of release that splashed with wet heat against my contracting womb.

When the light ebbed and our shudders ceased, when only little ripples of pleasure flowed through us now and again as if reluctant to leave us fully, he let my sore and sensitive nipples slip from his wet fingers and eased from my body. He carried me to his bed, and pulled me against the bigness of him, gathering me up in his arms, nuzzling the tendrils clinging damply to my forehead.

"God, Amber," I muttered, puffing hot breaths against his throat.

"What is it?" he rumbled.

"Nothing. Just . . . God."

Against me, beside me, I felt him smile.

ELEVEN

THE DELICIOUS SMELL of cooking food teased my senses awake. I crawled from Amber's bed, leaving him asleep, and made my way down the hallway to shower in my room.

Wondering where the others were, I opened my senses as I walked downstairs. There were heartbeats scattered around the house, but it was the ones beating more quickly, the ones gathered outside that drew my interest. I slipped out the front door, walked past the rounded corner of the east ballroom, and found what I'd suspected. Wiley had come back.

He was down on all fours, prancing around the lawn in a gentle canter. Casio was on his back, the skirts of her dress bunched up, her thin legs sticking out like sticks as she bounced on Wiley's back. She was giggling.

Tersa and Jamie watched them from beneath a hanging canopy of Spanish moss draped over the spreading branches of a giant oak tree, their red hair darkened to shadowy brown under the dim starlight as clouds covered the moon.

Wiley's face and limbs were smudged with dirt, and his hair once again tangled. But the clothes he wore were clean. Another set of Thaddeus's, I saw, the waistband loose, the cuff of the pants rolled up. He pranced to a stop beneath the towering oak and let his passenger disembark. She did so with clumsy grace, her eyes alight, her smile revealing dimples in her cheeks.

Wiley stood. Then with a casual shove, he sent Jamie toppling down to the ground and pounced on him. Pinning the larger boy to the ground, Wiley bared his teeth dangerously close to Jamie's throat and growled softly.

"No, Wiley!" I shouted, rushing toward them as Tersa said in a firm voice, "Wiley, no!"

Wiley looked up at me, gave me a smile—at least that's what I think it was . . . a lot of teeth but no growl—then lowered his face and snarling teeth back to Jamie.

"It's okay, Mona Lisa," Jamie said, making no attempt to move or fight back. He just lay there calmly, as if this was a routine they'd already gone through several times before.

"He's just establishing the fact that he's dominant," Jamie explained. "Something which I have absolutely no wish to challenge."

Only when little Casio put her hand on the Wolf Boy's shoulder and softly said, "No, Wiley," did he release Jamie.

"Likes you girls well enough," Jamie said as he got to his feet slowly. "Doesn't seem to like guys as much." He grinned, making his freckles dance. "But I think he's getting used to me."

"Jamie," I said, fear still a bitter taste in my throat, "you should have stayed inside. You shouldn't have put yourself at risk."

"It's okay, Mona Lisa," Jamie said, his voice soft, looking at me with that new maturity he'd acquired since his sister's attack. "I knew Wiley wouldn't hurt me as long as I didn't fight back."

You couldn't have known, I wanted to shout at him. His

freckles were a cheerful scatter across a face that lifted often and easily into a smile. But there was a budding strength beneath that sweet charm. He was a boy becoming a man. And I had to stand back and let him grow, let him make his own decisions, even though I wanted badly to keep him wrapped in safety.

Wiley came closer, sniffing me. I held out my hands and let him smell me.

"Thank you for rescuing me from that alligator," I told the wild boy, "although it was stupid to jump in and wrestle something three times bigger and heavier than yourself."

I doubted Wiley understood the words, but he certainly caught my scolding tone. He grinned up at me, much as Jamie had, unrepentant, making me sigh and smile. "I'm surrounded by fearless boys, it seems."

"They learn it from you," Tersa said.

"Maybe that's not such a good thing."

"But it is," Tersa returned, her voice a low, gentle, sure sound. "It's a good thing not to fear."

The awareness of a new heartbeat and the sense of a presence had me turning to my left. Wiley loped into the forest, disappearing as Miguel appeared.

"Wiley," Tersa shouted after him.

"Let him go," I said. "We know he'll come back now."

"Casio," Miguel said gently, "your mother sent me to find you. Who was that boy you were playing with?"

"Wiley," Casio said.

"And who is Wiley?" he patiently asked her.

"A friend."

Miguel lifted his head to look askance at me.

"A Mixed Blood," I explained. "He grew up wild and isn't used to men."

"Then he is dangerous," Miguel said quietly.

"No," Casio cried.

"Casio is safe with him. He would not hurt her," I said, and mentally chided myself. I was as bad as Jamie. But I knew with certainty that Wiley would not harm a child. It was just men he had a problem with.

"Come," Miguel said, holding his hand out to Casio, "your mother misses you."

We all trudged back toward the house.

"Who came up with the name Wiley?" I asked.

"Your brother did," Tersa said. "It sounds like what you called him, Wild Boy. Though he said something about a coyote and a cartoon that I did not quite understand."

"Wile E. Coyote," I muttered, smiling. Not quite the same thing as a wolf, but close. And Wild Boy did have a way of dashing off rather quickly like the cartoon character. My brother had a sly sense of humor, it seemed. "Wiley's as good a name as any, I guess."

I made a note to buy some new clothes for Wiley, clothes that fit him better. The way the boy was using them up, my brother was going to run out of clothes soon.

Speaking of my brother, I heard a car pull up the long driveway. They had returned, just in time for dinner.

I waited by the front door and watched my men climb out of the Suburban. "Where's Horace?" I asked.

"We sent the good steward on his merry way," Gryphon said.

"We have some of the coolest businesses, Mona Lisa," Thaddeus said, his eyes dancing, his usually calm face alive with excitement.

"Yeah? You'll have to tell me about them later," I said, smiling at his eagerness.

Gryphon scrutinized me carefully with his sharp falcon eyes as he climbed the sweeping steps, the others behind him. "You are well?"

It took me a heartbeat to realize he was asking about my injuries. "Oh, yes," I said, stepping back, letting them all enter through the door. "Janelle healed me up as good as new. It was amazing. And she said she was going to teach me and Casio how to do what she did."

"We will at least begin the process," Janelle said, coming down the front hallway, Prince Halcyon a golden presence beside her. "I have been sent to call you all to dinner." She gazed curiously at Thaddeus, and I realized that they had never met.

"This is my brother, Thaddeus," I said, introducing them. "Thaddeus, this is Healer Janelle and Prince Halcyon, High Council members. We are honored to have them as our guests."

Like the polite boy he had been raised to be, Thaddeus stepped forward and shook Halcyon's hand. Though Thaddeus glanced curiously at the long nails, there was no fear on his face. With the briefest pause, Halcyon carefully shook my brother's hand and released it, a slight smile on his face, and I realized it was the first time I'd seen any of them do that. Shaking hands seemed to be a human tradition, not a Monèrian one. Made sense among a people that had the casual strength to rip one another apart with their bare hands.

"A pleasure to meet you, sir," Thaddeus said.

"Likewise," Halcyon murmured.

"Your brother," Janelle said wonderingly. "You found him."

"Yes," I said. "I found him."

The healer held out a hand to my brother. But when Thaddeus reached out and grasped it, instead of shaking it, Janelle just held his hand in both of hers, a distant inward look in her eyes.

"Ah," she exclaimed softly, her eyes widening with surprise. "You also have the gift for healing. How rare in a male."

"I do?" Thaddeus said. His power flared out briefly as it did whenever he was frightened or threatened, and all present felt it.

And I knew what Thaddeus feared, what he was threatened by, because it was my fear as well. Whether or not

Councilwoman Janelle could sense his other even more rare ability: basking.

Gently, I pulled Thaddeus away from the healer, and she released his hand.

"How blessed we are," Janelle said, pleasure lighting her eyes. "Three new healing talents discovered in such a short span of time."

"How many do you usually discover a year?" Thaddeus asked curiously.

"One or two with the potential every ten cycles, if we are fortunate."

Ten cycles meaning ten years.

"That rarely!" I exclaimed. "So does that mean it will be hard to find a healer to come to our territory?"

"Healers are few and valued enough that they can pick and choose where they serve," Janelle said, confirming my suspicions. Which explained why my mother, Mona Sera, considered one of the worst Queens among the Monère, had not had a healer.

"I won't be able to get my hands on one, will I?" I said bluntly.

Janelle smiled, as if my quaint human phrasing seemed to amuse her. "If that means to lure a healer to your service, then no, not for the next several seasons, in all likelihood."

"Because I'm a Mixed Blood Queen," I said flatly.

"Yes," Janelle agreed gently. "You are an unknown. They will wait to see how you rule. You must prove yourself strong, stable, and prosperous first."

"To everyone, it seems," I muttered.

"In the meanwhile, the best you can do is to develop all your potential talent and you are richly blessed in that. You must allow me to instruct your brother as well."

"It seems we have no other choice," I said wryly. "How long does it take to learn to do what you did to me?"

"It varies greatly, but half a cycle of ten is most common."

"Five years?" I groaned. Which also meant that Janelle wasn't sure I'd be able to get my hands on a healer even a year from now. "How long can you stay?"

"No longer than a fortnight, I'm afraid. But we can continue our lessons thereafter every second new moon when you come to the High Council meetings."

I smiled grimly at Thaddeus. "Well, little brother, I hope one of us learns fast."

"So do I," he said, gazing down at my recently healed calf. "So do I."

TWELVE

THE NEXT MORNING ended up being a continuation of my long, long night. The plan was to enroll Thaddeus in the parish's local high school. Then I was hitting my bed. We were in a good school district, living as we were in the seat of old wealth. The other houses we drove past, while not mansions, carried the weight of their years with well-maintained dignity and expensively groomed lawns.

Thaddeus was in the back. Halcyon sat in the front passenger seat, looking as tired as I felt. The big SUV actually felt empty with just us three in it. Gryphon had been surprisingly agreeable when I had suggested that Halcyon accompany us to the school. In fact, Gryphon had been amazingly cordial and calm about Halcyon's presence thus far. But maybe that wasn't so surprising. Gryphon had asked for help, after all, and Halcyon had come to our aid, healer in tow. He seemed willing to entrust our safety to the Demon Prince's hands, satisfied that my brother's presence would be adequate chaperone.

I'd asked Halcyon to come along because, of the three

men able to withstand daylight, Halcyon would actually blend in the most. Amber was too strikingly big and Gryphon was just too damn beautiful. They would attract a lot of attention and curiosity, which I wanted to avoid. Prince Halcyon, the High Prince of Hell, actually wouldn't draw much human attention, believe it or not. He blended wonderfully, except for his long nails.

"Just keep your hands in your pocket or behind your back," I reminded him once again.

Halcyon just smiled and nodded.

"I said that before, didn't I?" I said, nervously tapping the steering wheel.

"Only four or five times," Thaddeus muttered.

"All will be well," Halcyon reassured me.

"I'm sorry," I said. "I don't know why I'm so nervous."

Thaddeus, looking curiously at the school grounds we were entering, obviously wasn't.

I pulled into an empty parking space in front of the three-story brick building. Two long rectangular wings flared back at forty-five-degree angles from either side of the structure so that it looked like a giant brick bird about to take flight.

"Don't worry," Thaddeus said, getting out of the car, "I'm not even starting school yet."

It was the last Friday before Christmas break. Our timing was almost perfect, as if we had planned it, which, let me assure you, we had not. It luckily had just worked out that way, like sometimes things did. School would be out for the next three weeks and the administration had decided that it would be best if Thaddeus started classes after the holidays. We were just here to register him and tour the school. Butterflies, however, still fluttered in my stomach as we stepped through the white double doors. The sight of long corridors, rows of lockers, and closed classroom doors brought back a wave of memories, many of them unpleasant. No matter where you are, schools smelled the same the world over, like waxed floors and disinfectant, the sweat of young bodies, still sweet, not yet pungent with maturity, the faint stench of gym socks, the whiff of old textbooks and new notebooks, girls' floral perfume, and the scent of forbidden bubblegum, chewed in hidden silence.

The registrar's office was to our right. A lady with tanned, wrinkled skin and obviously dyed brown hair sized us up in one encompassing glance, peering over the rim of reading glasses perched low on her nose with sharp, no-nonsense eyes. A veritable dragon.

I self-consciously smoothed the skirt of my dark blue dress under that piercing stare. It was the only short dress I owned. I'd bought it and worn it only once before, for my job interview at St. Vincent's Hospital. Tersa, acting like my lady in waiting, had French braided my hair neatly back away from my face, and had even applied some makeup with a surprisingly deft hand. When she was done, I almost didn't recognize myself. I looked older, more sophisticated. Pretty.

Now, I just had to act the part, which was easier said than done. Speaking slowly, calmly, I introduced myself. "Hello, I'm Lisa Hamilton. I'm here to register my brother, Thaddeus Schiffer, for next quarter. He's transferring schools."

The dragon's glance slid over me and moved on to Thaddeus, who was dressed neatly in brown corduroys and an oxford shirt. Then she looked pointedly at Halcyon; a woman who knew how to let silence speak for her.

"This is Albert Smith, my friend," I said, answering her unasked question.

Halcyon smiled charmingly back at her, his hands casually hidden in his front pockets.

"We've been expecting you," she said crisply and introduced herself as Mrs. Boudoin. She disappeared into the adjoining office for a moment. When she returned, she waved us in. "Mr. Camden will see you now."

Mr. Camden was a pleasant-looking man in his thirties

who smiled warmly at us in welcome, shook both Thaddeus's hand and mine and gestured for us to take the two
seats in front of his desk. He nodded congenially to Halcyon, who remained standing deliberately back against the
door.

"Your school has already forwarded your records and
SAT scores to us, Thaddeus. Both of which are very impressive. And you are just"—he glanced down at the
opened file on his desktop—"sixteen. Two years younger
than the rest of our seniors." And looking even younger,
more like fourteen. Social suicide in high school. I did not
envy my brother.

"Thank you, sir," Thaddeus said. "I started kindergarten
early and Hawthorne Academy was kind enough to arrange
a curriculum allowing me to complete high school in three
years instead of four."

Mr. Camden smiled. "The heavier course load does not
seem to have affected you adversely in any way."

"No, sir."

"Well, we can certainly accommodate you here as well,"
the smiling Mr. Camden said, looking at both Thaddeus and
I. "You only have one extra course per quarter to fit into
your schedule, which we should be able to do quite easily."

"We appreciate that," I said, and smiled for the first time
at him. He seemed stunned for a moment. Then his smile
became even warmer, and his eyes dipped down to gaze at
my bare left hand.

My smile disappeared.

"It's unusual for students to transfer in the middle of
their senior year. May I ask what precipitated this change?"
Mr. Camden asked.

"His parents were just killed in a car accident. My brother
has only recently come to live with me," I explained.

Mr. Camden murmured his condolences. "Do you have
any plans for college, Thaddeus?"

"I've been accepted into Harvard and Yale, sir."

Mr. Camden smiled. "Congratulations. But not so surprising with your scores."

"However," Thaddeus continued, "I have decided to attend one of the local universities instead."

Mr. Camden's brows rose with interest. "I have a friend who works in admissions at Tulane. You would be someone they would most definitely be interested in." He wrote down his friend's name and number and handed it to me with another warm smile. Then he got down to business and showed us the busy schedule he had tentatively worked out. With only a few minor changes Thaddeus suggested, the courses for the rest of his school year were finalized, and a locker assigned to him.

The assistant principal, a Ms. Emma Thornton, took us on a brief tour of the school. She was handsome rather than beautiful, a tall, elegant woman who seemed to smile with special interest at Halcyon. Made one wonder if the entire faculty here was unmarried.

Thaddeus's textbooks in hand, we left the building just before noon, finally sucking in air that didn't smell recycled. The sun—a hot, yellow ball hovering straight overhead—shot fiercely down upon us as we walked to the car.

Only in the car did Halcyon finally remove his hands from his pockets. "So that is a school. So many children," he murmured. "Over a thousand beating hearts I sensed in there."

"You've never been to a school before?" I asked, starting the car.

"The Monère do not have such a thing. Nor enough children to warrant such an institution," Halcyon said, a tinge of sadness in his voice.

"Are you feeling well, Prince Halcyon?" Thaddeus asked from the backseat.

My brother's question made me turn and look at

Halcyon. Really look. And what I saw alarmed me. He
looked haggard, sallow beneath the golden hue of his skin.

"What's wrong?" I asked sharply. Concern flared even
greater when he dropped his head tiredly back against his
seat. He'd never displayed any weakness before. Heck, he'd
never *been* weak before, and seeing a crack in that great
strength now rattled me completely.

"The sun bothers me," he admitted quietly.

"The sun?" I said, leveling him a hard look. "Halcyon,
you were walking in daylight when I first met you. The sun
was shining brightly down upon you then and it didn't
seem to bother you."

"I remember feeling as if something in the woods was
calling me," he said, smiling weakly in remembrance. "It
had been so long since I had walked the earth beneath the
sun's rays."

My knuckles tightened around the steering wheel until
they were white. "Shit, Halcyon. You told me when we first
met that the sun doesn't bother you."

He closed his eyes. "Not in short doses. Even these
lengthy hours today I could have withstood at my full
strength, but I have been long away from home." Home
being Hell, which I wasn't exactly sure if Thaddeus knew
just yet.

"I had already tarried seven days at High Court before
Gryphon called us here," Halcyon said.

"You should have told me that." I was angry and frightened, my voice harsh. "I would never have asked you to accompany us if I had known."

"I wished to come," he said simply. "I wanted to see
what a human school was like."

"Jesus Christ, Halcyon." I felt like smacking him for
taking such a foolish risk. "Are you going to burn or melt
or anything like that?"

Again that weak smile. "No, just bring me back to the
house. I will rest, then depart for High Court tonight, and

return back home. I will be fine once I am back in my own realm."

"I noticed that you hardly ate anything last night, sir," Thaddeus said.

"You are most observant, Thaddeus. I did not eat at all, actually."

I was getting an ugly suspicion here. "Let me guess. You cut up your steak and moved it around."

Halcyon sighed and admitted, "Foolish pride again."

"Why would you do that, sir?" Thaddeus asked politely.

"Because he doesn't eat food. Am I right, Halcyon?" I asked, spearing him a hard glance.

"Meat is not what I require," he said, closing his eyes.

"So this is even more my fault." But no one had told me. Still, I should have asked or at least guessed. Tersa and Jamie had been absent from dinner last night and now I knew why. Their mother had kept them hidden from Halcyon. She hadn't wanted them being served up as blood donors to the High Prince of Hell. Regret and guilt flooded me. "Halcyon, I would have provided what you needed, had I known."

He opened his eyes to gaze at me. "Would you have?"

"Yes." I reached out, touched the back of his hand. "And I would have trusted you to keep it clean, no hanky-panky while I did it."

"That I could not have promised to do," Halcyon said, smiling, turning his hand until his palm met mine. Carefully he closed his hand around mine, his long nails resting lightly against my skin.

"The fault is mine and of those under me," I said softly. Because they had known and hadn't told me, and I hadn't asked. "Forgive me. I will do my best to make amends for my breach in hospitality."

"There is nothing to forgive. The fault lies with my foolish pride," Halcyon murmured, his eyes a dark caress.

"What does he need, Mona Lisa?" Thaddeus asked.

I looked at my brother through the rearview mirror.
"Blood," I said, and saw his eyes widen slightly.

The Suburban jolted suddenly, as if something large
had hit it.

"What the—" My question was drowned under the
screaming groan of metal. Above us, talons punctured the
ceiling, the sharp claws popping through the fabric lining right above our heads. With a heart-stopping lurch,
the car was yanked from the small road we were on, and
then we were airborne for the distance of a dozen yards.
No other cars or houses in sight because this was private
property, my property. We were only minutes away from
home.

The talons disappeared, and we were dropped with a
lurching thud into a field with waist-high weeds. Before the
car had stopped rocking, I had the door open and was out.
A giant eagle came swooping down at me with razor-sharp
beak and lethal talons. I hit the ground, then scrambled
back up when it hurtled past me. For one terrible second I
thought it was Aquila, my guard, the former bandit I had
trusted and taken into my service. His other form was a
bald eagle. And then I saw that the plumage was less rich,
the black-and-white coloring different, the white of the
head extending farther down into the chest and the upper
part of the wings. Not an eagle—a vulture. And its presence felt different . . . jarring, abrasive.

"Behind you!" Thaddeus screamed and I ducked and
rolled, barely in time. A hard rush of wind blew over me
and the hunter's wings brushed against me, missing its
main target, but still striking me a glancing blow. Fiery
pain slashed my shoulder and the bittersweet smell of
blood filled the air as I tumbled to the ground.

A second large bird, a red-tailed hawk, shot past with an
angry shriek. Nope, not my people. The hawk was smaller
than the gyrfalcon Gryphon became, a muddy swirl of
brown instead of snowy white, with a chestnut-colored tail.

But still it was a deadly predator of the sky, a dark shadow of death winging overhead.

"Stay in the car!" I yelled to Thaddeus. He hesitated, then got back inside and shut the door.

"You, too, Halcyon."

"I think not," the Demon Prince said quietly and came around the car to crouch down beside me. Hard to order him around when he actually outranked me. Too bad. He didn't look too good. But if he insisted on playing . . . I offered him my silver dagger, my eyes scanning the blue sky.

"I do not need that," Halcyon said, and flashed his long nails when I glanced over at him.

"Oh, yeah. Forgot," I muttered. "Here they come."

The vulture hurtled down, dropping hard from the sky. The hawk was right behind it, a brown rushing blur. I sprang away from the car and stood, a clear inviting target, hands bare, daggers sheathed. With the barest adjustment, they veered toward me, diving like bombers.

"Mona Lisa, no!" Halcyon cried.

Just before the vulture struck, I called the daggers to my hands, one silver, one plain steel. I let the silver blade fly. A swift evading maneuver by the giant bird and I missed. I missed! Fuck!

The vulture came right back on target with a sharp angling of its wings, plunging straight toward me. With no time to call back the silver blade, I met talons with steel. I leaped up to meet it, striking it in the air. I had a fraction of a moment to savor my dagger sinking into the vulture's body, and then it struck me with the full momentum of its dive behind it. It felt like a freaking hammer hit me. Stunning force, a sharp tearing impact in my right arm, and not too much pain—not a good thing. It was better when it hurt like hell. When you didn't feel anything, that meant the wound was deep and the injury bad.

I think I dropped the dagger, couldn't tell. Couldn't feel anything in my right arm. And then I didn't know anything other than I was careening through the air, thrown by the impact of that motherfucking big bird. It shrieked with triumphant glee and swooped past me, red droplets dripping from its breast. I hit the ground with smacking force, eating dirt. The fall kicked the breath from my lungs and made me see stars.

"No!" Halcyon cried.

I turned my head in time to see Halcyon dive in front of me, using his lean body as a shield, and take the hit meant for me. The hawk struck him with an impact that I both felt and saw. The blow shook and reverberated through Halcyon's slight body. His blood splattered wide in a crimson spray as talons dug deep into his back. With a jerk that ripped a moan from his lips, the hawk heaved the Demon Prince upward into the air, carrying him away.

"Halcyon!" His name was a weak, airless gasp from my lips. Then my mouth opened wide in a soundless scream as sharp claws struck me, tunneling into my back, scraping against bone. The vulture jerked me into the air like a flopping doll, and hot, searing pain ripped through my body and sank me into darkness.

~⚬~

SEARING PAIN JERKED me back into consciousness. My back, of course. And my right shoulder throbbed like a screaming bitch. Chains were tight and secure around my wrists and ankles, giving me a hint that I was in deep shit, if the pain hadn't already clued me in.

I opened my eyes, then wished I hadn't. Silver chains I could have broken, but it was demon chains that bound me. And beside me, they bound Halcyon as well. He looked terrible. His tanned skin was almost gray, and his face and entire body was puffy, swollen. He looked like an overripe peach that would squish open with one careless squeeze. Rivulets of blood twined down his legs and side like crimson beads. I must have made a sound or some noise. Halcyon opened his bloated eyelids and tried to smile at me, but the movement cracked his dry lips and they split open, oozing blood and thick gooey liquid.

"Oh, my God, Halcyon." My voice came out dry and cracked. I cleared my throat, swallowed to moisten it. "What did they do to you?"

"Sun," he croaked.

They'd fried him, the bastards. Someone seemed to know quite a bit about the demon dead.

I felt the guilty sun innocently setting in the west. I'd been out for a while—several long hours had gone by. Relief welled up within me that at least Thaddeus wasn't here with us. I prayed that my brother had returned to the house safely. Did the others even know we had been taken? Or were they all still asleep and insensate in their daytime rest?

"Who took us?" I asked.

"Mona Louisa."

Somehow his answer didn't surprise me. She'd been my nemesis forever, it seemed, though it hadn't really been that long. Just felt that way. She'd tried to kill me twice already. Let's hope the third time wasn't the charm.

But it explained how Mona Louisa had gotten ahold of demon chains. From Kadeen, the same demon dead warlord she'd sicced on me. He must have served as her conduit to Hell and all its interesting supplies. Made me glad that we'd killed him. And made me wonder if she knew that her source had been gobbled down by Hell hounds and was no more.

"Where are we?"

"Mississippi," Halcyon rasped. "About a hundred miles east of New Orleans."

"What's Mona Louisa doing here?"

"She lives here. Part of her original territory. Louisiana went to you. She kept the western part of Mississippi."

It boggled my mind. They'd sliced up her original territory and given the bigger piece to me. Generous and yet incredibly stupid. Just begging for trouble, in fact. "You left Mona Louisa as my *neighbor*?"

Halcyon almost smiled, but managed to keep his lips straight so they wouldn't split open again. "Advised against it. Majority overruled me. Felt it was adequate punishment."

"And they thought she'd be okay with it? Live peacefully right next to me?"

"Yes. Trusted you to hold territory safe against her. And if not—"

"Yeah, I get it. Survival of the fittest, and all that stupid crap."

"Monère way."

"Frankly, I don't think much of that way."

He sighed. "Neither do I. They would never conceive of Mona Louisa making such an attempt. Even I did not think she would dare do something like this." This being not only trying for me but successfully snatching him as well, not just a High Council member but the High Prince of Hell.

The good news was that we were alone. The bad news was that I wasn't alone. Halcyon was here with me.

"Can you break free?" I know. Dumb question. He'd have broken free, already, if he could. And yet . . . I couldn't help but remember how easily, effortlessly, Halcyon had snapped the chains once before. Snapped them as if they had been nothing but thread.

"No." His voice was a low, dry rasp. He looked at me, all his great strength gone. And my ignorance, my lack of knowledge was mostly to blame.

"You?" he asked.

I shook my head, hot tears of regret and shame burning the back of my eyes because I lied. I could break free . . . if I shifted into my other form. But I couldn't risk doing so. I lost myself to my beast completely when I changed. If I were alone, I'd take the chance and trust to my beast's instinct to flee. But here, with Halcyon . . . I might very well fall prey to my own predatory instinct and eat him if I changed. I certainly would not have the presence of mind to break him free and take us both away from here.

Regret filled me. If I had not run from the darkness of my beast all my life, if I had been willing to free it more often, gain more control of it . . . but now it was too late.

"You shouldn't have helped me," I said helplessly.

"What else could I have done?" he asked, his once beautiful voice so terribly abraded now.

"You should have just let them take me."

"I could not."

"Oh, Halcyon. If I die, my people will continue without me. But if you no longer ruled, what would happen in Hell?"

He looked at me for a long moment, his thoughts turned inward, before finally saying, "It would not be good."

"Your father?"

"Would probably avenge my death. Kill many Monère. May even die himself doing so. It has been long since he has left Hell."

"You make it sound as if you have to build up a tolerance to Earth."

"It is very much like that."

"Oh." A long period of silence passed. "But say your father keeps his cool, doesn't go on a killing spree. He could take up his rule once again, and everything would be the same, right?"

Halcyon dropped his gaze to the ground. "He has existed for so long. You cannot imagine what that is like. For the last hundred years, he has withdrawn, lost interest in things, sleeps mostly. The only reason he still continues and does not go to his final rest is because of me. So that I will not be alone. If I were gone, there would be no reason for him to further exist."

"What about Lucinda, your sister?"

"Her relationship with Father is . . . complicated. And she has neither the strength nor desire to rule."

We both contemplated in silence the thought of an unstable Hell, of creatures even more powerful than the Monère battling for supremacy. If someone like Kadeen took over . . .

Kadeen had been a demon dead, a would-be warlord who had challenged Halcyon. But all he'd ended up being was would-be dead. *Dead* dead, this time. Back into the final darkness. But before he'd departed, he'd been a nasty, formidable creature who'd ripped apart Amber with stunning ease and drained Chami almost dry of his blood—two of my strongest, deadliest men. He'd taken a deep suck out of me, too. The demon dead seemed to gain power from drinking blood from living creatures. The thought of someone like that in power . . . I shuddered. Monère and humans alike would not be safe then.

"What can we do?" I whispered.

"Don't die," he said. "Survive until help arrives."

"Do you think it will?" So many things to do, to get right. They had to know we were in trouble, guess where we were, and then ride to the rescue.

His answer was not comforting. "We have no other hope."

THIRTEEN

THE DOOR CREAKED open as the sun dropped over the horizon and I knew that the time for fun and games was about to begin. For them. Not for us. All we'd do, unfortunately, was bleed and try very, very hard not to die. I just didn't know if we'd succeed.

Mona Louisa, the bitch, was looking pretty good. I'd labeled her the Ice Queen not only because of her stunning, icy beauty, but because ice ran in her veins and encased her heart. She'd given up one of her own men to the High Council without a qualm. He'd lied for her and then died for her. Miles had been his name, a nasty fellow who'd tried to rape me. Yeah, he'd deserved to go. But no more than she. She'd given the orders, after all. He'd just obeyed. But Queens were the tent poles around which the Monère gathered. They were too precious to kill. Of course, another Queen could kill a Queen in self-defense. But that law wasn't exactly to my benefit just this moment, chained and helpless as I was.

Mona Louisa's hair was a gleaming yellow cascade and

her pale skin was as lovely as ever. Only a thin, pink-silver scar above her right breast, where my blade had sunk into her, marred her perfection.

She was the vulture who had attacked us. Too bad my knife had been steel instead of silver. Her wound looked as if it'd had five days to heal instead of just five hours. Apparently she had acquired the ability to withstand the sun from Gryphon and had passed it on to at least one of her own men. Reason enough to keep me alive—the potential of passing it on to more of her men. But not if she killed Halcyon. Then she'd most certainly have to kill me. Couldn't risk leaving a witness alive if you murdered the High Prince of Hell.

Not wanting to, but having to, I assessed my own injury. My ripped shoulder was not nearly as neat and clean as Mona Louisa's nice little scar. I'd been sliced wide open: two long, gashing tears slashing through my bicep, curving behind to the back of my shoulder. With my arms stretched tight by the chains, the wound had stayed open. And had started to heal that way. So instead of knitting two pieces of pressed-together flesh back together, it had to fill in the gaping wound like a pit, from the bottom up. The deeper muscle and tendon damage had repaired enough while I'd been out so that I could move my arm now. But it was still a raw, ugly, healing mess. One quick glance was enough to churn my stomach and lighten my head. I looked away before I fainted. Wouldn't want to do that. Mona Louisa would no doubt find a painfully creative way to wake me back up.

Other bodies entered the room, a substantial number of them with healing slices and knitting wounds courtesy of Halcyon's nails. Even weak, they had not taken him easily, I noted with satisfaction. Many of them were faces that I recognized from High Court, her guards. Among those faces peering at me were Gilford, Rupert, and Demetrius, partners in crime to the late unlamented Miles. They'd been part of the original four loaned to me as my personal guards. But instead of protecting me, they had betrayed me. Their expectant gazes and Mona Louisa's glittering eyes shifted the feel of the place. As if it was about to become less dungeon and more torture chamber.

I caught sight of one other familiar face. This one made me catch my breath. "Dontaine?" I whispered as I stared at the arrogantly handsome face of the man I had nursed, the man I had appointed my Master of Arms. His lovely dark green eyes stared impassively back at me. I'd had my suspicions all along, but deep down in my heart, I must not have really believed them or wanted to believe them because the shock of his betrayal was like an unexpected punch in the gut, knocking the wind from me.

"Oh, good. You are awake," Mona Louisa purred. "Wouldn't want you to miss out on the fun."

Yup, still a bitch. But not quite the same. Something about her was different. Instead of icy aloofness, she was practically vibrating with emotion. A flux of eagerness and anger spun across her face, and a hot current of deep passion—hatred—burned in her dark pupils. Her diamond blue eyes gleamed with vicious satisfaction as she gazed at the Demon Prince.

She swished up to him, her long full skirt swirling about her feet in graceful peek-a-boo flutters. Coming to a stop before him, she lifted one perfectly manicured fingernail. She pressed the sharp sliver of her nail to his chest and, with eyes avidly fixed upon him, ran it lightly downward. His taut skin broke easily beneath the soft, cutting stroke, spilling blood and more of that clear viscous fluid.

"Cooked to perfection," she crooned. "How does it feel, Prince, to be the one suffering? To be the one being sliced open. Let us see how you hold up, shall we, when you are the one questioned." Once upon a time Halcyon had questioned her in private for the High Council regarding her role in her loaned men's lax protection of me. The Four

Colors, as I'd called them, had handed me over to a band of rogues.

Mona Louisa, it seems, had not enjoyed being questioned by him. Made me wonder what Halcyon had done to her. Not enough, apparently. Nope, she definitely hadn't liked the experience. And she didn't look at all willing to forgive and forget, to let bygones be bygones, and all that other good stuff.

"They're wrong when they say revenge is sweet," Mona Louisa said, raising her perfect oval nail once more, pressing it to another spot one inch over on Halcyon's chest. "Revenge isn't sweet. It's bloody," she whispered and ripped another slice down him. Her hot gleaming eyes watched Halcyon eagerly, disappointed when he didn't even flinch. Blood flowed out sullenly, as if his body were greedy to contain what little it had left.

It was hard to just stand and watch her literally slicing Halcyon's chest to ribbons. Delay. Wait for help. That just wasn't my forte. Depending on others could get you killed. Only now, I had no other choice.

Watching and waiting got a little harder when Mona Louisa uttered a name: "Dontaine."

The men parted, letting him step forward, and I got a glimpse of what was in Dontaine's hands. Whips. Two of them. One was a simple black bullwhip. The other had spiky silver barbs lodged in the long leather strips that flowed out like a horse's tail from the thick stock handle. It was a cat-o'-nine-tails, like what they'd used centuries ago to flog mutinous crew on the high seas.

"The bullwhip first, I think." Mona Louisa curled her soft white hand around the thick phallic-shaped handle and let the curled tail unfurl like a living, writhing leather snake. She caressed the butt against Halcyon's cheek. "Where is the nearest portal to Hell?"

Halcyon remained silent.

"Wrong answer." She stepped back. A flick of a wrist and the bullwhip hissed through the air like an angry serpent and bit into Halcyon. The fingernail had been bad enough. This slicing leather whip with full Monère strength behind it was much, much worse. The leather coil parted Halcyon's flesh like a hot knife cutting through soft butter. His chest was sliced diagonally open from left to right with a gush of soft weeping fluid. The white of his ribs was briefly visible before blood washed them darkly red.

Halcyon didn't make a sound. It was I who cried out. "Mona Louisa, you don't want to do this!"

"Oh, but I do," she said with almost wild gaiety.

"Do you want to call his father's wrath down upon you?"

"It is not I who his father will be seeking," Mona Louisa said with an unpleasant smile. "It will be you, your people, who his son was last seen with."

Shit. She was right.

"The nearest portal, my dear prince."

No answer again seemed the wrong answer.

Another whistle as leather cut through air, and then no sound as leather cut through flesh. This slice was in the opposite direction, from right to left.

"X marks the spot, they say." Mona Louisa threw back her head and laughed, a gay, vicious burble.

"Milady, perhaps the Demon Prince will be more inclined to talk if Mona Lisa is the one suffering," Dontaine suggested.

Something flickered in Halcyon's gaze as he turned his dark eyes to look upon Dontaine. Something that made the tall, fair Judas take half a step back.

"Why, Dontaine, darling. I think you are right," Mona Louisa said. "Although whipping her will not be nearly as much fun."

"Mona Lisa is a proud bitch. I was thinking of something much worse than the gentle kiss of leather." Dontaine glanced at me assessingly, and his handsome smile chilled me. "She reacts most unusually when I touch her in my Half Change form. It calls her beast forth against her will."

"What fun is calling her beast?" Mona Louisa demanded, pouting.

"Calling Mona Lisa's beast only partway, my Queen. Not all the way. Did not your steward report to you what occurred in the forest? She mates quite enthusiastically then, like the mongrel bitch she is."

"Does she?" Mona Louisa gazed at me with frightening consideration.

"I could make her willing, like a cat in heat, against her conscious choice," Dontaine suggested slyly, like a cunning devil. "And then I and all the other men here could take her, one after the other, in front of the Demon Prince while he watches, helpless and bound."

I tried to keep my face blank, but the tension in my body must have betrayed me.

"She hates the idea," Mona Louisa said delightedly.

I more than hated it. I wanted to kill Dontaine. Kill them all. I wanted to call forth my beast, rip out of these chains, and rip into them. I wanted to take my chances rather than submit to what he suggested. But however willing I was to gamble my life, I would not chance Halcyon's. Delay and survive. It was like a goddamn mantra looping around in my mind. Letting all the men here fuck me would certainly be a good delaying tactic. I just didn't know if I'd want to survive afterward. And the look on my face must have told her that.

Mona Louisa laughed like a gleeful child who'd just been told she was getting a present. "Yes, yes. Do it, Dontaine."

"Wait," Halcyon rasped, speaking up for the first time. "I will tell you what you wish to know."

"Too late, Demon Prince. Do it, Dontaine." Mona Louisa smiled wickedly at me. "Do her."

Dontaine tossed the cat-o'-nines into a corner, stripped off his shirt, and stepped out of his shoes.

"No!" Halcyon said, jerking violently against his chains, rattling the heavy metal. But they held fast and he collapsed, drained by the brief outburst.

"Dontaine, please," I choked out. "Don't do this."

The look on his beautiful betraying face was calm and peaceful. "I have to."

That odd electric energy began to ripple and pulse, and Dontaine began his transformation. He stretched, morphed, changed. Grew taller, broader. Muscles stretched, bones distorted, his jaw elongated into a muzzle, tendons popped, and dark gray fur rippled like a magical wash over his skin, covering it. He shifted and then arrested the change part way, taking on that monstrous form, choking the room with his power. He lifted his head and howled, a chilling primal cry of freedom as his wolf beast merged with his human form, a monster, a legend. Werewolf.

I shrunk back against the wall. I would have merged into the stones themselves had I been able to. But I couldn't. I could only stand there, cowering, trembling, shaking my head, as that terrible beast with Dontaine's eyes walked toward me with lurching, jerky strides on his partially bent hind legs. His gruesome claws reached for me and I screamed with horror, with fear, with helplessness.

But instead of touching me, he tore the demon chains free.

"Dontaine, what are you doing?" Mona Louisa shrieked.

"Freeing my Queen," came his deep, growling response. His claws slid inside my wrist shackles so that only his nails touched me, not his flesh. With a simple twist and pull, the silver metal broke and dropped from my wrists. He tore the chains from my legs, leaving the manacles dangling about my ankles.

A guard standing in front suddenly crumpled to the floor, his neck twisted oddly, his blood staining the floor.

Another guard screamed in pain, jerked, gurgled, and fell to the floor with his neck broken, stabbed from behind. His blood sprayed outward, the tail of the crimson arch stopped short by something right next to it.

Something invisible that became visible briefly upon the touch of blood. Chami suddenly appeared, two silver stilettos held in his hands, the long thin blades dripping with his victim's blood. The guards standing beside him cried out and leaped toward him. Chami winked out of sight—chameleon—and they caught nothing but air. One of them screamed and bent over, clutching his sliced belly.

"Dontaine, get Halcyon!" I cried and stretched out my freed hands. The Goddess's Tears buried deep in the heart of my right palm gave one deep throbbing pulse and a sword sprang free from a surprised guard's grasp.

Uttering a battle cry, I let it fly. The sword swung through the air, singing a song of death as the blade came down on the neck of one of the guards who had dived for Chami. It severed the man's head with almost sighing ease. The decapitated head flew from its body. Light shimmered out, and with a bright burst, scattered ashes rained down to the ground, and the man no longer was. His clothes fell to the floor, an empty shell, no longer supported by form.

"Off with their heads!" I shouted with savage glee, blocking a sudden vicious lunge with my sword. The sharp bite of metal striking against metal clanged like a clarion. But it was my right hand, my injured arm. I was barely able to hold my sword against the pressing force of my attacker's blade. He was overpowering me, and he smiled at my weakness.

It was Rupert, I realized, of the carrot-top hair. One of the betraying four who had delivered me into the hands of the outlaw rogues. The man who had spilled half a bottle of aphrodisiac on me and nearly killed me.

It was that smug smile of Rupert's that did it. That, along with the remembered agony of the aphrodisiac's hellish burning upon my body, and the ache of my right-shoulder wound now. It triggered almost a berserker's rage in me. My left hand pulsed once, almost painfully hard, and a silver dagger flew from a bewildered guard's hand into mine. With dizzying speed and an almost wild strength, I plunged the knife into my attacker. I sank the dagger deep, deep, all the way to the hilt, just under Rupert's sternum, and angled it up into his chest cavity, just like Chami had taught us.

Rupert looked at me with shock and surprise widening his eyes. One clean swipe left severed his aorta, and Rupert's eyes glazed and lost focus and his sword eased against mine. With an almost gentle push from me, his sword fell from his hand and clattered to the floor. Slowly he fell to his knees.

I took a step back and my entire torso turned as I lifted my sword up and back and then let it fly forward in a graceful downward swing with the full strength of my hips and back behind it. It passed through flesh and bone with slicing ease. And then flesh and bone was no more. Bright light scattered free, ashes fell, and clothes floated to the ground, empty.

I glanced around me. Half a dozen bodies lined the floor, Chami's work. Neck and high belly wounds. Spinal cords severed, aortas cut. They were still alive, would eventually recover, given time. Not as final as my ashes and light method. But it was an efficient way of putting down a lot of men quickly. Unfortunately, there were plenty more men still left standing, and some had shifted into their animal forms.

I caught sight of another bright flash of light. Ashes hazed the air and drifted down, coating Dontaine's furry feet. A huge spotted leopard screamed and pounced on Dontaine from behind, crashing them both to the floor. They rolled on the ground, a blurring mass of gray and orange fur, biting fangs, and striking claws.

Halcyon gave out a sharp cry, jerking my attention to

him. Dontaine hadn't managed to free him yet. The Demon Prince's back was arched, his neck tautly stretched. A look of horror masked his face and I felt a reflection of it grip my own. Mona Louisa was behind Halcyon, twined about him like a lover, embracing him, pressed tight against his back, her lips two crimson slashes pressed against the curve of his neck. Blood so darkly red that it was maroon trickled down Halcyon's golden throat as Mona Louisa's slender, strong neck worked obscenely. And I realized she wasn't kissing him, she was drinking his blood!

I gathered myself and leaped, soaring through the air to land beside them. They were too closely entwined to risk using blades so I dropped them. One of my hands twisted roughly in Mona Louisa's shiny bright hair. With my other hand gripping her neck, I ripped her from him, and flung her away. Only one bite mark on his neck. Almost innocuous looking. But Halcyon looked as stunned, as dazed, as frightened as if she had ripped his throat out. He collapsed forward weakly, held upright only by his shackles.

I couldn't break the damn chains. "Dontaine!"

With a heaving snarl, the leopard went sailing across the room to hit the far wall with a cry, and Dontaine was beside me. He snapped Halcyon's chains with four sharp pulls, freeing his arms then his legs.

"Get us out of here," I gasped, lifting Halcyon into my arms.

Dontaine did so with the simple expediency of turning and crashing through the very same wall where the chains were embedded. Stone burst outward, and I stepped through the jagged hole my wolfman had made with his body. I felt Chami, a shimmering presence behind us as we fled into the night. There were sounds of pursuit, startled cries, gasping gurgles, snarling animal growls as Chami danced with his invisible cutting blades and Dontaine ripped and slashed with his long deadly claws, both men guarding my rear.

My right arm burned like a howling banshee and I felt blood flowing down my forearm. My partly healed wound had broken open. But my arm was holding Halcyon's dead weight. I didn't drop him, and that was all I asked of my injured arm for now. I ran, breath coming hard from pain and exertion, and then cursed and stumbled to a halt as I felt the presence of others before me, blocking my path.

"Mona Lisa." It was Gryphon.

Amber, Tomas, and Miguel, Mona Carlisse's man, emerged from the darkness like pale shadows, flowing around Gryphon, passing us, rushing into the fray behind me. I almost dropped Halcyon from sheer relief. Gryphon carefully took the Demon Prince from me. A car screeched to a stop and Aquila leaned over and threw the passenger door open from inside. "Hurry!"

We tumbled into the car and the white Suburban pulled away, bumping roughly over the grassy lawn. It was terrain like this where four-wheel drives showed their superiority. The SUV navigated the grassy ground with the heft of a tank and an angry rumble, its tires throwing up clumps of grass behind it.

"What about the others?" I gasped.

"Gerald has them," Aquila said.

I looked back, turning in the front seat, and saw the green Suburban pulling away with the others inside. Amber was crouched outside, up on the roof, like a giant gargoyle of death, his great sword slashing away, cutting hands and limbs, discouraging pursuit, keeping them off the fleeing car. Other guards spilled outside, running to the front of the house.

We lurched onto smooth road and Aquila floored it.

"They're heading for their own cars," I gasped.

"Don't worry." Aquila smiled like the bandit he once was. "They can't come after us. Not with flat tires."

I felt like kissing him, then leaned over and did so, smacking him on the cheek. "You're brilliant."

Aquila's teeth flashed in a pleased grin, lifting his neat mustache. "I know."

"Thaddeus?" I asked.

"Safe back home with the others. He told us what happened. Dontaine led us here."

I watched with fear squeezing my heart as Amber swung himself feet first through an open window into the SUV. They hit the smooth pavement of the road and sped after us.

We'd lost all our pursuers. But relief was short-lived, triumph fleeting. Turning in my seat, I looked down at Halcyon. He had fallen into a shocklike stupor, lying limply on the second row where Gryphon had laid him out, his chest looking like raw meat slashed open, the flesh parted, not healing. His skin at both ankles and wrists had also split open when he had struggled against the manacles. A final insult, Mona Louisa's bite mark lay like a hideous kiss upon his neck.

"What did they do to him?" Gryphon asked.

"They put him in the sun," I answered. "He was weak but not like this, not until Mona Louisa bit him."

"I did not know that the sun weakens the Demon Prince as it does us," Gryphon murmured. "He needs blood."

I caught Gryphon's gaze. Held it with demand. "I know that now, but not before. Why did you not tell me?"

A glimmer of guilt, of remorse passed through Gryphon's eyes. "Who would you have had me ask to donate blood?"

It reminded me of when he had asked me which woman he should have asked to care for an injured, dangerous Dontaine.

"You would have chosen yourself again," Gryphon said, answering his own question, "and I could not bear the thought of him touching you."

Inwardly I sighed. I was merely mad when I should have been furious. This was even worse than Gryphon putting my hand on another man's groin, or keeping Wiley's chained captivity from me. This time we had nearly died. But it was hard to work my emotions up to furious when I understood Gryphon. He had been consistent in this all along, his fear and want of distance between Halcyon and me. Guilt and remorse shone in Gryphon's eyes as he gazed down at the insensate Demon Prince.

"Forgive me," Gryphon said softly.

"It's hard to keep forgiving you, yet again."

Gryphon bowed his head, frozen in that odd stillness that he was capable of achieving, as if he were inanimate, not breathing. As if his heart did not beat, so how could it break? Then he broke the stillness. A quick movement and he slashed his wrist with a blade, blood welling to the surface as I gasped with surprise. He pressed his opened wrist to Halcyon's mouth, his face once more serene, unreadable, blank.

At the touch of blood, the Demon Prince stirred. His mouth parted and his lips sealed around Gryphon's wrist, creating suction. Both of Halcyon's hands came up blindly to grasp Gryphon's arm and to hold it secure though his eyes remained closed. Like a baby, Halcyon sucked and nursed, greedily milking the cut flesh with firm lips for more of its red nectar.

Apparently it was not enough.

Halcyon's fangs lengthened and grew, a simple morphing that didn't even use a shimmer of power. It just occurred naturally, like breathing, lips drawing back. One sharp sinking bite and Halcyon pierced even deeper into Gryphon's flesh, drank down even richer blood, his larynx bobbing up and down as if it were a lever that could pump the blood faster into his mouth.

I wondered how much blood Halcyon was drinking down. How much blood could Gryphon continue to give? Gryphon looked pale, but I couldn't go by that: Pale was his baseline. But I could hear Gryphon's heart. It had kicked up its rhythm, a sign of his heart having to pump faster to meet its needs with a lesser volume of blood.

"Halcyon." I reached over the seat and touched the Demon Prince's hands. His skin was less sallow than before, not quite as sickly ashen beneath the tan. Those hands were wrapped tightly around Gryphon's wrist, holding him a willing prisoner.

"Halcyon, wake up."

Halcyon's eyes remained closed. He did not stop in his single-minded gulping of blood.

I slid over my seat into the middle row, crouching down in the floorboard space, a little alarmed at the strength I sensed in those golden hands. They were clamped down like cold steel. I couldn't pry them off Gryphon. Couldn't move a single finger, not even his pinky. When I tried, those slim, elegant hands only tightened even more, clearly unwilling to give up his food source.

Gryphon was definitely pale now. Sheet white versus lunar white. There's a subtle difference. Gryphon's eyes were closed as if lost to the giving, numb to his pain.

"Aquila, how do we get Halcyon off Gryphon?"

Aquila's concerned eyes met mine in the mirror. He shook his head. "I do not know, milady. Do you wish me to stop the car?"

"No, keep driving. Gryphon, can you get him to release you?"

"Not until he is ready to" was Gryphon's weak reply.

Well, shit. The Demon Prince didn't look anywhere near ready to do that. He looked like an innocent babe suckling, abandoned in his pursuit of more and more. Only he was gulping down blood, not milk. And babies didn't drain their mothers dry, usually.

Force hadn't worked, so I tried something different. I ran a gentle hand through Halcyon's hair, pushing it back away from his face. That gold-kissed skin was less puffy now. The blood was helping. He was healing a little.

"Halcyon," I whispered. He had to hear me at some level. "Halcyon, it's Mona Lisa, your hellcat." That's what he called me, even before he'd known what my other form was. I reached out with that other power within me—my aphidy, that inner allure that drew men to me. Deliberately I called it out and wrapped it gently around Halcyon, even though I wasn't sure it would work with the demon dead. I used it like an invisible embrace, an inviting stroke. *Come to me.*

I bent down, breathed against the shell of his ear. "Halcyon, I need you. Come to me." I pressed my lips to his tan cheek and kissed him for the very first time. "Open your eyes for me," I begged. "Please, Halcyon."

His long, gold-tipped lashes fluttered once, twice, and then opened. Confusion, comprehension drifted in and out of those chocolate brown eyes.

"Mona Lisa," he murmured and reached for me, releasing Gryphon's arm.

As if the strings that had been holding him up had suddenly been cut, Gryphon toppled soundlessly over, his body wedged back in the crack of the seat, curled around the Demon Prince's head, his heart stuttering, his breath shallow, his body still within biting range.

But it was not Gryphon the Demon Prince reached for. Halcyon wrapped those golden arms around me—still so strong even when he was weak—and hauled me up so that I was half draped over him, so that my breasts were crushed against his chest, so that blood from his open chest wounds wet my shirt, seeping through the fabric to dampen my skin like a liquid caress. With a sigh, a soundless murmur, Halcyon sank his long, sharp fangs gently into my neck.

And with that one bite, he took me over completely.

I was floating in a blue, blue sea. I was naked, and I was with my lover. Halcyon. His golden skin glowed in the waters, and his eyes shone like brilliant dark stars, his need, his want, glinting hard like black diamonds in their depths. And I wanted him. Oh, how I wanted him.

He was as wonderfully free as I, skin whole, sleekly

muscled, no cloth marring the natural grace and beauty of his body, his quiet strength, his rising passion. The ocean buoyed us in her comforting arms, safe. It was like a primordial time, when nothing else existed but the first man made, the first woman created from his bone. No need to breathe. Just feel. The touch of my lover's hand gentle upon the back of my neck as he drew me into his embrace. The brush of his soft, red lips against mine, tasting even better than the nectar of life. He let me sip from his cherry sweetness, drink down joy, swallow the seeds of passion. And as they slid down into my belly, I suddenly burned with need. Such need to feel that exquisite body pressed tight against me, in me. To feel that dark hard length of risen passion nuzzle between my thighs and bury deep inside me.

My bare breasts flattened against him, my nipples hard, stabbing into his chest, the twin peaks kissing his own flat brown areolas, their pointy aggression bringing a growl to his throat, turning sweet tenderness into something rougher, darker, more forceful, aggressive. Like stirring a hidden beast. His arms tightened around me, and with a shudder that racked that slender body, his arousal nudged against my notch, a lovely fit but not quite perfect yet. I swayed against him, swirling my hips enticingly, coating him with my honeyed juice, riding, sliding against that lovely jutting length. Sweet, but not enough.

"Come into me," I whispered.

"Soon," he promised and took my mouth with lips so luscious, so red, so smooth that they tasted even better than Eve's first apple, bursting with the bittersweet taste of something dark and tantalizing. A luring promise of more . . . more. And I was so hungry.

He delved into my mouth with an exploring tongue, sliding in like a sinuous snake, sweeping over my teeth, caressing the inner wetness of my mouth, slipping back out to lap and tease and nibble my full lower lip, catching it between his teeth and pulling it out, taut. A gentle press, a promise of teeth. The pull of pressure, the release. Sliding back in, sweeping his tongue against mine, tangling them together, stroke against stroke, twining, rubbing, and then sliding in that most intimate dance of push and retreat, promising a deeper joining yet to come.

My hands flew over him, touching, caressing, stroking that lovely smooth flesh. Feeling the resilient texture of soft skin, hard muscles, taut tendons. Seeing the beautiful contrast of white skin against dark, like the warm sun against the cool moon. His shoulders were broad ledges to explore. His back, hills to conquer, plains to venture over. His luscious bottom, small tight mounds of muscle to squeeze and pull against me. I slid my hands lower, trailing down the mysterious crack between his bottom cheeks, making him mutter, making him squirm, until I found him hanging low and vulnerable. I squeezed his balls gently, appreciating their thick, pouchy outer surface, their softer, looser inner roll. Their tightening, tensing, drawing up. So sweetly responsive, so wonderfully tight.

Halcyon gazed down into my laughing eyes and growled. His red, wicked mouth swooped down to plunder my vulnerable flesh and take its revenge. My nipple was engulfed in the dark wet cavern of his mouth and proved as responsive as his balls. They tightened, but instead of drawing up and inward, they speared out. He sucked and pulled and swirled a naughty tongue, tasting, laving me. A gentle swish, a rough pull, making me cry out. My other nipple was pulled and squeezed with agile fingers in rhythm to his sucking mouth. The twin assaults made me widen my legs and wrap them around his waist, squeezing down on his buttocks, pulling him tightly, grindingly against me. He swiveled against me in a graceful, wicked dance, rubbing his hardness against my softness. Then his hands caught my hips, angled them up so that my little pearl of hardness was caught against the base of his poling length and ground against it again and again as his hips swiveled and danced, a delicious bump and retreat.

And then all I felt was a hard, hard pressing as he bit down on my nipple, no longer gentle, squeezing my other nipple with his fingers to the point of pain, to the point of pleasure. I exploded outward, imploded inward. Shot into hard, shuddering ecstasy that shook my frame, within and without. His mouth covered me, swallowing down my cries, stealing my breath, emptying me until I was nothing, and then breathing life back into me, exhaling so that his air filled my lungs, so that his breath sustained me, brought me back. And as I revived, stirred, he slipped sweetly into me, a quiet, peaceful joining.

A moment of stillness. A moment to savor the fullness, the delicious stretching invasion. Then another breath into me, a gentle push into me, a fluid pulling back out. And all I could do was float in his arms, totally relaxed, utterly drained in the sated aftermath, wonderfully limp, held secure by him. All his. Unable to do anything but take whatever he wished to give.

My golden prince moved to the gentle rhythmic sway of the ocean. Ebbing, rising. Gentle, oh, so gentle movement. As natural as breathing, as necessary as life, as steady as the beating of one's own heart. He flowed in and out of me for a languid, unceasing time, kissing me, drinking from my mouth until my senses roused once more, lured by the gentle dance of his hips, his body brushing mine, inside mine. A stroking of hard flesh against soft. A giving, a taking, a receiving. An endless cycle of life.

He pulled back, stilled his motion, and looked down upon me, his eyes so hot, so glittery, so bright. So urgent with need, want, held back passion. And it was as if his eyes, his needs, sparked my own fervor so that the gentle passive pleasure was suddenly no longer enough. Not nearly enough. And I clenched around him hard and tight, making him cry out my name, "Mona Lisa!"

A stroke of my hand and I reversed Halcyon in the water, laying him flat, the water a firm cushion beneath him. I reared up and then back down, taking him.

"Halcyon," I sighed as he filled me. "You have the most beautiful eyes, like chocolate. I love chocolate."

I licked my lips, then leaned down and licked his. "You taste like it, too," I crooned with lust, with greed, and delved into the dark bittersweetness of him, lapping him up with my tongue as I rose and fell upon him, stroking him as he stroked within me.

"Don't hold back," I murmured, "don't hold back." And it was as if my urgent whisper released him from some invisible bond of restraint.

"Hellcat," he gasped. His hands clamped down hard upon my hips and he plunged within me, bucking beneath me like a wild bronco released from its stall, driving the very breath from me. God, he was strong.

He rolled up, twisting, and slammed me back against an immovable wall of water, pinning me there as he pulled back and surged into me again and again and then again, driving me up that liquid wall with each forceful, thrusting drive of his hips. His hands were on me, squeezing my breasts, thumbing my nipples. His mental constraint crashed and loosened, flooding me with a spill of sensation. I felt a tingling brush over my lips though he touched me there with nothing but his burning gaze. A stroking down my legs, a twining around my calves, a touch upon the balls of my feet. A greedy, total body caress down my arms, a meshing of my fingers with invisible ones to anchor me against that soft, firm liquid wall. Dark, stinging nips down my back, an edge of teeth against my round bottom. An arrowing, singing presence delving between my legs, tunneling deep to where we were joined, like invisible fingers thrusting alongside his heavy staff, all thrusting into me, and then going even deeper, burrowing deep, deep like a seed of pleasure, stretching my womb like a growing baby as he stretched and filled my tunnel, shooting sparks of growing sensation with each hard, thrusting rub, each sliding glide. Swivel, push. A different angle. An even deeper joining. Jolting penetration within me, shocking me with sizzling strength, igniting my senses as I felt him all around me, in me, touching every part of me. And most sharply of all, I felt that tingling pressure-pleasure stretching inside my womb, maturing, growing. When it ripened almost to the point of bursting, Halcyon lowered his mouth to my throat. I felt his hot breath against me, felt his teeth grow longer, sharper. Felt the tender, tantalizing brush of those teeth against my soft white skin and arched my neck farther, invitingly, wanting him, waiting for him to sink his teeth into me, whimpering with my need for him to join us even more in that one small way.

One long moment of stillness. And then he pierced me with his fangs. Deep down he sank into my flesh with his teeth. Deep down he sank into me with his long hot length, driving all the way home, tapping my womb, drinking my rich blood, tasting me with his mouth, with his male organ, with his invisible senses. Drinking me up, drinking me down, and delivering me into blinding rapture, into knowing bliss. Into a shaking, shuddering, jerking convulsion of sharp, painful pleasure.

My porous skin, my spasming sheath, my clenching womb—all drank him greedily down, and with a small cry he shot his sweet release into me.

My body was still quivering when I opened my eyes. My neck stung and I felt a thick droplet of blood trickle down to cradle low in the hollow of my throat. My breasts tingled and I felt soreness and wetness between my legs. But it wasn't the cool, cuddling ocean I saw. I was in the middle row of the Suburban, sitting on the floor, woozy and light-headed. I looked up into the startling awareness of Halcyon's chocolate brown eyes. He was still lying prone on the seat. Behind him, laid out in the opposite direction was Gryphon, his head resting on Halcyon's shoulder. Both of them stared at me, both sets of eyes punched black, pupils wide.

I transferred my gaze back to Halcyon. "Are you feeling better?"

"Oh, yes." His dark, richly satisfied voice whispered over me like a tactile caress, washing more tremors through me, setting off small, quaking explosions within me. Making me close my eyes until they passed like a hot, rippling rush, and released my body once more back into my control. My clothes were still on, but the wetness sopping my pants seemed more excessive than just my arousal alone could account for.

"Was that . . . real?" I asked.

"As real as you wish it to be."

I licked my lips. "You took me over."

"Not entirely. I was too weak for compulsion. I did not shade your desire. Your emotions were your own."

Great. I didn't even have "you made me do it" to fall back upon. Just my own horny little self.

I stared into Gryphon's pleasure punched eyes and wondered how much he had sensed or shared, pressed as he'd been against Halcyon. Then decided I might be better off not knowing.

Halcyon was better but still not well. His color more natural, his skin more taut, no longer swollen. The bruises on his wrist had disappeared. The deep wounds on his chest no longer gaped open like dead flesh, but had drawn together. Still, they remained deep, furrowing gashes, far from healed, and the bite mark on his neck was still there, Mona Louisa's violating brand.

"Do you need more blood?" My voice sounded hoarse, weaker than what I would have liked. I didn't know whether it was from the pleasure I had received—real or imagined— or the donation of my blood. Probably both.

"No," Halcyon replied. "More blood will not aid me further. Nothing will, other than returning home quickly."

"What's the quickest route home?" I asked.

"New Orleans."

Of course. "Aquila?"

"On my way," Aquila replied, and floored the gas pedal. The car shot into the night.

FOURTEEN

An hour later we drove past empty high-rises, steel skyscrapers and glittering hotels, passing through the Central Business District of New Orleans. It was my first glimpse of the infamous Crescent City and I looked eagerly out the window. Images of lurching vampires—whatever they may be—crossed my mind, and the screeching of darting bats was nearly audible in my ears. The seat of Mardi Gras. I could almost see the throngs jumping to catch the glittering beads they tossed from passing floats. This birthplace of jazz. I could almost hear the trumpets blaring away, the whispers of the night. But such was just illusion conjured up by the books I'd read and the movies I'd seen. Reality was reality. The tall buildings here looked no different than what I'd seen in New York City, and the sidewalks were as plain as those in the Big Apple. Some of my disappointment must have shown on my face.

"The French Quarter is much lovelier," Aquila murmured, gazing at me through the rearview mirror.

I certainly hoped so, but then again, sightseeing wasn't what we were about tonight.

We stopped beside a dark and desolate alley in the Warehouse District. It was quiet here, deserted until the Earth spun ponderously around and faced the sun once more. Then it would fill and teem again with life as the business bustle of daytime returned. But for now, in the dark quiet of night, not a soul was present. Life forms could be felt, heard, a short radius away, scattered in clumpings here and there where they slept, ate, lived.

Farther north, almost an immense mass of gathered humanity swelled, pulsing with the beats of thousands upon thousands of countless bodies. The French Quarter. But here in the deserted Business District, only the stillness of silence, the death of night, greeted us. The alley was bland, unremarkable, no different from thousands of other alleys dotting the city until with a flicker of will, a flexing of power, Halcyon called forth the portal. It shimmered then, brought to life, a glittering, white misty wall.

Making the portal appear seemed to use up whatever strength Halcyon had garnered from the generous donations of our blood. He would have collapsed had I not caught him. To my thankful surprise, I was stronger than I felt. My jellied knees managed to hold up both of us.

"You can't go back by yourself like this," I said.

Gryphon leaned weakly against the wall, letting it prop him up. "No," he said, vehemently shaking his head.

"No, what?" Amber asked. The green Suburban had followed us down into the city and the other men gathered about us now. Although gathered was too kind a word. Miguel and Gerald hovered back near the mouth of the alley. Even my men kept a certain distance, as if fearful of being drawn into the portal, fearful of being sucked accidentally down to Hell. They were wise to be fearful. If they were able to survive the trip down, they were dead upon arrival, nothing but dust upon hitting the other realm's hot atmosphere.

Monère and humans did not do well down in Hell; one unable to withstand the heat, the other too fragile to survive the trip. I, however, seemed to be the perfect sturdy mix of the two. Hell seemed to like me. I wasn't exactly sure what that said about me, but at least it didn't kill me. The trip, that is. And let me tell you, it is not a fun trip. Even though you don't die, it feels as if you will. After a while, you wish you had.

Nope, not fun at all. And not something I could believe I was going to willingly repeat. But goddamn it to Hell and back—which was going to be my goal here—Halcyon wasn't even able to stand on his own two feet.

"No, what?" Amber asked again. He and Gryphon stood the closest—stalwart, protective forces behind me.

"I'm going with Halcyon," I said.

A dangerous, frightening look came over Amber's craggy face. "No." In this, he and Gryphon were united. They stood there together looking at me with fierce, set faces as if they had a say in the matter, and I was both pleased and annoyed that they did so. Pleased because they were learning that they mattered enough to me that I would listen to them if I could. Annoyed because in this case, I couldn't.

"The damn portal isn't like an elevator you can just stick Halcyon in and trust it to bring him directly to his door. He has to make his way home, and there are a lot of dangerous things down there." Like other demon dead. "Just look at Halcyon," I said.

"We are looking," Amber said in a low, unhappy rumble, and he wasn't just looking at Halcyon. He was looking at me supporting Halcyon.

Which made me want to take back my last words. Not the most brilliant suggestion of the moment. Halcyon and I no doubt looked like we'd both topple over if anyone breathed too hard on us.

I hastened on. "Home—or rather Hell—is not a safe place. High Prince of Hell or not, Halcyon will be almost helpless once he arrives. And that is not a place you want to be helpless in, not if you want to continue existing." If not exactly living.

"Your men are right," Halcyon said quietly. "I shall be unable to protect you in Hell."

"Halcyon," I said almost gently. "It is *you* I wish to protect."

"And how do you expect to do that in your condition?" Dontaine asked, stepping forward. With his chest bare, his feet naked, his pants torn rags, he looked the primitive warrior that he was. My warrior now, I thought with satisfaction. Not hers.

My eyes softened as I looked at him. "You, too, Dontaine?"

"Milady, I did not save you to watch you kill yourself now. No one who has gone down to the other realm has ever returned."

"Except me."

Dontaine's eyes widened with surprise.

"I'm the only one here who can do it because I did it before. It has to be me."

"Prince Halcyon," Chami asked. Blood splatter covered the chameleon. None of it, however, was his. "When you arrive, will your friends help you?"

Halcyon smiled slightly. "I am the High Prince of Hell. I do not have friends. But, yes, there are those who will aid me if I can call them."

"Can you not send down a message to have them waiting for you when you arrive?"

"That is a good suggestion, Chami," Halcyon said kindly. "But I do not have any way of doing that other than to return myself. Nor could I delay going back even if I did."

"Why can you not delay?" Gryphon asked.

"I will just get weaker. Mayhap become even too weak to make the journey."

A sobering thought.

"I have to go with him." I was growing desperate, because if I stood here arguing much longer, I might just collapse, and then none of them, Halcyon included, would let me go. "I'm his only chance."

Sad because it was true. Sad because it meant our chances of surviving this were not good.

"We have to try," I said. "It will be bad for us all if Halcyon dies. Not just us but for all Monère."

Surprisingly, it was Tomas, good loyal Tomas with his plain face and simple, true heart, who finally spoke with the voice of reason. "Mona Lisa is right. I do not wish to lose her either . . . but milady is right. They have to go now. Further delay will only worsen their plight, and in the end, ours as well."

A heavy silence.

"If you must go," Aquila said, "then, at the very least, you both must first change so that you do not arrive smelling of blood, smelling like prey."

"That makes sense. What?" I muttered as they all looked at me. "I'm always willing to listen to reason when I can."

Aquila and Gerald, the two drivers—the only two not bloodied or smelling of blood—ended up giving us their clothes. They stripped down before us, comfortable in their nakedness. I seemed the only self-conscious one, the only one averting my gaze. Chami left and miraculously returned with a bottle of water that I didn't know how he had procured but was very thankful for. I took a drink, and saved the remainder to wash us down with.

"Okay," I said, my hand going to the button of my jeans. "Everyone turn around."

"A modest Queen?" Dontaine said with surprise.

"She is not like other Queens," Gryphon and Amber said together, their faces grim.

I grinned at them, immensely pleased. "You guys are learning." I circled my finger. "Your backs, guys."

"A pity," Dontaine muttered, turning around.

"Yes," agreed Chami with a wry smile, but he also presented his back and the others followed.

Propping Halcyon against the wall, I stripped down to my underwear, washed the blood off of me with my water-dampened T-shirt, and quickly dressed in Gerald's clothes, the slenderer of the two. When I was done, I hesitantly reached for Halcyon's pants.

"I can do it," Halcyon said softly, loosening and pushing down his pants. No underwear. It must be a Monère guy thing that carried over even when you became demon dead.

I watched Halcyon from the corner of my eye to make sure he didn't fall on his face. But had to turn and look at Halcyon fully in order to wash him. Except for his injuries, his body was as I had seen it in that vision or dream or whatever it had been. A sleek, strong build with nice shoulders, trim waist, slender hips, powerful thighs, and a rising erection at half-mast. The latter made heat rise in my face.

You could have said he was injured but not dead. But that wasn't true. He *was* dead. His heart didn't beat, his lungs did not take in air. And yet . . . he wasn't really dead as humans defined it. He still . . . existed, would be the best word. And I was going to try my damn best to see that he continued to exist.

Halcyon, gentleman that he was, said and did nothing to worsen my discomfort. He stayed still and quiet as I found a clean spot on my T-shirt, dampened it, and used it to lightly scrub the bite mark on his neck. I started from the top and worked my way down, pouring water directly onto his chest wounds and patting the slivers of raw meat gently dry. He didn't make a sound, even though it must have pained him. Didn't say anything, mindful of nearby ears. But his face was soft, his eyes warm, his expression tender as he watched me minister to him. When I was done, after I'd helped him step into Aquila's clean clothes, he brought my hand to his lips and kissed it gently. No one did it as naturally, as gracefully as Halcyon accomplished the gesture, like something sweet and natural. But then he'd had over six hundred years of practice.

My shoulder throbbed like a bitch, leading to the twenty-thousand-dollar question: Where was a healer when you needed one? Ding, ding, ding. The answer: Back home, protected like the prized resource she was. But, hey, at least I could use my arm.

The men came up to me, one by one, offering their treasures. Amber gave me his great sword, his precious baby, his faithful companion for over a hundred years. The gesture touched me. How could it not? But his sword was too big for me to heft, too awkward to swing with my injured arm. I ended up taking Tomas's shorter, more manageable sword, and Aquila's curved hunting knife, its silver blade almost a foot long; big enough to take off a head if I needed to, a nice backup for the sword.

There was only one way to kill the demon dead that I knew of. Hack them to pieces. And even then they didn't die. Of course, that was assuming I'd get to them first before I, myself, was hacked to pieces by them. And, come to think of it, they didn't even need to hack. Just tear me apart, limb by limb. They were strong enough to do it.

I felt like a kid being sent off to summer camp. You know, one of those sleepaway thingies, parents all teary-eyed, the kid all clingy. I'd never been away on one, but every kid watched television. Only the tone was much more somber, funereal even; they weren't expecting me back. I was going to try to surprise them.

I hugged Amber, felt his big arms engulf me, surrounding me all too briefly in warmth and safety. Being held by him always felt like home.

Gryphon, my heart, gave me a gentle kiss, so at odds with his terribly tormented eyes. "Come back to me," he whispered.

"I will try. With everything that is within me," I promised.

Chami, Aquila, and Tomas—my people, all so dear to

me. I hugged them, kissed their cheeks, gave them a wavering smile. Even managed to ignore Aquila's nudity. The trick, I found, was pretending that he wasn't naked.

Tears threatened and I blinked them back. "Watch over the others for me until I return."

They bowed, said as one, "Yes, my Queen."

I saw in Chami's eyes his personal promise to me to protect Thaddeus.

My eyes softened as Dontaine stepped forward last. "Dontaine, it makes me so happy to know that I chose the right man for the job." I squeezed his hand softly and smiled warmly up into his beautiful green eyes. "Thank you for not disappointing me."

"You are a Queen worthy to serve." He bowed and stepped back.

I sought out Gerald and Miguel next. "Thank you for your aid this night and for caring for your Queen so well. Please communicate to Mona Carlisse my deep gratitude."

Miguel dipped his head.

Gerald gave a courtly bow, executed as gracefully as if he were fully clothed.

Goodbyes were said. Enough time had passed for eulogies to have already been written and recited. Morbid thought.

I took a deep breath and turned to Halcyon. "Shall we?"

The Demon Prince nodded. Together we hobbled toward the wall of mist, arms around each other. My knife was clutched in the hand wrapped around Halcyon's waist, and the sword gripped by my right one.

I stepped into that nasty white fuzz quickly. It was like pulling off a Band-Aid. Some people did it slowly, stretching out the hurt. I preferred ripping it off in one bold tear. Same thing with this portal. If I were alone, I wouldn't have entered it so eagerly; they'd have had to drag me into it. But I had an audience; people I wanted to spare. I didn't want to start screaming horribly like I was being torn apart while they were still watching. A lousy last impression, you know.

It sucked us in, swallowed us up, and started stinging like a fucking son of a bitch. White stabs of agony, lancing jolts of pain, like I was being zapped by something with more juice than Chernobyl and its twin sister. It was a terrible, punishing force.

Then we were falling. And I was screaming and screaming.

FIFTEEN

THAT GUT-PUKING, NAUSEATING pain miraculously stopped halfway down and I knew that Halcyon was somehow insulating me from it. Let me tell you something: The absence of pain is a wonderful thing. And let me tell you another thing: People were wrong. Hell wasn't what waited for you. It was the trip down. Once you got there, it wasn't really that bad.

Then we hit the ground with a jarring crash and I had to revise my opinion. The good news was that I hadn't accidentally stabbed either Halcyon or myself in that teeth-rattling landing. Jesus Christ, I hoped touchdown wasn't like this all the time or I wasn't coming down here again. No, sirree. The bad news was that my right arm was numbed by agony for a moment. Yeah, numbed. When white-hot pain rips through your shoulder and bursts out like an exploding supernova through the rest of the body, you don't feel anything but the pain. It becomes so great that your nerve endings shut down and stop transmitting, sort of like throwing a breaker switch.

I couldn't tell if I'd dropped my sword or not. I looked down and realized that I still held it in my right hand, even though I couldn't feel myself gripping it. But okay, sword in one hand, numb or not, knife in the other. We were good to go. And as soon as I got my breath back, I'd get us to our feet. In a moment, or two, or three.

The thing you noticed about Hell, other than the pain—but that was internal, my own injuries, my fault, you know, not Hell's—was the heat. Dry heat, almost smothering, like in the desert. The next thing that you noticed was the odd, muted lighting. It was forever twilight down in this other realm. And muted was another good description. There were no sounds, other than my heart that seemed to beat as loudly as a dinner bell, and my harsh breathing, the rush of air in and out of my body. The sounds of life. There were no other sounds of life but for my little loud self. In the deafening silence, I could hear the rush of my blood, the pumping of my heart spurting that rich red liquid into my arteries, pushing it through my veins. Even my pale white skin glowed like a neon "come and eat me" sign.

And come they did. Various faces emerged out of the twilight darkness, all in shades of brown, from light tan to dark brown. Male and female. I felt like a Pale Face surrounded by Apaches—about to be scalped. Only these were demon dead. They were going to do far worse than scalp me. Fangs emerged, saliva glistened, dark eyes gleamed, light eyes glittered. I could feel their unthinking hunger for my tender, living flesh like a beating presence, could almost taste their dry thirst for my fresh red blood.

"Uh, Halcyon." With great effort, motivated by a strong survival instinct, I got us both to our feet. To say Halcyon didn't look too good was a vast understatement. His head lolled against my shoulder and his eyes were closed, as if the trip down had worn him out. As if he'd used up all his energy to shield me from the pain. A heroic gesture, that, but I'd have rather taken the pain and had him a little fresher and stronger while meeting his subjects. They didn't look too loyal at the moment. Just hungry. Hungry enough to tear me apart, gulp me down, and then start on him afterward for dessert.

We were in the middle of nowhere. Nowhere to hide. Nowhere to run.

"Halcyon." I shook him a little.

Halcyon roused, opened his eyes finally. Blinked them, looked around.

"See any friends or anyone likely to give us a hand instead of take it?" I asked.

Halcyon didn't bother answering me. The answer was obvious. Anyone wanting to help us would have stepped forward by now. Instead they were creeping forward slowly, sniffing as if scenting the delicious aroma of fresh blood, their saliva dripping, circling around us like jackals, gathering for the kill.

The High Prince of Hell threw back his head and released a blood-curdling howl that lifted to the nightfall sky, outward and beyond. A calling, a beckoning that was answered by a fierce, joyous baying in the distance that rose on the hot wind like an utterly anomalous sound, inhuman. Howls that crawled over my skin and creeped out my flesh. That made me want to run far, far away.

I wasn't the only one. The faces surrounding us turned as one toward the eerily triumphant cries, then slipped away, disappearing like dark sand shadows, leaving us alone to face what was coming.

"Uh, Halcyon, do you think calling the Hell hounds is a good idea?"

"They are one of the few things the demon dead fear."

"For good reason, no doubt. I don't know if facing them is any better than what just left us."

"It cannot be any worse."

My skin rippled in an involuntary shiver as the first big

shadow appeared. "I happen to disagree. Uh, can you control them?"

"We shall see." His answer was far from comforting. "When I call them, it is usually to feed."

"It would have been nice if you hadn't told me that." My arm around Halcyon's waist became more clutching than supportive as more and more shadowy forms appeared. They had the eyes of night creatures, reflective, glowing. Cold eyes gleaming with frightening intelligence.

They came forward and my first clear vision of them almost made my knees buckle. I firmed my wobbly joints urgently, desperately not wanting to be down on the ground when they reached us. Down on the ground would make us appear less master and more food in their eyes.

Hounds was the wrong word for them. *Hounds* made you think of dogs. And let me tell you . . . these things were not dogs. They were giant beasts on four legs, their heads as tall as we were standing. The sheer size of them made the sword I held feel like a flimsy toy. They were death come calling, with a tail. But the tail was wagging back and forth, as big as a sturdy branch *whoosing* through the air. But it was wagging. The biggest creature, pure black like the complete absence of light, came forward and nudged Halcyon's outstretched hand.

"Shadow," Halcyon murmured, petting that massive head. The great jaw yawned open in a happy grin, showing razor-sharp teeth and a long pink tongue. A pulse of power and Shadow was shrinking, growing smaller. Although smaller was a relative word: In this case meaning shoulder-high instead of head-high. He became an animal form more like the canine species he was named for. Black, sleek, still powerful. Still more than capable of ripping your throat out and swallowing you down in a few big gulps. Still frightening. But less . . . monstrous.

More pulses of power like batteries discharging around

us. Other transformations. There were over thirty of them, of all different colors and fur patterns. A solid gray Hell hound came forward, nudged Halcyon's other hand, snuffling me curiously.

"This is Smoke, Shadow's mate."

Halcyon deliberately lifted his arm around me and gazed into the eyes of the great Hell hounds before him. "This is Mona Lisa." He laid his golden hand against my pale face in a gentle claiming. "My mate."

Their intelligent eyes studied me as if they understood what Halcyon had said. I let them sniff me, take in my scent, even snuffle my crotch. I'd washed but some scents you couldn't wash completely away. Their mouths opened up in gleeful doggy grins. I tensed, but they didn't take a chomp out of me. Shadow's long pink tongue swiped over the back of my hand—my right one holding the sword—and it felt like the roughest grade of sandpaper rubbing over me. I gave a startled yip, and his uncannily intelligent yellow eyes laughed up at me.

"Shadow, stop playing with her," Halcyon scolded him affectionately, "and take me to my father's house."

Father's house turned out to be quite a trek away. I walked. Halcyon rode . . . hunched over on Shadow's back, with his hands buried in the thick pelt of the hound's powerful neck. The midnight black beast was gentle, careful in his stride, as if he knew how weak his master was and how injured. But even so, pain carved deep grooves in Halcyon's face with each soft jostle.

I seemed to have found a second wind. Maybe from almost being eaten twice, first by demon dead, then by the demon dead's version of a dog. My sheathed sword and hunting knife jostled against my side as we passed thatch-roofed huts built of wood, and ramshackle abodes constructed from rough-hewn stone. Hidden demon eyes peered out at us through the windows, but none ventured outside as the Hell hounds swelled the fairway, sweeping me along in their midst. The shelters disappeared and we traveled alone on an empty path for a stretch of time.

Then the fairway widened and rose, leading to a rise upon which loomed a dark tower built of smoothly chiseled black rock, with twin spirals reaching mournfully for the twilight sky. Grand it might be, but it seemed empty, full of gloom, as if no life stirred within its stony interior. Like a giant, elaborate mausoleum or an avoided monument.

And yet, life, it seemed, did reside here. The metal doors, black like the color of demon chains, creaked open to frame a demon dead male of imposing height though lean of build who wore a neat white shirt, waistcoat, and—can you believe this?—a duck-tailed jacket. All spruced up with nowhere to go. The odd thought that the attire had to be tailor-made flitted through my mind before the man strode down like a lurching tree, fearlessly wading into the pack of Hell hounds toward Halcyon. The action jerked me out of my reverie. I didn't know who he was, only that he wasn't Halcyon's father. I sprung in front of Halcyon and drew my sword.

"Don't come any closer," I said, baring my teeth in warning.

"'S okay. Winston. Dad's butler," Halcyon slurred.

"A butler named Winston. Down in Hell?"

The big man eyed me imperturbably. "No odder than a Monère Queen down in Hell named . . ."

"Mona Lisa," Halcyon supplied.

The thin, severe mouth didn't even twitch, but some spark of humor leaped into Winston's mirror-dark eyes. "Mona Lisa," he repeated blandly. "Like the painting."

I bristled. He was the first one to reference it . . . a demon dead butler, at that. "What of it?" I challenged.

His eyes laughed at me, quite a feat to accomplish without moving a muscle in his stiff face. He simply brushed by me, ignoring my sword, giving me his damn back— hmmph!—as if I were no threat to him. But his long arms were gentle as he picked up Halcyon, cradling him against his lean chest.

I turned to the watching Hell hounds. Shadow's and Smoke's intelligent feral eyes swung from their master to me. I swallowed under their intense yellow gaze.

"Thank you for your help," I told them, feeling foolish talking to them. But Halcyon had spoken to them as if they'd understood, and oddly, they seemed to know what I wished to convey.

Their jaws opened in wolfish grins. Lifting their muzzles to the sky, they howled, a chilling, primal sound meant to stir man's deepest fears. The rest of the pack joined in the baying, a lonely but joyous sound. With startling bounds, they loped off into the woods, fleet-footed shadows of death, to hunt other prey.

"This way, milady," Winston said. He pushed open the heavy front door, carrying Halcyon inside. There was nothing to do but sheathe my sword and follow them into the gloomy tower. Inside was even less inviting. The looming corridors seemed empty and windy. The grand stairway spiraled along the interior, reaching for its infinite pinnacle. Winston's footsteps echoed hauntingly in space rarely trod by others. It was hollow and dark, a prison with only two lonely inmates trapped inside. Upon closer inspection, the interior was immaculate, spotless. Furnished in wood tones, accented with dark forest green and heavy gold. Some might even call it stylish, if you liked that old gothic, monolithic look. The school of doom and gloom, not your typical *Town and Country* look. It was a man's abode. Not my cup of tea.

Via the windy stairway, Winston took Halcyon to a spacious bedroom on the second floor, and laid him gently on the bed. "I will awaken the High Lord," he said and left, moving with a curious silence and grace for one so tall and gangly.

I moved to Halcyon's side and smoothed his soft black

hair back from his face. "I thought returning home would make you better, not worse."

Halcyon smiled. "The trip down did that, not being here."

"Ah, yes, the trip down. You shielded me. That's what drained you so much."

"You were in pain."

"I can take a little pain," I said softly.

"It was not a little."

"I can take a lot of pain, then."

"I could not," he said, eyes tenderly stroking my face. "I could not bear to see you in such pain."

"Oh, Halcyon." My fingers stroked his hair gently then moved down to cover the gaping wound slashing down his chest. It had started to bleed again, either from the rough landing or during the ride on Shadow's back. Dark red blood seeped out sullenly, wetting my hand, coating the pearly mole embedded in my palm, making it tingle, warm, come to life. Pain called my power forth and I let it pour out of me and seep into him. I moved my other hand down, swept both my hands across his chest, my palms strumming with energy as I moved them over his slashed chest.

Halcyon's eyes widened. "What are you doing?"

"My question as well." A dangerous voice came from the doorway.

I gasped and stepped back from Halcyon to stare at the High Lord of Hell. Standing framed in the doorway, he looked like the portrait I had seen once at High Court. Like the spitting image of his son. Or perhaps it was the other way around. The same long straight nose, narrow high cheekbones, full wide mouth. The same quiet elegance, trim and slender build. But he was darker than Halcyon, bronze rather than golden, and wore unrelieved black: a black silk shirt, tailored black pants, black diamond cuff links. The dusting of white hair in the portrait had become solid wings of silver flaring his temples while the rest of his hair remained dark.

The greatest difference, however, between father and son was in the eyes. The High Lord's eyes were the same dark brown color, like bittersweet chocolate. But it was the expression in them or rather the complete lack of expression in them that so differentiated them. They say that the eyes are the windows to your soul. These eyes were blank, empty. Completely neutral eyes that I had only seen once before. In the Queen Mother. Eyes that weighed and measured you and passed judgment. Eyes that did not care if you lived or died. It was more unsettling looking into those unemoting eyes than to stare into the hungry yellow eyes of a Hell hound. At least you knew what compelled *that* animal.

"Father," Halcyon said, his voice a weak whisper from the bed. "Mona Lisa. My friend."

"Your friend?" The High Lord arched a brow, an identical echoing gesture of his son's. "Your blood coats her hands," he observed, and silky menace coated his voice, thicker than the blood staining my palms.

I glanced down at my incriminating hands, at the guilty blood gleaming so darkly red against my white skin. "I was only easing his pain."

Halcyon nodded. "She brought me here."

"Winston said Shadow did."

Halcyon smiled. "Him, too."

"And he brought her here as well instead of ripping her apart and feasting on her tender blood and delicate body parts."

I shivered at the gruesome image those cool words conveyed. It took great effort not to fidget under that cold, cold stare.

"I claimed her as my mate," Halcyon said. "Shadow would not comprehend the meaning of friend."

The dark brow winged up again. "And he accepted her as such?"

"He smelled my scent upon her."

"I see."

I wondered if the High Lord did and felt a blush rising in my face.

"Call me Blaec." The High Lord flashed me a sudden white smile, wielding charm as effectively as did his son.

I blinked. "Blaec? What an unusual name."

"It means 'darkness.'"

"Oh." I swallowed. "And yet your son is named for joy and happiness."

A fleeting shadow of memory and regret chased over the High Lord's face, then was gone. "A mother's wish for her son," he said quietly.

Procuring a pristine white handkerchief from an inner pocket, the High Lord offered it to me.

I gratefully wiped his son's blood from my hands. Not knowing what to do with it now that it was stained, I left it on the small bedside table.

Blaec's eyes swept over Halcyon's torn chest with almost cool detachment. But when it alighted on the bite mark, a ripple of dark power pulsed, thickening the air, filling the room. Making it suddenly hard for me to breathe.

"Who dared?" Blaec hissed, leaning down to catch the scent.

"Mona Louisa," Halcyon said.

"Does she still live?"

"Yes."

Something unspoken passed between the two of them. Lightly, Blaec ran his fingers over his son's neck, just above the skin. When those fingers lifted, I gasped. The marks were no more.

Blaec swept his hands slowly down Halcyon's chest, floating over the surface, healing the torn flesh. And it was healing so effortless, so unfelt. Always before, with Janelle, with myself, you could feel the power flowing from one to the other. But not so here. I stood only a foot away and did not sense anything. No pulse of power or strumming of energy. He just moved his hands and tissue was healed. And the complete absence of effort spoke more eloquently than words of the vast power he must wield in those hands. What one could heal, one could also destroy.

Even knowing this, when Blaec turned to me and pushed open the collar of my man's shirt to reveal my own jagged wound, I did not flinch or draw back. I just looked into those cool chocolate eyes with the knowledge of his power clear in my eyes as he lifted a hand and ran it over my torn shoulder. He did not touch my skin, but a feeling of tingling warmth, of heat, fell from the shadow of his hand and balmed my flesh.

"You have no fear." He removed his hand.

"There is nothing I could do should you decide to hurt or heal me," I said quietly.

Blaec's dark eyes glinted. "You'll do," he murmured. "Come."

"Where are we going?" I asked.

"Back to your people."

"You are taking me back to the portal?"

Blaec nodded. "I will await you at the front entrance."

Alone once more in the room, I looked down to find Halcyon's gaze warm upon me.

"You are well?" I asked.

"And will be even more so in a few days."

The sting of tears bit the backs of my eyes. "I am so sorry that you were injured this badly."

"Shhh," Halcyon crooned and grasped my hand. With gentle pressure he brought me down to him. Lifting his head, he met my lips for the first real time with his. Soft. A tender brushing. A sweet pressing of tender flesh to tender flesh. A searching, discovering. A knowing, now, of the shape of my mouth, the feel of his. A light stroke over the seam of my closed lips asking for entrance, for a greater knowing.

I drew back and looked down at him, my lonely prince, wondering why he drew me so. Wondering if his warm eyes would grow cold like his father's as the centuries marched slowly by.

"This attraction between us is now endangering you," I said. It had almost gotten me killed before. Now it had almost killed him. "We must end it. For both our sakes."

He shrugged, gave a wry smile, and answered simply, "I cannot. I cannot stay away from you, though I truly tried."

"Oh, Halcyon."

"You have so much love within you," he said quietly, his eyes searching mine. "Can you not spare a little for me?"

My heart twisted at his words. I did love him. And not just a little. But telling him this would only worsen things, not help. Wouldn't it?

"You are my only friend." Halcyon sat up suddenly and folded me into his arms. "My chosen mate," he whispered against my lips. "Do not leave me alone."

I closed my eyes, unable to resist his plea otherwise. "I cannot stay here."

I felt a sad smile curve those soft red lips. "I know. And I cannot be long away from here." A soft releasing sigh, a promising kiss. "But I shall see you when High Council meets. And perhaps upon occasion at Belle Vista, your home, if your invitation still remains open to me."

I gazed into his eyes, into those bittersweet eyes so like his father's and yet so different. They swirled, alive with emotion. It was those eyes that helped make up my mind. I could not bear the thought of those eyes growing cold, detached. Becoming neutral. He'd been alone for so long. I knew how precious love was; it did not matter how long or short a time you held it for.

I sighed and smiled and yielded. "You are always welcome, Halcyon. In my home and in my heart." And I kissed him, sealing my soft pledge.

"Mona Lisa," he murmured and crushed me to him. I

opened my mouth to him and he stole in, a sweet marauder, plundering what I offered and giving so much more in return. His tongue sought mine out with rough passion, glided sensuously against my tongue in a sweet wet slide. He trembled against me, broke the seal of our lips, and laughed softly against the sensitive hollow of my ear. "Ah, Hellcat, you make me ache when I am too weak to do anything about it."

My hand slid down to stroke his bold length, to measure his sweet arousal. He groaned and shifted against my hand as I savored the lovely fullness of him. "You don't feel weak," I purred.

He gave me one last hard, almost husbandly peck and set me away from him. "We will not put it to the test." His eyes grew heavy-lidded, slumberous. "Until later, when I am fully recovered."

"Until later." I echoed his promise with a sultry smile. "Heal quickly." One last glance at the son, and I closed the door behind me and made my way downstairs to the waiting father.

SIXTEEN

W ITHOUT A WORD the High Lord led me outside. My attention was caught immediately by the two horses on the front lawn, if that was what they could be called. I stared at them with both wonder and apprehension.

Suddenly the dark tower groaned. The walls shook and the ground quaked. I whirled back to catch the High Lord calmly removing his hand from where he had pressed it against the smooth black wall. The trembling ceased.

"What was that?" I said.

"I set the wards. Nothing can enter now."

That sounded nice. It would keep Halcyon safe until he regained his full strength. "What about getting out?" I asked.

"The stones of Darkling Tower are keyed to Halcyon's hand as well. He will be able to leave when he is ready." Darkling Tower. Another edifice with a name. And how appropriately named.

Once that task was accomplished, Blaec seemed like a different person. His eyes were no longer empty but filled with energy, with purpose. He strode down the front steps, fairly strumming with impatience, as if he couldn't wait to be off. Or rid of me. I trailed warily after him. Wary because he headed straight for those giant demon horses.

I was getting a bad feeling about this and was trying to find a polite way to tell the High Lord that I didn't ride, in case he was getting any ideas that way, when he plucked me up and swung me onto the back of one of the animals, completely ignoring my sputtering sounds of protest. Blaec's hands lifted from me and then I was alone on the terrifying beast. I squeaked as I felt myself sliding sideways and instinctively tightened my hold on the flowing mane, but it was the gentle unseen power shifting me upright like an invisible pushing hand that really kept me from falling.

"Was that you, High Lord?" I managed to squeak out.

Blaec leaped gracefully onto his own mount, a jet-black stallion that neighed and snorted, eager to be off. And I noticed then that it wasn't only its greater size that set the demon horse apart from its equine brothers up on Earth. It was also the eyes. They flared to life, a fierce, fiery red then faded slowly back to dark brown. Sharp intelligence glinted in those knowing eyes.

"No, that was Mary, your horse," Blaec said.

I gazed down at Mary with surprise. Whereas the stallion was ebony black, she was pure white, like fresh-fallen snow. "Er . . . thank you, Mary."

The mare tossed her head in acknowledgment and gave a polite little neigh. Her eyes, I noted thankfully, were not glowing red. No doubt they would, though, if I aggravated her enough. I tried not to do so. I tried to hold real still as Mary took off in a gentle canter after the stallion, as if by not moving, I wouldn't imperil my perilous balance. It sounded good in theory, but like many good theorems, did not work out in application. I continued to shift and tilt and slide sideways, and Mary continued to patiently push me back upright with that invisible hand.

The stallion snorted in disgust, prancing in place, waiting for us to catch up with them. His rider snorted in equally impatient disgust.

"Hell fire," Blaec said, not bothering with charm anymore. "You're stiff, like an iron poker's shoved up your ass. No wonder you keep falling over. You've got to relax, girl, if you want to keep your seat."

"Why didn't you say something sooner!" I said. He wasn't the only one disgusted. "This is my first time on a horse."

"Really?" Blaec said dryly, "I couldn't tell. Oh, just pretend that it's my son you're riding."

I gasped in outrage but the High Lord turned and galloped off before I could come up with a scathing retort.

"Stupid, arrogant male," I muttered. Mary neighed. Her eyes laughed kindly back at me, as if I amused her. "Well, he is," I said to her and groaned as I slid sideways once more. Gently, she shifted me back.

"Let me just walk," I called ahead to Blaec.

"I told you before, no time."

"What's the rush," I muttered, and grimly concentrated on relaxing, letting my upper body roll with the easy rocking motion of my mount. Surprisingly, it did help me keep my seat, and the fact that the High Lord was right only served to rankle me more.

We passed a scattering of shabby abodes. The demon dead were out and about. Men, women, but no children. They bowed to the High Lord, eyed my white glowing skin hungrily. They made no effort to approach me, but their hot gazes itched my back.

When I finally seemed to be getting the hang of staying on Mary, Blaec said, "Hang on." With that one warning, he murmured something to the stallion. The great beast

gathered itself and sprung up, stretching out, soaring into
the air, floating up, up, and then down in a long effortless
arc, covering well over a hundred feet.

I only had time to say, "No!" and squeeze my knees
tightly around Mary's barrel sides, and then she was also
springing up, airbound, dropping my stomach down into
my feet and choking a gasp out of my throat as she landed
a soaring distance away. Her feet barely touched the ground
before she sprang up again in another giant leap after the
High Lord's stallion. "Goddamn it! You're supposed to be
horses, not leap frogs."

But my protests seemed not to matter to them. When
Mary finally came to a halt, I slid off her, falling into an
ungraceful heap beside her dainty hooves, thankful once
more to be on solid demon ground. She eyed me sadly, as
if sorry for one so clumsy.

Blaec dismounted with a natural fluidity that I was beginning to despise. Walking over, he offered me a slender,
elegant hand. Grudgingly I took it and he lifted me to my
feet with hardly a pull.

"Showoff," I muttered and he grinned. He grinned, the
bastard.

"No wonder he calls you his hellcat."

With a gentle murmur of thanks and a light stroke on
their powerful necks, Blaec sent the demon horses on their
way.

I assumed there was a portal here. Couldn't really tell. It
looked just like an ordinary clearing. But when I turned my
head, looking around, I caught sight of it: a shimmering
white force, barely visible, like a blurring of reality you
could only see from the corner of your eye. If you looked at
it straight on, it disappeared.

I stepped toward the portal. "My thanks for escorting
me here, High Lord," I said grudgingly. I still had manners,
even though his had apparently completely fled.

"My duty is not yet done, child." Blaec took my arm.

"You don't have to bring me up."

"I will accompany you. Then you will bring me to Mona Louisa."

I halted. "You're going after her," I said flatly.

"Yes."

I regarded him calmly. "What if I told you that I will take care of her?"

Blaec shook his head. "I must see to the matter myself."

My shoulders and the back of my neck were already tense from that harrowing ride-flight. Now they were tightening even more—great big knots of tension that threatened a pounding headache if they continued.

I did not want to be responsible for Blaec's safety. No, that wasn't true. I really did not want to be responsible for his death. Halcyon had said that his father had not walked the Earth for a long, long time. And the longer you'd been away, the harder it would be to play.

"Look," I said, "the night is already more than halfway spent. Wait until tomorrow and I will bring you to her then." My plans were to take care of the blond bitch Queen before it was time to fetch him.

"It cannot wait."

"Damn it, Blaec. I didn't do too well keeping your son safe. If you get dinged up, as well, it's going to suck something major."

He smiled for the very first time and it lit his face up the same way it lit Halcyon's: flashing light over darkness, brightening up his whole face. Making me wish he hadn't smiled. Potent weapon, that smile. It made you want to please him, to coax out another smile from him.

"Somehow, I managed to understand what you said," Blaec said with amusement. "Do all Queens talk as you do now?"

"Nope, just me. I'm one of a kind." Wasn't that the Mixed Blood truth.

"Do not worry for me, my young Queen."

"Can't you contact the High Council? Let them punish her?" Of course, they hadn't done such a good job of punishing her the first time around. But hopefully he didn't know that.

"It is no longer a Monère matter. By laying hands on my son, her judgment has passed into my realm."

Desperately, I tried to think of another deterrent. "You should think of how your son will feel if you get hurt."

"Halcyon knew that I would seek her out. Counted on me, in fact, to do so."

"He did?"

"He came to me," Blaec said simply, "when he could have easily gone instead to his own residence to rest and recover."

I flashed back to that stupid look of understanding that had passed between the two of them. "Ah, Christ." God, I was so tired. I just wanted to crawl into my bed and close my eyes for a few hours. It would be so much easier to face things with a little rest. Although perhaps it was all the weight on my shoulders making me feel so tired.

Sighing, I glared at Blaec. "I will never forgive you if you die."

A hint of a smile. "I will do my best then not to die."

Great. Just freaking great.

Taking my hand, Blaec pulled me to that shimmering haze of biting energy.

I hesitated. You can't really blame me for that slight pause. I'm the first one to admit I enjoy a little pain; in the right context it spices my pleasure. But even the worse masochist wouldn't enjoy this much pain. Pain that pulsed through you until you thought your blood would boil and burst out your veins.

Unfortunately, it was the only route up.

Taking a deep breath, I stepped into the portal and . . . sweet bliss. No pain. Blaec was shielding me. I almost collapsed against him in gratitude. He kept me upright with a light supportive hand.

Descending down to Hell felt as if you were falling. That was the only real impression I'd had while ripping pain had threatened to tear me apart. That and the fact that it seemed to take forever. Of course, being in horrible agony would tend to make even a second feel incredibly long.

Ascending was quite different. Nope, gravity didn't seem as if it were squashing you, and there was no sense of shooting up or being lifted. There was only an impression of speed, of movement. The direction of that movement was not specific, though, just a whirling sense of motion around you, as if you were in a spinning tunnel that passed you from one continuum to another. And time sped by swiftly like the movement. In what seemed a mere moment, we were stepping out of the wall of mist.

SEVENTEEN

THE SMELL OF blood gave me the first inkling that something was wrong. My sword and knife sang from their sheaths and flew into my hands as I stepped in front of Blaec. There was only time to realize that there were four Monère warriors in front of us, and that they weren't mine, before a heavy net woven with the same dark alloy that comprised demon chains was descending on us. I caught the net with my sword before it could touch us and used its momentum to heave it over and past us.

Terror slashed me like a knife, sped up my heart. The blood. Whose blood had been spilled? Would I find a scattering of ashes somewhere near the mouth of that dark alley?

Two of the warriors I recognized. Gilford and Demetrius. Half of what I had once called my Four Colors for their various shades of hair. If I recalled it right, Gilford was the brunette and Demetrius had the jet-black hair. They'd been part of the four betraying guards loaned to me by Mona

Louisa once upon a time. The other two of the original quartet were dead. Just two more to go.

I bared my teeth and stepped forward only to come to a sudden halt as Demetrius held up something in his hands. Silver moonlight glinted off a gold medallion chain, unmistakable in its uniqueness and symbol of power.

"Come with us quietly or Lord Gryphon will die," Demetrius said.

Gryphon had waited for me. Alone, it seemed.

"Where is he?" I demanded.

"With Mona Louisa." Demetrius leered. "We will be happy to take you to your lover. In fact, we must insist."

I took the opportunity to quickly scan the rest of the alley beyond them. No scattering of dust. No empty clothes. A passing quaver of relief weakened me for a moment.

"You are a fool, Halcyon, to have returned," said one of the warriors I didn't recognize.

Halcyon? Could they not tell the difference between father and son? I shifted a little so I could glimpse Blaec from the corner of my eye. Then was so surprised that I turned and looked fully at him, keeping my other senses attuned to sound and movement.

Gone were the white wings at the temples. And bronze had lightened to a golden hue. Blaec even gave out a sense of weakness, his face drawn and haggard, looking exactly like Halcyon had with a few exceptions. There were no chest wounds and he wore a black shirt instead of white. But even I would have been fooled were I to come upon Blaec as he was now.

I shivered. It had to be some sort of glamour or mind control. But for the life of me I couldn't sense it. I whipped my attention back to the four jokers.

"You should go back, Halcyon," I said with clenched teeth.

"When they wish to take us to Mona Louisa?" the High

Lord of Hell said smoothly. "How can we decline their kind invitation?"

I hoped to hell Blaec knew what he was doing. In fact, I was betting our lives on it. I sheathed both sword and blade in a smooth, abrupt motion. "All right, we'll go with you."

Gilford approached with demon chains in his hands. I tensed and the hunting knife was back in my hand. "No chains," I said.

"You have no choice, bitch," Gilford said with venomous hatred.

I drew the sword. It slid free of its scabbard with the joyful ring of steel. "I have every choice, you stupid fool, or have you not learned that yet."

"We'll kill Gryphon," Demetrius threatened.

"Go ahead. And your Queen will probably kill *you* for failing to bring us in. Would you like to put that to the test? Would you like to see who prevails? Two against four. How shortsighted of you. If there were but two more of you, it would have almost evened the odds."

"Bitch," Gilford spat at me.

I flashed him a cold smile. "Always."

"You must surrender your weapons if we do not chain you," Demetrius negotiated. "And give us your sworn oath that you shall come with us peacefully."

I hated the idea. But our hands would be free. "Agreed, as long as you keep your hands off of us."

I tossed them my weapons, blades naked, keeping the sheaths buckled at my sides. "Don't worry," I said. "I'll get them back later." The sword and dagger weren't mine, after all, just loaners. Had to make sure I returned them to their rightful owners.

Gilford glared at me, clutching the surrendered weapons in his fists like he wanted to run them through me.

I smiled sweetly at him, knowing he wouldn't dare. "After you," I said. "Or should I say: 'Cowards first.'"

"Gently," Blaec cautioned quietly. "No need to tweak their tails further."

"Oh, but it's so fun," I whispered back, eyes glittering. I was furious at Blaec for stubbornly coming with me. Furious at the whole goat-fucking situation. Furious at Gryphon for having waited for me. Furious at him for leaving himself vulnerable. I even knew how it had happened. Gryphon would have sent the other men back home to protect the others, in case Mona Louisa decided to retaliate. Instead, she had somehow tracked Gryphon here and had taken him. But beneath that white, cleansing fury was the sour taste of fear. Gryphon could have been killed instead of captured. Might still be.

A dark minivan was parked at the curb, probably stolen because their damaged cars had to still be back home. Nothing open. No place to have changed their slashed tires at this time of night.

The warrior who held Gryphon's medallion got behind the wheel.

Demetrius opened the front passenger door. "Prince Halcyon," he said politely.

Blaec slid into the seat without demur, like a welcomed guest instead of a prisoner.

Not a bad seating arrangement, splitting us up, the High Lord in front, me in the middle row. The fourth warrior sat in the third row. Demetrius moved to sit in the far corner of the second row. "Milady."

Reluctantly, I sat next to him. Gilford entered last and shut the door, sandwiching me in between the two of them. But having an angry, armed Gilford sitting beside me was far better than having him sit behind me where I couldn't see him. That I would have protested. Demetrius was smarter than he looked. He hid his dislike and fear of me rather than show it like his bristling friend. It took more deviousness in a person, more smarts, more control to do that.

I breathed easier when we got on the interstate and

headed east toward Mississippi. Nothing would have
changed had we gone west toward Belle Vista. Yet at the
same time, everything would have changed. I'd have sat
there, let them take me there. But something inside me
would have died a little knowing that they had taken over
my home, conquered my people. And more guilt would
have been loaded upon me. East told me that Mona Louisa
hadn't made a move on her old territory yet. She was hoping to take out the new Queen first and reclaim her old
Queendom. A simple, elegant plan, actually. And she knew
me well enough to bait her trap with a lure I could not resist.

So I sat there docilely, surrounded by enemies, and let
them take us where we wanted to go. Blaec was my hidden
ace. I prayed that he knew what he was doing. I prayed that
his strength did not ebb. I prayed that we even reach our
destination faster. Time, now, was our ticking enemy. The
night was passing quickly and the coming of dawn could
destroy us.

Mississippi did not seem much different from its bor-
dering sister, Louisiana. We passed patches of marshy wet-
lands along the highway, drove past rolling farmlands, and
finally pulled into a long drive. The house was a two-story,
pillared affair, but not as grand, not as big as Belle Vista. A
lovely old property, but not a mansion. Not something
meant to be the opulent residence of a Queen. How being
forced to come here must have eaten away at Mona
Louisa's pride. The crumbled wall where we had burst free
was a lovely eyesore, as were the deep, slashing tire tracks
ripping up the immaculate lawn.

Gilford leapt out of his seat as if sitting beside me had
burned him. I scooted over and pulled myself out of the van.
Blaec and I stood there surrounded by a score of men—a
little less than twenty. We'd killed several in our last skir-
mish. Too bad it hadn't been more. The ones we had injured
were healing or already healed.

I glanced at Blaec. His camouflaged appearance still

held, and he looked uncannily weak. I prayed that it was mere illusion and not truth. If it was his true state, we were in big trouble. I was good, but not even I could take on seventeen men alone and hope to win.

The group welcoming committee was nice and flattering and all that, but they weren't who I wanted to see. I unfurled my senses, let them fly free.

Inside. What I sought was inside. A Queen's presence and a second slow heartbeat that I knew as well as my own, the smell of my mate.

We moved as one up the stairs, as if Blaec and I were the core, and the ring of guards the outer steel rim. They kept a respectful barrier of space around us. It might have been because of me. The natural attraction between a Queen and a male, any male, was felt more strongly with close intimate contact. Then again, it might have been who they thought was the Demon Prince, moving free of chains. An unbound demon dead, even weak and injured, was still someone to be greatly feared.

Without direction, I entered the spacious receiving room to the left. Mona Louisa reclined on a plush butter-leather couch, a pleased cat-that's-caught-the-canary look on her smooth porcelain face. Evil was worse, somehow, when it was so beautiful. Gryphon sat beside her, bound in silver chains, his arms behind him and his mouth gagged. She stroked his bare chest unthinkingly, the way one would pet a dog, not caring for the body she stroked, but keenly intent, rather, on my reaction.

I kept my face inscrutable, my reaction blank, even though I raged inside with fury and relief.

Gryphon was injured low in his left side, as if a sword had been thrust through him there. It was almost the exact spot where he'd once rotted from silver poisoning. It was a gut wound that would have killed a human, but Gryphon was already beginning to heal. The sword hadn't been silver.

Gryphon held obediently still under that insulting,

caressing hand. But his eyes were most eloquent. They were frightened and urgent, desperate almost, as if he were trying to convey an important warning to me.

"My dear Halcyon," Mona Louisa exclaimed with saccharine delight, her eyes glittering with that same heated fervor. The feel of her, though, was oddly less abrasive. "How nice of you to join us once more. Although it was very, very foolish of you to return. It is truly a wonder that you ruled Hell for so long."

Blaec didn't respond. She didn't seem to expect him to. I wondered for a fleeting moment if the High Lord hadn't spoken because he couldn't disguise his voice. Father and son's tonality was the same, but Blaec had a slightly more arcane rhythm and flow to his words, reflecting his greater lifetime of existence.

"How stupid of you to fall so easily into my little trap, my dear," Mona Louisa sneered at me. "It is almost beyond comprehension that one would do something so utterly dull-witted. No other Queen would have done as you. Come as docilely as a lamb led to the slaughter. But then I expected nothing else from a weak mongrel. So sentimental. So unwise. So . . . human. Ruled by your heart, not your thinking mind. The taint of your Mixed Blood weakens you." She tsk-tsked in mock pity. Then her eyes hardened to ice. "But my men seemed to have carelessly left you unadorned. Where are the demon shackles?" Her voice cracked like a whip, making her men jump.

"Here, milady," Demetrius said, his voice tremulous as he held up the dark chains he had carried in.

"Why are they not on them, you fool?"

"They agreed to come without resisting if we left them unbound, milady."

"Some things, it seems, only a Queen can handle." Mona Louisa's cold look promised later retribution for her poor foolish men.

She turned her considering eyes to me, then said lightly,

almost gaily, "A wager, Mona Lisa. A test of strength. If you lose, Halcyon will agree to be shackled without resistance. *You* need not be held by such promise. Am I not generous?"

Gryphon tried to speak but only muffled sounds escaped the cloth gagging him. He shook his head, his eyes anxious and urgent.

"And if I win?"

"Why then, both of you and the beautiful, talented Gryphon here will go free. My word upon it."

It was almost too easy, if you trusted her word. And I didn't know that I did. But the possibility that it could end so easily, so bloodlessly, was too great a chance to pass up. "What specific test?"

"Something basic, I think." Mona Louisa cocked her head and thought for a moment. "How about arm wrestling? Something that primitively human and masculine should appeal to you."

Bitch. I glanced at Blaec. He nodded. I had to trust that he'd be able to break free of the demon chains. But hopefully he wouldn't even have to. I was almost certain I could take her. I was stronger since Basking and being gifted with some of Amber's great strength. I was as powerful now as a Full Blood, if not a little more.

"One arm only, seated," I said. "No trickery. Just pure physical strength. Agreed?"

Gryphon shook his head again and tried to struggle to his feet. Mona Louisa's slender hand pressed him back with disdainful ease.

Mona Louisa dipped her head in agreement, a little smile curving her lips. "Agreed."

A small rectangular oak table and two high-backed chairs were brought in. Mona Louisa and I sat opposite each other with only the narrow width of the long side table separating us. Again I was struck by that odd lack of abrasiveness. I felt her presence, but it was only a faint echo of the annoyance that it should have been. Our skins should have been crawling with the urgent need to put distance between us by now, two Queens this close. But they weren't. She was different somehow.

I braced my right hand on the solid wooden surface, hand cupped, waiting. With a smile of satisfaction, Mona Louisa clasped my hand in hers. She possessed a lady's hand, all cool pampered softness and smoothness. A lady who had never known a day of labor in her long life.

"On the count of three," I said. "One, two, *three*!"

Mona Louisa's soft hand firmed, gripped me like a vise as I lunged with all my strength, trying for a quick, decisive win. I threw my entire weight behind that downward pulling motion. Her hand dipped back a couple of inches. Then slowly, inexorably, came back up to starting point. Without visible effort, with that amused glee as if she were in on a joke that only she knew about, Mona Louisa levered my hand over to her side. Down two inches . . . three . . . four. The wooden surface loomed near and none of my straining effort was enough to withstand her strength. I grimaced, pulled, sweated, and grunted to no avail.

Mona Louisa's eyes gleamed like twin icy shards, an intimate distance away from me. Her face was unlined, unmarred by exertion, smiling. She was unbelievably strong.

"How could you hope to ever be my equal?" she asked with serene disdain. "A mongrel bastard. How could you even dare dream of rising up to become one of us? Your human-infected blood can only weaken you. It is my royal duty to rid us of your taint before it stains more of us with your inferiority. Let everyone here bear witness to how weak you really are. So pathetically weak."

She slammed my hand down, crashed it through the wood, sprawled me on the floor, and smiled. "Winner takes all." Mona Louisa pinned me down and her small, smooth hands closed about me like shackles. And I was helpless to break free of her iron grip. Jesus Christ, how had she gotten so fucking strong?

"Your promise, Demon Prince," Mona Louisa said to Blaec.

Without demur, Blaec held out his hands and Gilford quickly clamped the demon chains about Blaec's wrists, closing them with a loud and heavy clang.

"Bring the other pair of demon chains here," Mona Louisa ordered and Demetrius jumped to do her bidding.

I gazed despairingly up at Blaec as I lay there pinned to the ground, Demetrius only steps away from binding me, too. Dear God, had I been wrong? Had I gambled and lost everything? Goddess help us.

Like an answer to my prayer, the demon chains binding the High Lord broke with a snap. Blaec tore the manacles from his slender wrists with two easy motions and straightened his cuffs. As the chains dropped to the ground, his glamour fell away. White wings flared once more at Blaec's temples. Gold skin darkened to bronze. There was a moment of frozen silence where everyone stopped and stared, where all eyes were upon him, all breaths held, where time itself was suspended. Where some recognized who they truly faced and others did not. Then all Hell broke loose.

Death came not with blood or violence. But with almost gentle grace. With nothing but a look, just the weight of the High Lord's gaze, Gilford flashed into light, puffed into dust. The next closest warrior standing next to Blaec almost immediately followed, so that they were like twin strobing lights going off next to the elegant bronzed man, illuminating the High Lord of Hell. A *flash, flash* of brilliant light and they were gone before the brightness had faded.

Mona Louisa screamed with rage, loud enough to deafen the entire room. "Cut him, slash him! Make him bleed! That will weaken him."

Even facing living death could not counter a warrior's strong inborn instinct to defend his Queen. And she sent them all to their sure death without remorse, without thought, with an ice-cold heart. Sacrificing her men to buy time for herself.

Mona Louisa pulled me up to her like a rag doll in her strong grip and buried her teeth, her fangs, in my neck. I felt a sharp pain, a tearing bite. She was pressed so closely against me that I felt her slender throat work strongly as she gulped down my blood like a demon dead creature, pulling it from me so fast that I was dizzy.

With the last ebbings of my draining strength, I stretched out my right hand. A silver blade harkened to my call, leaped into my grasp. I buried the shaft deep down to the hilt in her back. Mona Louisa tore her mouth away and screamed in painful outrage. Letting me drop, she clawed the dagger from her back and threw the bloody blade at me, a blinding whirl of silver. I rolled and the knife sank into the floor where I had lain.

Her eyes spewing with molten wrath, Mona Louisa sprang to the couch where Gryphon lay bound. Her men acted as a living barricade of flesh between her and the Demon Lord so that I couldn't see Blaec, only the *flash, flash, flash* of bursting lights. Could only hear sounds and screams. Could only see swords and daggers rising and falling in a cacophony of vicious sound and stabbing motion.

With her left hand, Mona Louisa yanked Gryphon to his feet, hissing her blood-stained fangs—*fangs!*—at me. "I told you once before, mongrel bitch. If I cannot have him, then neither shall you."

I scrambled to my feet, but it felt as if I were wading through thickened air. I stumbled and watched helplessly as Mona Louisa pulled back her hand as if pulling a tautened bow. Then with terrible finality, she unleashed her hand and plunged it straight into Gryphon's chest, tearing through flesh and bone as if she were ripping through paper. With a vicious grabbing twist, she yanked his heart out, so that it was a bulging, quivering organ gripped tight in her first. She threw it into the air.

"No!" My horrified scream echoed loudly in my ears as I leaped up to catch it. Slowly, so slowly, I watched that precious tumbling heart fall into my hands. Felt the warm wetness of fresh blood, the squish of firm and tender tissue. Felt one weak throb against my palms. Felt myself shudder with the reality of it, and then time resumed its inevitable fast march forward. I landed at Gryphon's side; he had fallen to the ground. With sobbing haste, I rolled him onto his back and aimed the throbbing heart at the gaping hole in his chest. Carefully, I reinserted that still beating organ back into his broken chest cavity and held it in place with a trembling hand. I ripped the offending gag from Gryphon's mouth and screamed, "Blaec! Blaec!"

There was an almost endless ripple of exploding lights and then the High Lord was at my side, his face drawn and sallow with the effort of his kills.

"Heal him, High Lord! Please!" I cried. "I'll do anything, give you anything, if you'll heal Gryphon."

"I'm sorry, child." Blaec's words tolled with bitter finality. "No one can heal such a wound."

"No! There has to be some way of helping him." Frantically I covered Gryphon's torn chest with both of my hands. Desperately I called up that power deep within me as I looked down at him. "Don't leave me," I whispered.

My palms throbbed, ached with burning heat, and I poured that hot rushing energy into Gryphon. His eyes, those beautiful blue eyes, stirred, fluttered open as if he were awakening from a sweet dream. Our eyes met.

"Gryphon . . . please don't leave me."

"My love." It was the barest of sounds on a last sighing breath. A gentle smile shone on Gryphon's beloved face. Beneath my hands, his heart lay coldly still, no longer beating. Then Gryphon shone one last time, a glittering eruption of light released, no longer held. Before my eyes, his flesh shimmered, dried up, and started to crumble, collapsing into a cascade of powdery residue. He gave off one final flash of his essential light, then he was free.

And was no more.

EIGHTEEN

ASHES SCATTERED TO the ground, dusting over my knees, coating my bloodstained hands. His clothes lay on the floor like an empty shroud. *Dust to dust. Ashes to ashes.*

Silence filled the room like a tomb, broken only by my shuddering breath. Carnage had swept the room with a clean, ruthless hand, piles of ashes all that remained of so many. I was surrounded by death and felt as if I had died also. Wished that I had, since living hurt so much.

Then the sweet, clean burn of rage filled my empty shell, giving me a driving purpose to focus upon, so that I thought of only one thing.

"Mona Louisa is mine," I rasped harshly, jerkily, looking up at the High Lord.

He crouched down beside me so that his dark compassionate eyes were level with mine. "She is much stronger than you now," he said gently.

"Mine," I reiterated with a flat, trembling voice.

"She will kill you," Blaec said.

My eyes held his gaze fiercely so that there would be no misunderstanding. "After I die, she's all yours. But she is mine until I depart this earth." I stretched out my shaking hands, coated with the dark redness of Gryphon's blood, and the words came to me from somewhere deep inside, some place old, long before my birth, a hazy past filled with the most base, primal instincts: desire to own, to possess, to conquer. The words came tolling out of me. "I claim Mona Louisa's life as my blood right."

The words echoed, trembled in the air. *Blood right.* A claim that seemed to hold meaning for the High Lord. Bowing his head, Blaec nodded.

We left that house of death and stepped into the dark whispering night, tracking our prey where she had fled into the woods. I smiled with cold satisfaction. The stab wound in Mona Louisa's back had prevented her from flying away, from taking her vulture form. She was grounded until the torn tissue knitted together.

Deep in the woods, ahead of us, Mona Louisa's slow heartbeat sounded in the distance and the scent of her blood drifted to me like tracking beacons. We headed north after that heartbeat, after that obscene sound of life that still was and should not be. So many dead because of her. It was only just that she join them.

I threw myself into mindless pursuit, trusting to instinct, to primal senses to find my way, leaping over trees and bushes, springing blindly after her, after that beckoning heartbeat, landing wherever I landed, on fallen logs, on the moist rich ground, in clawing brush, soaring over rocks and boulders, only to spring up again, throwing myself blindly forward, ever onward at full speed, letting that unthinking, natural part of myself that was more animal than human guide me on to paths unknown.

The High Lord was a silent shadow beside me, pure

movement, no sound. No betraying breath or pumping of blood to mark his presence.

We were gaining on her. She'd been spoiled by the ease of taking wing and soaring high in the sky. On the ground, Mona Louisa moved more cautiously. She made her way carefully in the thick woods, less experienced in the forest than above it. She moved not with the dangerous speed I forced upon myself, the blind leaps of faith I took. And why should she? She wanted to live. I did not care if I did or not. All that filled me was that single driving purpose, that pervading anger.

Cold rage. I'd never understood the term before. Never thought that rage could be anything but hot. But rage can be cold. Like flames that burned so hotly they edged from orange to cool blue, from rash heat into cold fire. It was thinking rage. Anger, pain, sorrow did not fill you, overwhelm you. You were dispassionate, detached from your emotion, as if you were already dead. My heart was. When she had ripped Gryphon's heart out of his chest, it felt as if mine had died as well.

Almost there. I closed in on that slow, slow heartbeat, my only goal to make that beating stop. I drew my sword, called the dagger from its sheath. "Face me, bitch," I whispered and knew that she heard me.

With one last bounding spring, I fell down upon Mona Louisa, her blond hair glowing bright under moonshine, waving in the darkness like a beacon of light. She turned her face up to me, and I fell upon her with a soundless cry, aiming my sword at her neck, my dagger driving for her heart.

At the last possible moment she turned fully and, with blinding quickness, heaved a melon-sized boulder at me that she had hidden in her arms. Going downward, I was unable to avoid it. Like a cannoned missile, it struck my drawn sword aside, knocking it from my hand. The heavy rock smashed into my chest with crushing force. The pain was blinding, breath-stealing. Hot, searing agony ripped through my torso from the blow, and then once again as I hit the ground with jarring force. Before I could catch my breath, I felt her hands on me, gripping my hair, grabbing the back of my pants, lifting me up, and heaving me into the air. I crashed against the trunk of a giant cypress tree, the rough bark shredding my cheek, my arm, my entire left side.

I hit the ground, half of me numb. I'd lost my dagger and wondered for a moment if I'd stabbed myself. My chest felt as if it were on fire, as if purgatory had decided not to wait until I died and was roasting me now. I glanced down to make sure. Nope, no dagger sticking out of my chest. Just felt that way. Broken ribs tended to do that. They hurt like the dickens.

Mona Louisa's battle shriek tore through the quiet of the night as she rushed me with blinding quickness. She may have been strong, beyond Monère strong, but she'd obviously not had much fighting experience. Experienced fighters didn't scream and warn you that they were coming.

I lay there waiting for her to come to me and she did. She threw herself at me, reaching for me with clawed fingers. I took a trick out of her own book and waited until she'd almost reached me. When it was too late for her to check her rush, I brought both legs up and donkey-kicked her in the stomach and chest. The jarring impact of stopping dead all that weight and momentum ripped another fiery pain through my chest, but the satisfaction of hearing that *whoosh* of breath and glimpsing the surprise in Mona Louisa's face was worth it. Seeing her go flying back and smash up against a palmetto tree, hearing the groaning wood crack and tilt as she hit it, was even better.

The stunned look that swept across her face and the twisting rage that flushed into an ugly red mask made me think that it was the first time she'd ever been hit in her life. Made me want to hit her again.

Pushing back against the tree that had broken my fall, I climbed back onto my feet, hunching over a little. "Did that hurt, bitch? Why don't you come back for more?" I taunted, mainly because I couldn't rush her. Heck, I doubted I could even take one step toward her.

With a screeching cry, she flew at me again. I got in one good swing that snapped her head back nicely before she grabbed me and tossed me up so I soared twenty feet in the air again. I was getting used to the feeling of flying. Landing, though, was a real bitch. Sure enough, a tree trunk tried to break me in half again. Holy sweet mother of God . . . I almost passed out from the pain.

I saw Blaec, or I thought I did, in my wavering vision. A hazy bronze shape peeping out from beneath the shadow of a tree, a question on his face.

"No." I shook my head stubbornly to clear my vision, to shake off the pain. "She's mine!"

And then she was on me, her breath in my face heavy with the smell of my own blood, imprisoning my arms, crushing them to my sides as she lifted me up with almost effortless ease and slammed me back against the heavy, solid tree trunk with pounding force, her teeth drawn back in a furious snarl. "You are nothing!" she screamed. *Thunk! Thunk!* Beating me like a board she was trying to break. "Nothing!" Rough bark tore into my back, snagged my hair. Blood trickled down, soaking into my pants.

"You are as weak as your lover!" she hissed. "Killing him was so easy."

The blackness that had been edging my vision cleared at her words, and I began to struggle in silent, fierce earnestness, twisting in her grasp.

Mona Louisa laughed and slammed me upright, back against the tree, pinning my wrists low with her shackling hands, restraining my legs with the press of her lower body against me. "Killing you will be even easier," she crooned, her breath warm against me. "And much sweeter."

Her teeth lengthened. Rearing back, she struck hard,
her fangs sinking deep into the left side of my neck, the
clean, unbroken side. I screamed as she drank me down.
Tried . . . tried so hard with everything that I was to break
free. But I could not. She was too strong. All I could do was
twist my hands, wet from Gryphon's blood. They slid
barely, just barely in her cinching grasp so that my palms
turned outward, facing toward her.

Her loud swallowing sounds echoed in my ears as I
reached out with that other part of me, with a willing, *Come
to me.* My palms throbbed, but either the distance was too
great or I was too weak. The lost silver dagger, the dropped
sword did not fly to my hands. They remained empty, im-
potent. My vision was hazing, sounds growing distant as
more of me flowed into her. All I could see above me now
was the moon, three-quarters full, a neutral presence in the
sky, a silent witness. *Help me, Goddess. Hear your daughter's plea.*

I forced my last conscious will into my hands, into those
mounds of pearls embedded deep in my palms. The Goddess's Tears. I angled them up to the dark, velvety sky and
begged: *Give me strength. Renew me.*

I didn't just open myself to the moon, welcome it, and let
it flow down. I pulled it down, called it to me, demanded it.
Give me justice! But it wasn't the moon's rays I pulled forth.

The Goddess's Tears trembled, gave one giant throb.
Then another. They began to glow, twin pearls of light
breaking the darkness of the night. Heat filled me. Power
swept into me like a gentle spilling light. Mona Louisa's
head suddenly jerked up, her eyes panicked and wide.
"What is that? What are you doing?"

A light radiance sparked deep within her, like a candle
lit by a match, the wick catching aflame. My hands pulsed,
my entire body throbbed with the power, with the calling.
And I drew more light from her. Pulled it into me.

She released me as if touching me suddenly burned her. She tried to draw away, step back. But I held her now. Energy rushed through me, her radiance spilled into me, filling me, renewing me, siphoning her power, making it mine. My palms pressed against her arms, imprisoning her, holding her to me gently like a sweet lover as I drained her of her power, of her beauty, of her youth and vitality. As I drained her of life itself. And the power that rushed into me and flooded me, stretched me with seductive heat was better than Basking. Better than sex.

Her essence filled me, poured into me, kept coming in a steady streaming, a steady draining. My skin felt as if it had become porous. Her energy, her aura, her force flowed over my skin like thick honey and then seeped into every open pore. Was sucked in. And I watched her ebb, fade away. I watched myself grow stronger, brighter.

Power streamed into me until I felt as if I were a paper lantern. As if I had swallowed down the moon and it glowed within me, spilling from me with such blinding luminescence that the forest was ablaze with wild, glorious splendor, lighting up the night.

I watched Mona Louisa shrivel before me, her skin becoming tight, thicker, leathery, all moisture wrung from her. Her flesh melted, was sucked away until she was nothing but thin wrinkly skin draped over dried bones. Youth and beauty vanished. She became an old crone who had lived too long and yet still clung to life, her bulging eyes white and terrified. All that remained of her old self was her bright yellow hair, still shiny and silky and long, like a wig worn by a mannequin. Even her screams had dried up, as if all moisture in her vocal chords had vaporized and all she was capable of emitting now was a high keening sound. A wailing that did not stop.

I extracted the very last drop of her light into me like a final drop of sticky molasses. And yet she still was . . .

screaming, keening, crying, always crying. "Why won't you die, bitch?"

She lay there on the ground where she had fallen, too weak to move, a drained bundle of sticks, an undying corpse.

"She has become more than Monère now." The High Lord's quiet voice came from a careful distance away. His eyes were neutral once more, his face inscrutable.

"Because she drank Halcyon's blood," I said. "Demon dead blood."

"Yes."

"Even demons can be killed." I stretched forth my hands, palms out. But still my weapons did not answer my call. Not for lack of power then. Simply too far away. My eyes fell to some nearby rocks and narrowed in thought. It wasn't just knives that could cut.

Smashing one heavy stone against another, I broke them open. One large piece of stone had fallen apart with a sharp glistening edge six inches long. Picking that up, I walked to where Mona Louisa lay. She rolled her eyes sideways to look up at me, and the movement of her eyeballs shifting in her sockets made a dry sucking sound. Dropping to my knees by her head, with her terrified eyes wide upon me, with that unceasing high, dry wailing buzzing in my ears like an irritating gnat, I raised the razor-sharp piece of stone up over my head with both hands. "Die," I muttered. "I want you to die."

The knife-sharp stone edge came down hard with my full shining power behind it. It sliced through skin, broke through bones. I looked down upon my work. The dried-up hag was three-fourths decapitated.

"Oops, my aim was a little off. Once more, shall we." The rock blade came smashing down again and her severed head rolled off and came to rest a couple of yards away, the base of her head rocking in the dry leaves, her long blond hair spilling around her like a yellow cape, part of it wrapped around her lower face and bloody, sticky neck stub. That high keening had stopped. Her mouth yawned ajar as if on silent hinges. No sound emerged. Her blue eyes were open and aware.

"What does it take to kill you, bitch?" I asked, breathing heavily, gazing down into those frightened knowing eyes. There were no handy Hell hounds here to feed her to.

"If I may?" Blaec asked, polite and distant.

I looked up at the High Lord of Hell, gazed at that dark, inscrutable, elegant face. He, of all people, would know how to kill that demon dead part of her.

"Go ahead." I stepped back and let Blaec come around to the front of Mona Louisa, the head part of her, that is.

He crouched down, his shirt torn, his pants ripped, with the smell of blood on him. But his skin beneath was whole, healed, even though his face was strained with fatigue. One bronze finger reached out and touched Mona Louisa as her eyes rolled toward him in terror, as her mouth moved open and shut in a mute parody of speech. The tip of his sharp fingernail came to rest lightly on Mona Lisa's forehead, between her eyes so that they crossed together as she tried to watch him. But all that lethal nail did was touch her. And I wondered if physical connection made it easier for the Demon Lord's power to flow.

A pulse of power so strong that I felt it shake the air reverberated through me, and Mona Louisa's rolling eyes closed.

I spoke softly. "What did you do?"

"Destroyed her mind. That psychic part of her."

He'd killed her mental power, that part of her that would have allowed Mona Louisa to become demon dead and exist in Hell for as long as that power continued. "What becomes of her now?"

"Now she will simply fade back into the darkness."

Another pulse of power and her head exploded into ashes, and her body puffed into dust.

Blaec stood as I moved next to him to stare down at the twin pile of ashes, her severed head and her body.

"You've killed Mona Louisa and all her guards," I said, my voice empty as I turned to look at him. "Will you kill me now, High Lord? I am the only one remaining who knows the value of a demon dead's blood. That drinking it can multiply a Monère's power, endowing them with demon dead strength."

"And if I wished to?" Blaec asked. He looked tired but still strong.

"I would not fight you" was my quiet reply, even though I still gleamed with my stolen light, my stolen power.

He smiled at me with a kindness that would have made me cry had I any feelings left. "There is no need, child. Your secret should be ransom enough to keep mine."

"What secret?"

Blaec gestured to my hands with a long nail. "Your Mortal Draining. An ability I had heard only in tales as a child. I had thought them merely that. Tales. I will keep your secret if you will keep mine."

"Why would I want to keep this ability secret?"

"Because nothing then will stop the other Queens from killing you or your brother."

It was the mention of my brother that made me flinch. "More than they want to kill me now?"

"Oh, yes. Now you are a mere inconvenience. If they knew that you were capable of Mortal Draining, of taking their power, their very life into yourself, then you would become the gravest danger to them. To them all."

I sighed. Secrets. So many of them to keep. They seemed senseless, with no meaning at the moment.

Blaec turned, put a comforting arm over my shoulder, and we started walking back. "Come, child. My task is complete. I am old and weary and eager to return home."

WITH MONA LOUISA dead and gone, my focus was lost. She'd said that revenge was not sweet, that it was bloody. She was wrong. It *was* sweet. For one fleeting, glorious moment you felt incredible satisfaction. Then it was gone, empty, and you had to go on living. The power high that filled me with her light had faded, and all I tasted now were bitter ashes.

I drove Blaec in Mona Louisa's stolen van back to New Orleans as dawn beat back the darkness. At the white misty portal, I turned to the High Lord. "Let me come with you."

His tone was kind but final. "No."

"Is Gryphon down in Hell?"

"I do not know, child, but he felt strong. He should have made the transition."

I clutched the High Lord's arm. "I have to see him."

Gently, he disengaged my hand. "You cannot, for his sake. Think, child. Gryphon has just experienced a tragic loss, of life itself. Those newly dead have no desire to see the living when their loss is so keenly fresh. It takes time, sometimes a great deal of it for them to adjust to their new existence. Seeing those they once loved, who are still alive while they are not, would be painfully cruel."

My eyes clung to his. "I have to know if he made it."

"I will send you word," he promised.

I would have to be satisfied with that.

Gryphon's medallion chain slid out, clinking, as I pulled it from my pocket. It was the only thing I had retrieved from that house. I pressed it into Blaec's hand. "Give Gryphon this for me."

"I will." Taking the necklace from me, he walked into the mist. It swallowed him up and both winked out of existence.

I waited a few heartbeats, then went to where the portal had been. Felt for it, tried to sense it. But nothing was there. I felt along the walls, walked back and forth across the spot where it had been in that deserted alley. But it was gone, truly gone, and I could not call it forth.

Nothing left to do now but go home.

NINETEEN

❧❧

THEY SAY THAT time heals, but that's a lie. All it does is allow you to hurt. And I was so tired of hurting. The sun was shining brightly when I pulled up in front of Belle Vista. I shut off the engine and sat there looking at it. The people I loved were all in there, sleeping. Except one of them was missing and would never come back. I wanted to return to the sanctuary of my chamber, but to reach it I'd have to pass Gryphon's room. Empty now, forever. I couldn't face it. Not yet. So I just sat there until Amber came out the front entrance and flowed down the steps.

Concern flared in his eyes when he saw me—concern that I was alone in a strange car. "Mona Lisa, where's Gryphon?"

"He's dead," I said numbly. "Mona Louisa killed him, and I killed her. She sacrificed her men. They're all gone."

He opened the door, spoke gently. "Come inside." But I refused to get out. I felt so brittle. I was okay just sitting here, but if I had to go inside, pass Gryphon's empty room and smell his scent, it would break me. I didn't know how to tell Amber this, other than to say, "I can't."

Amber knelt, took my limp hands, engulfed them protectively in the largeness of his own.

"It hurts, Amber. It hurts so much. I don't want it to hurt anymore. I don't want to think or feel anymore. Come running with me."

In the knowledge of his eyes, I saw that he knew what I desired. "Wait for me. Let me tell one of the others."

I sat there in the car, unmoving, until he returned.

Amber led me to the edge of the woods. There he stopped and undressed, neatly folding his clothes, then removed mine. I stood passively and let him, concentrating fiercely on the birdsong, on the feel of the sun on my skin, on anything other than my feelings, my thoughts, my memories.

"Mona Lisa, when you are ready," Amber said quietly, bringing my attention back, and I realized that I was completely nude and unembarrassed. What did it matter now?

I dropped that shielding, that control, those mental chains that had bound my beast for so long that it felt a natural part of me. Nothing happened, and for one moment I felt despair. Was I too consumed? Was I too spent? And then I felt my beast roaring out of me, exploding from me, and caught its thoughts for one fleeting second . . . *Unleashed. Finally unleashed* . . . Before it took me over completely and I ceased to be. In my receding consciousness, I heard only the panting of my tiger. Felt it leap with its great paws touching the ground ever so lightly, racing toward the heart of the deep forest.

⤫

WHEN I CAME back to awareness, it was dawn or dusk, I could not tell. I did not know how much time had elapsed, remembered nothing. I was in a bed of leaves in the shelter of a shallow cave, in Amber's arms, my head pillowed on his chest. I was covered in an acrid scent I did not recognize and the tang of old blood was a coppery taste in my mouth. My stomach churned and I scrambled on all fours out of the cave. Only a few feet from the entrance, I could hold it back no longer, and heaved and wretched up bloody chunks of raw meat. And then heaved even more when I saw what was spewing out from me. Amber held back my hair, supporting me, crooning in wordless comfort.

⁓

IN THE DAYS to come, we nestled in the forest. Amber roamed free as a cougar, and I as a Bengal tiger. My beast became my escape, my salvation now. And it reveled in its newfound freedom, unchained, unbound.

Every day I awoke to other unfamiliar scents on me, and the tang of old blood in my mouth became a familiar aftertaste. But I always woke with Amber's arms, large and secure around me, with his heart beating slow and strong beneath me. I no longer vomited, and there were memories now. Flashes of running through the forest, my head low to the ground, stretching out. Bits and pieces of the hunt. Different ones, so many different ones. The rush of bringing prey down, that final soaring spring, the tearing of flesh, that sweet hot spray of blood filling my mouth.

And then one day, I didn't just remember. I was aware. I saw my paws stretched out before me, felt the bare impact as I touched lightly upon the ground, and I came to a sudden stop, letting the deer I was chasing dart away, its bobbing white tail a teasing allure that I resisted though my beast still wanted it. I felt my beast's silent half-hearted snarl at me for stopping. But it was well fed. The deer had simply come along while it had been resting and it had given chase because that was what it did. I turned, and through my tiger eyes saw the tawny mountain cat that had been my constant companion, saw it watching me with intelligent amber eyes.

Are you in there? he asked.

Yes.

I changed and it was an easy, natural thing to do, to resume my human form, to stand and watch as the cougar shimmered, as fur became skin, and Amber once more stood before me. "Welcome back."

"How long was I gone?" It felt odd to talk.

"Almost a fortnight." Two weeks.

"What day is it?" I asked.

"The second day of the new year."

I'd missed Christmas then.

Thoughts of the holiday made me think of the others and I found myself missing them, my family. "Let's go back home."

Amber smiled and extended his hand. I took it.

"Home," he said. "That sounds nice."

EPILOGUE

IT SEEMED CHRISTMAS hadn't passed me by entirely. Warrior Lord Thorane, Speaker of the High Council, had called and left a cryptic message: Halcyon had given the necklace back to its rightful owner.

Gryphon was in Hell.

His scent still lingered in his room. Soon it would fade completely. I felt sadness at that fact, but not despair. I knew where to find him now. He hadn't left me completely. Just gone to another realm. In time, I would see him again.

The others had held my little Queendom for me while I'd been gone. Thaddeus and Aquila had overseen the various businesses, Chami had arbitrated the disputes. Dontaine and Thomas had gone to Mississippi, cleaned up the house, and even returned the stolen minivan. Its owner found it one morning innocently parked in front of his lawn. The registration had been in the glove compartment.

The adjoining Mississippi territory that had been sliced up and given to Mona Louisa became mine by default. To the victor the spoils. Horace, the nasty steward, came along with the new province. He was just as slimy but much more humble now, more eager to please. Slimy or not, Horace was efficient at his job. Amber and I ended up sharing the little steward.

At my insistence, under protest, Amber ruled the new Mississippi slice. He didn't want to leave me but I made him. Who else could rule it on my behalf? I had asked him. Since the answer had been, "No one else," he had gone.

I felt lonely and a little guilty for making him leave. I had refused to join the two territories back under the single rule they had once enjoyed. Everyone thought it was because Gryphon had died there, and that was a small part of it. But the greater reason was because Amber was a Warrior Lord. He should have ruled his own territory but had chosen to stay with me, in service to me. This way, we could still have both. Amber could rule as he was meant to rule, and still continue to serve me. But having both came with a price. I could no longer fall asleep in Amber's comforting arms and wake up with the reassuring beat of his heart beneath me.

Thaddeus began his final semester in the new high school, and Jamie and Tersa made plans to take the GED and enroll in college next fall. We never did get around to lessons with Healer Janelle. Mona Carlisse, her daughter Casio, and Janelle had all returned to their homes. Perhaps we'd see each other again at the next Council Meeting. Finally get in a lesson one of these days.

My beast and I were one now. I ran with Amber in the woods once a week during the precious one day and night I got to be with him. But our lack of a healer and my limited healing capacity was still a problem. Mona Louisa's healer had fled back to High Court after discovering the carnage in Mississippi. She still trembled at the mention of my name. Rosemary had come up with some creative ideas, ingenious bribes, really, to lure a healer into my service. We'd see how well they worked come next Trade Festival.

Until then, life went on. It really did. And some life goes on to become demon dead.

ABOUT THE AUTHOR

A family practice physician and Vassar graduate, Sunny was finally pushed into picking up her pen by the success of the rest of her family. Much to her amazement, she found that, by golly, she actually *could* write a book. And that it was much more fun than being a doctor. As an award-winning author, Sunny has been featured on *Geraldo at Large* and *CNBC*. When she is not busy reading and writing, Sunny is editing the works of her husband, literary novelist Da Chen, and being a happy stage mom for her two talented kids.

Mona Lisa Darkening, the fourth book in her acclaimed Monère series, will be released in January 2009. For excerpts, contests, and other news, please visit www.sunnyauthor.com.

Turn the page for a preview of the next
Novel of the Monère
by Sunny

Mona Lisa Craving

Now available!

THE CRESCENT MOON gleamed bright in the star-studded sky, a beacon of light in the darkness. Not chasing it away. No, darkness was fine. Darkness was our domain, the time when we roamed and played and hunted. We slept the days and roamed the evening twilight. And when the sun fell over the edge of the Earth, that was when we rose. The lunar rays didn't chase darkness away, so much as crown it. Make it glisten and glow with shadows and light.

We weren't vampires. We were something older, much older than those legends. We were what begat those first whispers that eventually wound their way into folklore: The Monère, children of the moon, a people who had fled their dying planet over four million years ago. Supernatural creatures faster, stronger, more beautiful than mere humans.

I was the exception to that. The beauty part, that is. I was the pigeon among all the peacocks. Plain, with straight dark hair and shadow-danced eyes. The exotic almond tilt of my eyes was my only attractive feature. At five feet

eight, I stood as tall as the shortest of my men, and was
built more like a long-distance runner—lean, pared down
like an athlete, with a light, modest bosom. I hadn't inherited my mother's lushness, which was fine by me. It was a
body I was comfortable with. And my simple looks . . .
well, the plainness was not so surprising. Not in a Mixed
Blood, which is what I am. A quarter of me is human, the
other three-quarters of me is Monère, a people I'd only just
come to know existed. And the reason for that? My mother,
Mona Sera, a Full Blood Monère Queen, had tossed my
mongrel self away at birth, like garbage. I'd been raised
among the humans. Grew up thinking of myself as such
until puberty hit and the moon's gifts of greater strength
and sharper senses, far more acute than any human's could
ever be, made it clear that I was more.

I was more than even what I had first suspected. I was a
Monère Queen, the newest one crowned. The first Mixed
Blood Queen to ever exist in their long and bloody history.
Unfortunately, I was doing more than my share of adding
to the bloodiness of that history. I'd just returned from
High Queen's Court, called before the Council to explain
my role in Mona Louisa's death, the Queen who'd ruled
here before me in Louisiana.

Mona Louisa of Louisiana. Had a ring to it now that I
rolled the words together, didn't it? No longer. She was
dead. Not by my hand, though I'd done my best to kill her
after she'd torn my lover's heart out from his chest and
killed him. When Gryphon died, I had wanted to die, too.
But not before ensuring that Mona Louisa departed this
Earth first. After I'd seen that goal accomplished, I'd been
grief-maddened and had submersed myself in my Bengal
tiger form—something I'd suppressed, ran from all my life,
that dark, dangerous beast chained inside me. In my grief-
storm of pain and loss, I'd finally embraced that animal
part of me. Lost myself wholly, mindlessly, in my other
self, roaming the forests for a fortnight until my human and

animal minds had merged, come one into the other, and I found myself once more aware of who and what I am—a part-human Monère Queen who had abandoned her people for half a month.

One of my people ran beside me now. An enormous wolf with a beautiful, lush pelt of silver-gray, and autumn brown eyes that gleamed as if a light shone within him. And it did. Lunar light. He was not a true wolf but a Full Blood Monère warrior shifted into his animal form. He romped with me now in joy of the night, and I ran with him in celebration of our time, of our strength, of our being, lithe and light in my human form, springing ahead of him, veering sharply aside so that he leaped in front. I followed then, chasing after him. We danced like that for a time, like children playing, or in our case, like living creatures who still had life, who should celebrate that life while it yet remained in them.

Life and death were fickle, sometimes bleeding one into the other. Gryphon, my first love, had died but he'd made the transition to demon dead. He resided now in another realm. In Hell. I would see him again one day. Mona Louisa, the bitch Queen I'd tried so hard to kill and had failed to, was also dead but not entirely gone. She'd drank demon blood and had become more than Monère . . . and I had sucked her light and essence into me. That part of her, that demon-tainted part, resided in me now.

I ran in human form because, now that it was triggered, that demon essence within me partially blocked my tiger self, preventing it from coming out fully. I wondered if the opposite were true, if my animal self prevented the full manifestation of that demon sliver that lurked within me like a dark, insidious shadow.

Others thought I ran the night in my animal form with my master at arms by my side to keep me safe. But I'd really come here, away from the others' keen ears, to speak to him privately.

Deep in the midst of the forest, we came upon a small clearing. Nestled there was a small hut. The west cottage, it was called. I'd never been here before and looked upon the charming little structure with pleasure. It was a tiny thing with yellow siding, a green sloping roof, and matching green trim. The door was unlocked. I pushed it open and stepped within. It was a simply furnished but comfortable abode, used as a hunter's cabin. A place where Monère warriors shifted back into their upright forms. A place to clean up and wash off the blood after hunting in their animal selves. There were several other cabins like this spread out among our vast acreage.

Nails scraped the wooden floor as the wolf entered the cabin and crossed over to me. A natural wolf, *canis lupus*, stood thirty inches tall at the shoulders and weighed 150 pounds. *Canis Monère*, on the other hand, was much bigger. Or at least the one before me was. His weight was closer to 250 pounds. And his shoulders topped a natural wolf's height by more than half a foot. No wonder the timber wolf that I'd encountered at High Court, a wolf that had looked upon me as food, had backed away beneath Dontaine's growling threat.

A shimmer of light, a pulse of power, and Dontaine stood before me naked and unadorned, breathtakingly handsome with hair as blindingly bright as sunshine, and eyes a lush and deep verdant green in his human form. He was tall, and what I would have called of average build. But average was not a word you used with Dontaine. With broad shoulders, arms roped with sinewy strength, a chest sculpted with rippling muscles that flowed like flesh-silk beneath his pale, flawless skin, he was more heavily muscled than Gryphon, my beautiful, dark, departed angel, and much less massive than my towering Amber, my Warrior Lord, my other love.

Dontaine's hand reached out and I felt that electric, jolting dance upon my skin, a sensation that came from him alone. He touched me. And his touch was not like that of a guard but of a new lover—my new lover.

"Mona Lisa." He whispered my name and title both. The emotions that crossed my face when I looked at him, truly looked at him and saw him—not just the surface beauty but the generous, valiant heart that lay beneath it—made his eyes swirl a deeper green.

He was achingly handsome with bold and noble features, like a blond sun god. And like most men blessed with fair face and exquisite form, he had the confidence, the touch of arrogance that usually came with the looks. And he wasn't just beautiful but powerful, even for a Full Blood Monère warrior. He had been Mona Louisa's favorite, before she had tried to kill me, her territory forfeited to me as punishment. She'd tried to regain it, and one of the means she had used was the tall, sumptuously handsome man who stood before me now, looking at me with soft wonder in his eyes. He'd been left behind to spy and betray me, but he hadn't. He'd saved me instead. Not just once, but again at High Court when I had been questioned there for Mona Louisa's death.

I'd taken him not just into my body but into my heart. In the midst of sadness and loss, I'd found love again, unexpectedly. It was because I loved Dontaine that I needed to talk to him now. So that he did not continue to look at me that way—with love and happiness.

It had only been one day since we'd returned from my testimony at High Queen's Council. And we'd spent most of it reassuring my people here that I would not be blamed or punished for Mona Louisa's death, that everything was okay. But that was a lie. While things may be okay Council-wise—or as much as it could be after a stir like that—*I* wasn't okay. And only Dontaine knew the truth of this.

I stepped back from my lover's touch. Dropped my eyes from his compelling male beauty, from the tempting loveliness of his form, from the raw and tender heart he offered up to me with those expressive green eyes. I took a hard step back from it all and said, "We need to talk, Dontaine."

A beat of silence. When he spoke, it was with quiet tension thrumming in his voice. "That never bodes well."

I guess that was a rule that held true not only for humans but for the Monère also.

"I will dress," he said quietly, and I retreated to a corner chair as he opened the armoire and began to pull on clothes. I would have stared out the window had there been one, but there was none in this simple cabin. I passed the time instead with an intricate study of the wood-planked floor.

I felt his presence as he neared and sat by my feet. There were no other chairs. I would have felt better had he stood instead of seating himself on the floor below me, a gesture that placed him lower than I, made him even more vulnerable to me.

My eyes lifted from my perusal of the floor, met his, and flicked away. I couldn't say what I had to say to him while looking into those unshielded eyes.

"Dontaine." Just his name for a moment, so lovely upon my lips. Then came the blow. "We cannot be lovers."

He didn't say anything, so I rushed to fill in the pregnant silence. "I care for you. You know that." It was a truth that he'd seen in my eyes. "But you also know that there is something very, very wrong with me. You've asked no questions."

"There has been no time. No opportunity."

"There is now. Do you have any questions for me?"

A strained silence. Then he asked not what I would have asked after all that confused madness that had occurred two nights ago, but what was most important to him. "Why can we not be lovers?"

His hands, long-fingered and elegant, an aristocrat's hands, were folded neatly around his bended knees as he sat there on the wooden floor. I focused on those hands, remembered how they had felt on me, in me, caressing me, and looked blindly away.

"You and I know that it was not my beast's hunger that almost overwhelmed me at High Court." Though that was what we'd told everyone else. Even Tomas, my other guard who'd been there that night, believed it to be true. "It was bloodlust, Dontaine. Demon bloodlust."

"It is because of Halcyon, the Demon Prince. When you accompanied him." Dontaine's words, more of a statement than a real question, referred to the time when I had returned with Halcyon to Hell. When my Demon Prince had been so severely injured because of me . . . always because of me, it seemed . . . that he could not make the trip safely home by himself. Hell was a dangerous place, even for its ruler.

I closed my eyes, picking my answer carefully, tiptoeing among all the lies to pick a truth that I could tell him. "Not in the way you think. I wasn't infected then. But you're right, it does involve Halcyon." It certainly involved his blood, which Mona Louisa had taken from him against his will, breaking one of their greatest taboos—drinking a demon's blood. She'd blood-raped Halcyon. And I, in turn, had light-raped her. Now both of their essences dwelled within me. And all of this had to remain a secret. Unknown.

Blaec, the High Lord of Hell, Halcyon's father, had killed a score of Monère warriors and their Queen—Mona Louisa, the demon blood violator—to keep this secret: that drinking their blood can multiply a Monère's power, endowing them with demon dead strength. I did not want the next blood bath to be that of my men.

"It involves Mona Louisa, too," I said, and told Dontaine nothing he did not already know. He'd seen my brown eyes turn blue, turn into Mona Louisa's eyes. "How, I cannot say. Only that it was the reason why the High Lord of Hell killed her."

"But he spared you. Does he know that you have some of their essence in you?"

A good question. The High Lord had seen me drain Mona Louisa of her light, her energy. He had spared me, believing that keeping my Monère secret—my extremely rare, extremely dangerous gift of Mortal Draining, that light-drinking thing I had done—would ensure the keeping of his demon secret. But the real reason he had spared me was because his son, Halcyon, had named me as his mate. Because after six hundred years alone, he had found love.

Still . . . that was before Blaec knew that his demon secret dwelled as a living presence within me. That it had infected me. That it evidenced within me everything they tried to keep hidden from the Monères. Would he still have spared me had he known this? I would know soon enough. Lucinda, Halcyon's sister, had been at High Court, and her presence there had brought out the demon taint in me. There'd been no hiding it from her. She knew what existed within me—what was changing me—and would have reported that to the High Lord and to Halcyon. Death resided within me, most likely lay before me.

"Lucinda will have told them by now," I said. "If the High Lord, or if Halcyon . . . if they come to kill me, you are not to try to stop them or seek revenge."

Dontaine froze into a stillness that unnerved me.

"They will be within their rights, Dontaine. Do you understand?"

He shook his head, his voice sounding harsh and strained. "No. I do not understand."

"It was something that *I* did. Something I brought upon myself. I'm sorry to lay this burden on you, but if anything happens to me, you are the only one who knows. The only one who can testify before the Council that I hold Halcyon and the High Lord blameless."

"For executing you," he said. "If two of our Queens are

killed by demon hand, even if it is by the High Lord himself again, it will not sit well with the High Queens Council."

"What will they do? Go to war with them?" My laugh was short and bitter. "They would be slaughtered. As would you, all of you here. Everyone I love and hold dear." I closed the distance between us, gripped his hand tight. Felt his electric touch dance with shocking little jolts upon my skin. The sensation was sharper, more painful than normal, betraying his leaking distress. "Dontaine, promise me that you will not lift your hand against them if they come for me."

A hard, painful jolt shot from his hand to mine, making me gasp. He drew his hand away so that we no longer touched. "Are you asking me, or ordering me?"

I searched his eyes, those green tumultuous depths. "You are my master at arms. With command comes great responsibility. You hold our people's safety in your hands. Would you see your mother, your sister, killed for no purpose? Would you throw away their lives—your life—so easily? I ask it of you but if I must, I will order it. Must I, Dontaine? Must I demand it of you?"

His eyes dropped away from mine. "Mona Lisa . . . What you ask of me . . ."

I went into his arms then because I loved him. Because I was hurting him, and I did not want to. I went into his arms because the torment I glimpsed in his beautiful eyes just plain broke my heart.

Contact with him lanced me for a sharp, electric second before he brought his forceful presence back under control.

"Please, Dontaine. I love you. I want to keep you safe. All of you—Jamie, Tersa, Rosemary, Thaddeus, Chami, Tomas, Aquila, and Amber. You are my family. The most important beings to me in this world. Please, help me keep you all safe. I could not bear it if I lost someone else I loved."

His hands cupped my face, lifted it up to his so that I saw his brilliant, gleaming eyes, the chiseled lines of his face fierce and raw with emotion. Perhaps he would have kissed me then. Perhaps I would have let him. A foolish thing to do when it was infinitely safer to push him away. Safer for him.

I don't know if I would have given in to that momentary folly. I don't know what would have happened afterward. All I suddenly knew was that my gums were burning as if fire had set them aflame. That my teeth were aching. That I had a sudden thirsting urge for blood, to feel it sliding hot and sweet down my throat.

This was what had happened to me at High Court—the promise of fangs. That promise suddenly became reality. My teeth elongated and pushed upward and outward through my gums like small mountains erupting. I gasped because it hurt like hell. Then gasped again when I felt a sharp sting and looked down to see blood welling from the hand I'd drawn up to my mouth and pricked. I'd accidentally cut myself on the sharpness of my own teeth . . . on my *fangs*.

"Dear Goddess," Dontaine whispered. Cold fear skimmed the surface of those two words.

I pushed away from him and stumbled out the door. Away. I had to get away from him. I fled outside into the cool night, and in the breeze that glided over my skin, I felt him—the demon presence outside that had brought forth the demon presence within me. And not just any demon, but one I knew intimately. "Halcyon."

He came to me out of the darkness, my elegant Demon Prince. I sensed him as I'd never sensed him before, like a heartbeat. Only his heart did not beat, he did not breathe. He—like the other demons—was dead, demon dead, and we were not supposed to be able to sense them this strongly. That was what made them so dangerous—that they could approach us almost undetected. That and their far greater strength, both mental and physical.

The last time I'd seen Halcyon, he'd been weak and bloodied, his chest ripped to shreds by a whip. He was not weak now. Others would have looked upon him and seen an average man in looks, height, and build. He was only a bare head-tilt taller than I, slender and trim, with dark hair, dark eyes, just like me. He had a quiet presence rather than a shouting one. A reserved air. An air of loneliness. An apartness from others that had pulled me to him since the very first time I became aware of him in a sun-dappled meadow.

A Monère warrior who did not know the Demon Prince would have seen him and dismissed him in strength, and power. Never would have guessed that before him stood the ruler of Hell, someone far stronger than our greatest Warrior Lord.

I'd never feared Halcyon as others did—his great strength, those lethal nails. He'd been kind to me from the very first, and not just kind but a friend . . . and then a lover in a dream or a vision—you might call it a dream reality. Whatever it had been, the feelings between us had certainly been real.

Even when I'd seen Halcyon shift into his alternate demon form—huge, monstrous, ugly—and kill another demon in battle over me, even then I had not really feared him. But now I did. Because I didn't just feel Halcyon's presence, I felt his emotions. He *ached* with sadness. Almost overwhelming grief.

The cabin door opened. Dontaine stepped out, a silver dagger gleaming with naked threat in his hand, and I felt Halcyon's grieving sadness flash into anger.

"Dontaine, leave us," I said, my voice carefully calm.

My master of arms, my lover, did not obey me. Instead he came to stand beside me. "I'm sorry, I can't."

"I'm sorry, too." With a blow that took Dontaine unaware, I struck him, careful with my strength because I was more than just Monère strong now. I caught his unconscious body as it went lax, and carried him inside to the cabin, laid him gently down on the bed.

One last secret touch of that sun-bright hair. Then I straightened and stepped out to meet my fate.